THE PLAYROOM

THE PLAYROOM

GLORIA MURPHY

DONALD I. FINE, INC.
New York

Library of Congress Cataloging-in-Publication Data

Murphy, Gloria.
  The playroom.

  I. Title.
PS3563.U7297P55   1988   813'.54   87-45108
ISBN 1-55611-043-X

Library of Congress Catalogue Card Number: 87-45108
ISBN: 1-55611-043-X
  Manufactured in the United States of America
  10 9 8 7 6 5 4 3 2 1

This book is printed on acid free paper. The paper in this book meets the guidelines for permanence and durability of the Committee on Production Guidelines for Book Longevity of the Council on Library Resources.

This novel is a work of fiction. Names, characters, places and incidents are either the product of the author's imagination or are used fictitiously. Any resemblance to actual events, locales, organizations or persons, living or dead, is entirely coincidental and beyond the intent of either the author or publisher.

*Dedicated to
my brother, Phil Walter,
and his wife, Maureen.*

*Thanks to my editor,
Rick Horgan and my children,
Dan Gitelman and Kate Murphy.*

CHAPTER ONE

VICTORIA'S teeth dug slightly into her lower lip, creating temporary indentations. . . It was one of those peculiarities she had picked up as a kid and though she'd shown remarkable willpower kicking other vile childhood habits, she still sometimes chewed her lips so hard she actually drew blood.

She might not have realized what she was doing but for the white-haired lady staring at her across the narrow bus aisle. Should she thank the woman for calling it to her attention or glare back? She did neither, running her tongue soothingly across her lip and turning to look out the dirt-smudged window into the darkness: they were in Boston—the Charles River was coming up on her left. She checked her watch. The bus trip from Manhattan had taken nearly five hours.

Though she had tried to calm herself down, she still couldn't help feeling a little nervous. Six years away, and now she was heading home. Her home . . . Rosalie's home. There she went again, separating herself from Rosalie as if they weren't the same person. The doctor had done an elegant job on the outside—she had chosen one of the best cosmetic surgeons in Manhattan—but sometimes she wondered if, one of those times when she was under the knife, he hadn't scooped out some of her brain cells as well.

Victoria rummaged through her gray leather shoulder bag, pulled out a hand mirror and examined her face, then tilted her head to the side, studying the profile of her nose and chin, all the while aware of the eyes from across the aisle still directed at her.

"The chin is fine," the doctor had tried to convince her before surgery, but she had remained adamant. "Not good

1

enough," she'd said. "It's small and weak, it needs to be built up more to go with the rest of my face."

She had leafed through hundreds of pictures. "It's like shopping for a face in a Sears Roebuck catalog," she'd told the girls in the secretarial pool. "Or like . . . ," she had smiled at the thought, "like putting together a Mister Potatohead." But they never did appreciate her dry humor.

"Personally," one of the more outspoken girls came out and said—the others always preferred to air their opinions about her privately—"I don't know how you can go through with such a change. To look in the mirror and find a total stranger staring back at you. I'm sorry, but it strikes me as kind of ghoulish."

But it had never struck Rosalie that way. She'd gone through with the surgery anyway and voilà: the demise of Rosalie Salino and the birth of Victoria Louise. A new face, a darker hair color, contact lenses, even elocution lessons to give her voice a deeper, more mature quality. And best of all—a new body. She'd lost ninety-nine pounds in less than a year. If only mama could see her now.

Mama . . . She had never really approved of her daughter's move to New York after graduation from high school, but then again, she hadn't had much say in the matter. Victoria was determined to leave all that childhood pain behind, not that she ever really managed to do it. She soon found out that ugly and fat stays ugly and fat wherever you take it.

She had seen hundreds of commercials on television—"Even if you don't like you, we do. Let us show you how much."—but it wasn't until mama had suffered a massive stroke and died a little more than a year ago and Victoria had received all the money, that the idea to make herself over took hold. And then, of course, once it did, it followed that she would come back home. The strange part was, if not for the money mama had left, Victoria might never have come back at all.

The house and more than two hundred thousand dollars . . . She'd had no idea . . . in fact, she nearly keeled over when mama's attorney phoned to tell her the bottom-line figure.

Apparently her father's insurance had left them well fixed when he'd died, but mama hadn't touched a penny. Instead, she kept on a boarder, Mrs. Mills, and lived off the modest rent.

Victoria dropped the mirror back into her purse, then pulled out a black leather-bound book from her overnight bag and opened it. Her expression tensed as she studied the group photograph neatly cut and taped to the first page. Faces. Eleven of them. Each one belonging to an elite member of the Bradley Class of '81. The captain of the football team, the head cheerleader, the prom queen—no member of Bradley's finest was missing. They were gathered around The Thinker, the massive granite statue that stood in front of Bradley High School. Under the photograph, in bold print, it read, "A party . . . did we hear someone say a party?"

Victoria looked up, eyes staring blankly ahead. Yes, she thought, there will be a party. Only this time, *she* would be the one throwing it, and it would be different from any of their other parties. She'd make sure of that. Her eyes focused on the one face in the group circled in red and her expression immediately softened. That is, except for you, Rusty, she had other plans . . .

Out of the corner of her eye, Victoria saw the old lady's neck stretch—ironing out its wrinkles—as she tried to get a peek at what Victoria was looking at. Victoria turned, facing her. "Would you like to look?" she said, handing the book across to her.

The woman shrank back, her neck folding back into her shoulders.

It was nine o'clock when the Greyhound approached St. James Street and pulled into the depot. Victoria's nosy and now nervous traveling companion scurried off the bus out into the cool October night as soon as the doors wheezed apart. It hadn't taken much to put the woman in her place, just a calm, confident, direct approach, something that had taken Victoria years to master. As a youngster, she had always been the meek one, the one whose face would redden or vocal chords would suddenly clamp shut at the least provocation. Of course with Mrs. Mills, their ever-present boarder, she would react just the opposite: the littlest interference from Mrs. Mills would throw Rosalie into a rage, and almost always she responded sharply to the woman's comments. It still amazed her that Mrs. Mills never seemed to take offense.

Victoria slung her purse over one shoulder and her overnight bag over the other. She hurried into the crammed terminal, squinting momentarily as her new extended-wear contacts adjusted to the bright fluorescent lights.

There were rows of wooden benches, mostly occupied: drunks, derelicts, unkempt mothers with drooling, wet-nosed babies, blacks, Puerto Ricans. Lots of Puerto Ricans. One bus station was like another—she should have flown. It would take a while until she got used to having so much money.

A man with a dirt-smeared T-shirt, suspenders and bare feet tapped her shoulder, gesturing to an empty space on one of the benches. "Sit?" he said.

She still wasn't used to having men offer her seats—even seedy men like this one—but she declined gracefully, then backed away, redirecting her attention to the glass door. A man with a red cap was pulling the last of the luggage from the bus's belly, lining it up along the curb. She opened the door, then spotting her suitcase and brown cardboard box, reached into her pocket and retrieved her claim checks. The man with the red cap took the stubs from her and helped her maneuver the luggage to a nearby taxi stand. Bradley was a full forty minutes north of Boston, but she would take a taxi.

Seventeen Valley Road. Victoria set her luggage on the ground then watched as the yellow cab sped down the street and disappeared. Even for mama's funeral, she hadn't been able to bring herself back here. Slowly she turned, forcing herself to look up at the darkened three-story house, and for a split second her mind went blank and she was aware only of the fine, electrically charged hairs elevating along the nape of her neck. Then suddenly the familiarity: the multipeaked roof, the sagging second-floor balcony, the ornate porch banisters stretching like withered arms down the front stairs. And the windows. Seventy-six windows, in all—Rosalie had counted them once.

Hefting her belongings, Victoria climbed the chipped cement stairs leading to the house, then the porch stairs. Finally she slid the key in the lock, pushed open the door, and reached inside, flipping the entry hall light switch. Nothing. Damn—the electricity! She had forgotten to have the power turned on.

Guided only by the flames of a dozen or so matches, Victoria felt her way to the dining room china closet. She ran her hands along the shelves. Candles . . . mama had always kept candles here. They should be—she stopped. A squeaking sound was coming from the stairwell. She spun around, staring into the blackness. "Who's there?" she called out.

Silence.

Victoria backed herself against the wall, listening . . . More silence. It must have been her imagination, she thought. Old houses, strange noises—another thing she'd forgotten. She had just reached back into the china closet when she saw the light coming toward the dining room. Her hand touched an object—a wine decanter—and she wrapped her fingers around it, lifted it . . . waited. The beam came closer, bouncing shapeless shadows off the walls . . . Then there was a dark figure standing in the doorway.

She swallowed hard, then again, "Who's there?"

"The lady of the house, that's who."

Was the voice familiar? Victoria moved closer to it. Now only a few feet away, she could make out the face: wide deep-blue eyes dominating small, bland features. Pale brown hair with gray seeping in from the hairline . . . This time Victoria knew the answer when she asked, "What's your name?"

"Agnes Mills. And who may I ask are you?"

"Victoria Louise." Victoria took the lantern from the woman's hand and held it up to her own face, holding her breath. But the woman showed no signs of recognition. "What are you doing here?" Victoria asked finally.

"I live here . . . alone . . . now that Mrs. Salino is gone."

"But Mrs. Salino's daughter sold the house to me."

The woman's eyes narrowed. "Rosalie? You know Rosalie?"

"Not really. I met her once."

"Where is she?"

"New York, but—"

"Tell me about her," the woman asked. "Is she well?"

"I'm afraid there's nothing to tell. As I said, I saw her only once, and that was simply to sign papers. To give me deed to the house."

The woman shook her head. "No, I don't believe it. Rosalie would never put me out. She would never sell this house."

Victoria opened her purse, unfolded a copy of a deed listing Victoria Louise as the owner (she had prepared it herself), then held it up to Mrs. Mills. "Of course the original has already been filed."

Mrs. Mills studied the paper, then sighing deeply, looked up at Victoria. "And me . . . what am I to do?"

Victoria shrugged. "Well, I hadn't expected . . . that is, I'm willing to give you some time to find suitable quarters. Perhaps a week . . ."

The woman's chin tilted upward and her voice choked. "Of course . . . that will be sufficient. I'm sure I'll find a place by then."

She turned and headed upstairs, her gait unsteady and her shoulders hunched forward, adding twenty years to the fifty-nine she already was. For a moment, Victoria wondered if the woman's labored movement was an attempt to gain sympathy. Well, if it was, the act wouldn't work on her.

Victoria bit down on her lip, running her teeth along it . . . What was it Mrs. Mills had said . . . that Rosalie would never put her out? Why would she say that . . . why would she even think that? Surely *she* hadn't forgotten how badly Rosalie had treated her . . .

Victoria lit three candles, and with a drop of melted wax poured into saucers, stood them in place. Then, tossing her overnight bag over her shoulder, she headed downstairs. To the playroom.

She walked around the damp basement, holding the candles. There were a few old chairs and a sofa . . . yellowed stuffing seeping out of the furniture edges. No, it wasn't much of a playroom, at least not yet. But soon it would be just the kind of room her father had planned for her. She remembered how he had called her his "little princess" and how he had told her over and over again how magnificent the playroom would be when it was finished. She looked at the one small, paneled wall at the far end of the cellar. He had gotten only that far before he died . . .

She reached down, unzipped her overnight bag, took out the black book and studied the eleven smiling faces on the first page. She glanced around the room, remembering where each of the boys and girls had stood eight years before when mama had surprised her with a sweet sixteen party and stupidly invited them.

Victoria could even remember the expressions on their faces as they mocked her over and over again with their cruel gifts. Even mama didn't know what was really happening . . . only she knew. And of course, them. Victoria drew in a deep breath, then slowly let it out. No, this party would definitely be different. She looked again at the red-circled face, at the strong chin and wavy blond hair, and her lips pressed against the photo's glossy surface.

Victoria dug again into the bag and took out the tattered rag doll that had shared all of her childhood secrets. She touched the blue eyes that were now chipped and the knotted black yarn hair, and the tiny hole in the doll's chest, remembering how beautiful it used to be when its name was Victoria Louise. But that was a long time ago. Now *she* was Victoria Louise and Rosalie . . . Rosalie was gone forever.

Or was she?

"Are you still here, Rosalie?" Victoria said to the doll, but the doll didn't answer.

CHAPTER TWO

"GOD, Rusty . . . are you deaf?" Carol said as she ran past the sofa bed and snatched the phone up. Her voice became suddenly more civil. "Hello." She waited, then repeated herself. Nothing. "Who is this?"

"Hang it up," Rusty said, his deep voice muffled into the pillow.

"Whoever this is, please say something," Carol said.

Still nothing.

"I can't hear you."

Rusty turned onto his back. "Just hang it up!"

Carol sighed, then put down the phone and looked at her brother whose eyes still hadn't begun to focus. It seems as if someone's on the line but the connection isn't working."

Silence.

"Maybe it was something important. I should have waited longer."

"Why?"

"To see who it was, naturally."

Silence, then, "What time is it, Carol?"

Carol looked through the doorway to the kitchen clock. "Five to nine almost." She ran over to the side parlor window and pulled open the curtain. "Sunny, clear and cold. An excellent day."

"How do you know it's cold?"

A lock of Carol's honey-blond hair fell across a flushed cheek, and she pushed it aside. "Just a guess. Mr. Lyman's designer jeans are hanging on the clothesline and they look like he's still in them."

Rusty threw his legs over the side of the bed and sat up, yawning, his arms resting on his knees. "Saturday . . . I get the

9

chance to sleep late, and we've got some jerk playing telephone games."

Carol picked up Rusty's empty beer can and tossed it in the kitchen pail. "It's weird, isn't it? Why would a person keep calling—"

She stopped and Rusty looked up at her. "This happened before. Why didn't you say something?"

Carol shrugged. "It was no big deal. Besides I know you, you're like daddy, you read something crazy in the newspaper and then you think it could have been me and then you go spastic, blowing the littlest thing out of proportion."

Rusty stood up. "What kind of calls were they?"

"Like these two. You think somebody's there, but either they're not talking or what they're saying isn't coming through."

"And what do you do . . . carry on a one-way running conversation?"

"Yeah, right." She put her hands on her hips. "What do you think I do? I hang up naturally."

"Yeah, naturally. Listen Carol, I know you have a hard time cutting connections, but if it happens again, you hang up right away. No need to encourage this guy, whoever he is."

Carol had picked up a dirty towel from the floor and was heading to the bathroom hamper. She stopped and turned back to Rusty. "What makes you think it's a he?"

"Did I say that?"

"Yes you did."

"So hang me. What is this—a complaint against sex discrimination?"

"Well, you do have some chauvinistic tendencies." She grabbed the corner of the soggy towel she was holding and swung it at him.

Rusty raised his hands to ward off another blow. "Quit it, will you."

Carol's almost colorless brows arched over green eyes. "What's the matter? Can't take it?"

Rusty leaped forward, yanking the towel from his sister's

hands. "No fair!" she screamed, scrambling away and lifting a pillow cushion from the floor. She tossed it—the cushion edge grazed his head, then flipped over onto the kitchen counter, toppling a half-empty can of Pepsi. The brown liquid streamed onto the linoleum.

Rusty grabbed for the can. "Shit."

"Now, now, Russell, we will have no cursing." She edged away from him . . . then ran. Rusty followed behind, snapping the towel at her back. She reached the bathroom, ran in, and slammed the door in his face. The lock clicked into place.

Rusty was heading back to the kitchen when the phone rang. He turned toward it. It rang again. The bathroom door cracked open and Carol peeked out. "Well . . . aren't you going to answer it?"

"Yeah, sure." He went to the phone and picked it up. "Hello." Louder than necessary.

"Mr. Erlich?"

"Yes, speaking."

"You *are* the Erlich that does construction work, carpentry, that sort of thing?"

"Right. Who am I talking to?"

"Oh, you don't know me. I got your name from the directory, the yellow pages. My name is Victoria. Victoria Louise."

The pancakes Carol had served tasted great—just like mom's. Unfortunately, just like when mom made them, Rusty had eaten way too many. He turned the ignition of his 1976 Chevy C-10 pickup and it sputtered to life . . . thanks to the four-hundred-dollar valve job he had just sunk into it. He crossed his fingers that the heap would hold out one more year, enough time to get his business off the ground.

He threw the shift in reverse, backing out slowly—no point in dumping the transmission in the driveway—then glanced back at the three-story house, his eyes drawn to the side kitchen window of his first floor apartment: Carol stood in a short flannel nightgown—her long legs exposed—stacking breakfast dishes at the sink. She was tall and graceful, looking less and less like the tough little tomboy he had teased mercilessly when growing up. Her long blond hair, usually worn in a single thick braid, was now flowing free down her back. He blew out a stream of air—he'd pick up a cheap pair of curtains for those windows on his way home. This was the kind of thing that never worried him before September, before his father's emphysema forced his parents to a drier climate. And he became sole guardian to a sixteen-year-old.

He smiled. Actually he was happy Carol had insisted on staying with him and finishing her senior year here. It hadn't bothered him much that his folks had decided to pick up stakes—mom and he got along fine, but there had always been friction between him and his dad. If his kid sister had decided to go, though, he would have really felt lost.

But—that was it, the big *but*—he did worry about the responsibility of it all, and his dad's initial reluctance to trust him with Carol's well-being didn't help matters. Not that Rusty needed to be reminded of the scrapes high school kids could get themselves in. It wasn't that long ago he was in high school himself. But sometimes problems occurred even when you were on guard against them.

Rusty thought back to his own high school years—no drugs but a lot of drinking and partying. Compared to most, he supposed his jock friends would have been considered mild. All of them came out of it okay. Only one drunken driving incident—eight in the car, him one of the passengers. Luckily no one was hurt beyond a couple of sprains and bruises. It was enough, though, to make him wonder if it wasn't just luck if you made it through high school in one piece.

He thought about the telephone calls again as he pulled his truck into the parking area of Line Lumber. Was it just some friend of Carol's playing dumb games or could it be . . . what? He was obviously taking this too seriously.

Rae Lemkin had been shopping for most of the morning before she took stock of her shopping cart. She loved do-it-yourself items and could wile away hours just browsing through hardware sections. But today she had done more than browse. Jammed next to the six traverse rods that had brought her into Line Lumber to begin with, were three five-foot pine boards— perfect bookshelves for her new apartment, a can of wood stain, brackets, a bunch of white lightswitch plates to match the newly painted walls, and an unassembled stereo cabinet that, judging by the completed version pictured on the box, was a steal at twenty-six dollars.

Having decided she would splurge and take it all, she shoved the cart into the main aisle, toward the registers. "Watch it!" Rusty called out just as the steel grate plowed into him.

Rae jumped to the side of the carriage. "Oh, I'm so sorry, I didn't mean . . . Did I hurt you?"

Rusty rubbed his side and shook his head. "Shit. You ever think of moving those boards aside so you can see where you're going?"

Rae flushed, instantly blotting out the few freckles sprinkled across her nose. She pushed the slats of pine to one side of the carriage. "I am sorry . . . Did I hurt you?"

Rusty straightened up, and his voice lost its edge. "I guess I'll survive."

"Good. In that case, if you'll let me pass?"

Rusty reluctantly moved aside. "Hey, wait a minute. There's no reason to get nasty. I'm the one who almost got run over, right?"

"And I apologized."

Rusty shrugged. "Yeah, you did."

Silence.

He tilted his head to the side and squinted his eyes, studying her: thick flame hair pulled back and secured carelessly with a purple clip in back of her head. She had a redhead's fair complexion, even a few well-placed freckles, but it was the color of those eyes that was unexpected . . . Like chestnuts. "I know you, right?" he said.

"I doubt it."

"No really, I'm sure I've seen you before. I'm Rusty Erlich."

She nodded. "I guess we do know each other." Then, "I'm

Rae Lemkin, you hung around with my cousin, Bobby Cole, in high school."

Rusty smiled. "I remember now. I only met you once or twice."

Silence, then, "Where's Bobby been lately? I haven't seen him around. Usually I run into him during the week . . . at a diner or something."

Rae shrugged. "I don't really know myself. I've been trying to reach him since I moved in."

"Well when you do, tell him to give me a call. I think I might have a lead on a job for him. Some people who want a couple of sketches done of their house. Nothing fancy, of course, but it's money."

"Did you hear the good news: Bobby got a picture of his accepted in Raneer's. It's supposed to be the best gallery in Boston."

"You mean, his Marathon man. Yeah, I heard." Then, "What about you . . . you stayed with Bobby's family awhile, even went to school here, right?"

"I came to Bradley in eighty-one, our senior year."

"Why don't I remember seeing you around more?"

"I guess we hung out with different people."

He stared at her a moment, then looked in her carriage. "Redecorating?"

"Setting up an apartment. I've been away."

"Yeah . . . where've you been?"

"School, then a couple of years nursing at Beth Israel in Boston With the expansion of Valley Hospital and the shortage of nurses, I decided to come back to Bradley. Besides I missed having family around."

He ran his hand over the cardboard box in the carriage. "Who's going to put this cabinet together?"

"Me."

"Those aren't as easy as they look, you know."

"I know you don't think much of my ability to drive shopping carts, but I'm pretty good with a screwdriver and hammer."

"Well, if you get stuck—"

"Not to worry," she said, cutting him off, "I won't."

Rae watched Russ head toward the tool section. The truth was she had known who he was the minute she saw him. Why hadn't she just come out and said so? It was so unlike her . . . What *was* typical of her was that independent streak that would flare up seemingly out of nowhere. He was just about to offer his help and there she went and cut him off cold. She hadn't meant to be so blunt—after all, he was a friend of Bobby's. But she did know how to put together a simple cabinet. She smiled to herself: she hadn't put up with the hell of being the only girl in high school shop class for nothing.

She pulled her wallet from her purse, hoping she had brought enough cash with her. If not, she could always put it on her credit card, though she hated to use those things. She flipped through a bunch of plastic-covered pictures, stopping momentarily at a recent one of her cousin. Bobby's receding hairline seemed to be getting more noticeable. She thought again about her inability to get hold of him. She had spoken to him several times before the move—in fact, he had been the one to locate the apartment for her. It *was* odd that he hadn't stopped by yet or called.

Well, as soon as she got home she'd get in touch with Aunt Sara and find out where Bobby was hiding himself.

CHAPTER THREE

GNES Mills had been told in no uncertain terms that her time was up. After twenty-five years of living under one roof, her home, the only thing she had left of her past, had been snatched away. Agnes could hardly believe it was happening—the Salinos had never prepared her for this; indeed, they had promised that Rosalie would never put her out. And although she knew how self-centered . . . and yes, insolent the girl could sometimes be, Agnes had believed it.

In the last week she had been thumbing through real estate ads, searching for apartments . . . apartments that she could afford. Of course, if not for the small check she received monthly from the Salino Trust—not enough to always cover utilities—even that would have been impossible. But as it was, she had managed a small deposit on a one roomer with kitchenette, less than a block away. It comforted her to know that she'd be living in the same neighborhood.

Until she moved down the street, though, Agnes had to deal with Victoria, and if the truth be known, the girl did intrigue her. Without a doubt she was beautiful, even charming in a peculiar way, but there was something strange about the girl that Agnes found unsettling. It wasn't what she said, it was more the intonation in her voice or the expression in her eyes. For instance, the way she'd stared at the artist fellow whom she'd summoned to do her portrait. Victoria had sent Agnes off to her room the moment he arrived, but she had seen enough . . . Some might have simply called the look seductive, but no, Agnes knew a seductive message when she read one.

What intrigued Agnes most was the habit the girl had of chewing her lip, sometimes causing the flesh to become puffy

17

and sore. Whenever Rosalie had been agitated, she had done that very same thing.

Mrs. Mills folded the last of her sweaters and placed it into one of the cardboard boxes over the photograph albums. She looked around the room at all the pictures thumbtacked to the walls. They would be packed next. But before she brought herself to do that, she'd go downstairs and brew a pot of tea. Lemon tea always had a calming effect on her. She glanced once again at the room and sighed deeply. By tomorrow it would be like she had never lived here at all.

Victoria locked the door of the second-floor bedroom, then opened the closet. She stepped over the cardboard box on the closet floor, then reached up, pulling the doll off the shelf . . . She felt bad, keeping it in a dark, dusty closet, but once Mrs. Mills left, she wouldn't have to. She dragged a chair over to the window and sat, sitting the doll on the windowsill facing her . . .

Her hands were cold . . . freezing. Nerves, she guessed. She took hold of the doll's pink fingerless hand, then sat back in the chair. She couldn't believe this was really happening . . . Rusty was coming here to see her—something that had only happened before in her dreams. For awhile, it seemed as though she would never get through to him with that girl always picking up the telephone, but finally she had.

Not that she still wasn't upset by the fact that he was living with someone . . . Not Elaine either—she would have immediately recognized *that* voice. But Victoria had to be reasonable. She could hardly expect someone as handsome as Rusty to live in a tomb while she was gone. She hadn't yet figured out how to get rid of the girl, but she was confident she'd come up with something. She reached down and squeezed the doll's hand, imagining that its small fingers had wrapped around hers. "Trust me, Rosalie," she said to the doll. "Rusty is not going to get away from us now. Not now, not ever."

Bradley was about fifteen square miles, held twenty thousand residents and abutted southern New Hampshire. The Merrimack River ran straight through the center of town, separating Bradley proper from West Bradley, an area whose residents in some misguided fit of snobbery saw themselves as being the better side of the parting waters. Although Rusty himself lived in the west end, it was the other side of the bridge he found to be more interesting. Mostly because of the architecture: Georgians, farmhouses, saltbox colonials, Queen Annes, some of the houses going back to the 1800s. Sure, many were in shambles, but there was a definite trend of young couples moving into the area, buying up some of those eyesores at bottom dollar and restoring them. What he wouldn't do to be in a position to buy, fix and resell.

Since high school, he had taken a couple of liberal arts courses and a dozen architectural and design courses at Boston University night school while apprenticing days as a carpenter. In spite of his dad's continual harassment, as well as a respectable show on his SATs, he had opted not to get a college degree. He didn't need a sheepskin to build, and though that argument fell on his dad's deaf ears, building was what he had wanted to do ever since he was a kid. Finally, last year, he had felt sure enough of his skills to go out on his own. And while he hadn't yet contracted for any major jobs, he wasn't exactly starving.

He stopped the truck in front of Seventeen Valley Road, killed the engine, and stared up at the dilapidated Queen Anne set back about fifty feet from the street. He was sure he'd been here before . . . .But he couldn't place when. He got out of the truck and leaned against it for a moment, his gaze traveling to a second-story window. Was someone staring out at him? He looked again, then smiled . . . Maybe he ought to have his eyes checked out . . . A closer look revealed it was only a rag doll sitting on the sill.

A lady with sharp blue eyes set in a worn face greeted him. Was she also familiar?

"Yes?" the woman said loudly, as though it wasn't the first time she'd said it.

"Sorry, ma'am. I'm Russ Erlich, here to see Victoria Louise."

She pulled open the door. "Won't you come in?" He entered a foyer . . . maybe nine by fourteen. Against the far wall set in an alcove was a handsome scroll-edged mirror with a bench beneath running from one side of the wall to another. He studied the delicately carved molding that ran along the top of the walls. Trim, doors . . . all of it was enameled white. No doubt hiding solid pine beneath. It always amazed him: why would anyone spoil the luster of natural wood by dumping a bucketful of paint over it?

He had hardly noticed that the woman had left, but now she was descending the staircase, and a young woman was moving to greet him: good looking . . . smooth sable brown hair swept lightly under, barely touching the shoulders. Her dark sculptured features—almost too perfect—were softened somewhat by magnificent wide-set eyes. Gray? She came closer to him. No, not gray . . . blue.

She held out her hand to him and stared into his eyes. "Mr. Erlich, I'm Victoria Louise." Long, dark lashes fanned down, then up again.

"Rusty will do fine." Returning his hand to his side, he looked around the foyer, then back to her. "You know, it's funny, I remember this house, but I can't quite place when I was here."

"Really? Did you grow up around here?"

"Just across the bridge . . . I take it you're not a native. I think I would have spotted you."

"Oh, no, I'm from New York." She smiled. "That is, I was from New York."

"How'd you end up here? Not that it's really my business."

"No, that's okay, I don't mind you asking. Actually it kind of just happened. I visited New England a couple summers ago and fell in love with it. As for Bradley . . . I guess it was the house that drew me. I saw it advertised in the Boston *Globe* and then when I saw it . . ." She shrugged. "There's just something about old houses."

"I'm pretty hung up on them myself."

"Don't you think they have character ... personality? I know it's going to sound a little nuts—" She stopped.

"Go ahead, what were you about to say?"

"Well, I like to think that old houses have memories. Every single thing they see and hear through the years gets sorted and stored somewhere and it all becomes part of the house's personality. And in turn, each new person that lives in it takes a little from the house, becoming bonded in a way to the people before him."

Russ crossed his arms at his wide chest, angled his head toward her, then nodded. "I don't know, it sounds like a bit of a stretch to me. But maybe you're right."

Victoria smiled winningly. "I can see you're just humoring me."

"No, no, not at all." There was a short pause, then, "From your phone call, I gather you have a lot of plans for this place. Why don't you show me around, I'll take some notes of what you want, then I'll come up with some estimates for you. How does that sound?" He uncrossed his arms and plucked a pad and pen from his shirt pocket.

Victoria continued staring at him, her eyes flashing seductively. "Great. It sounds great. I guess I really lucked out when I went to the yellow pages this morning."

Jesus Christ ... his face felt hot. Was he blushing? He hadn't done that since he was a goddamned twelve-year-old.

Mrs. Mills kept discreetly out of sight, though at the dining room table sipping tea she was within hearing distance of Victoria and the young man. He was good-looking, tall and muscular, with sprays of gold running through his hair and shaggy brows. Like he spent a good deal of time out in the sunshine. And nice green eyes ... The kind of eyes that you trusted the minute you looked into them.

"Mrs. Mills."

The woman looked up at Victoria. The young man was standing behind her. "Yes?"

"I thought you mentioned some packing left to do?"

"Oh, it's mostly done. All except for the photographs."

"Then perhaps you ought to take care of them. I wouldn't want you to forget anything." Victoria leaned across the table, laying her hand over the woman's hand, subtly applying pressure with the heel of her palm.

Mrs. Mills stood up quickly, and with her eyes riveted to the floor, sidled past the two of them. She grabbed onto the banister with her freshly bruised hand and began the two long flights to her third-floor bedroom.

If there had been any doubts before in Agnes's mind, there were none now: nice sweet words or not . . . the girl's intentions were anything but nice. And again came the question that seemed to make little sense but had plagued her from the moment the girl walked through the door: who was Victoria Louise, where did she really come from, and why had she bought the house on Seventeen Valley Road?

By the time they got to the outside, Rusty already had two pages full of items to repair. The structure, he had decided, was solid: only one lolli column was needed in the basement to crank up the sagging living room floor. There were a couple dozen spots where dry rot necessitated replacing floor boards. Then a bunch of minor jobs: plastering holes; repairing or replacing a dozen or so windows, doors, and doorknobs; replacing spindles and repairing three steps in the staircase. In addition, all the trim on the first two floors would be restored to its natural wood state, including the built-in china closet in the dining room.

"Well . . . what do you think?" she asked after walking with him around the yard. She crossed her arms over her chest as if to warm herself.

"I think you ought to put on a jacket before you catch cold."

She smiled. "You know what I mean, about the outside of the house."

He looked up again at the shingles. "Well, from here it looks like you're going to need a new roof. I suggest we put that off till spring, along with the painting."

She nodded.

"Also, there's some rotted boards we're going to need to replace. Gutters . . . wrought iron rails . . . chipped cement stairs." He gestured with his pad toward the front porch supported by two thick, round columns and the balcony overhead. "The columns and steps need work and the banisters need replacing. Then we'll give a little more support to that balcony."

"That's it?"

Rusty shook his head, tucking the pen behind his ear. "I've gotta say, you certainly don't scare easily."

Victoria stared at him. "Oh, no. I've planned for all of this."

Rusty pulled his eyes from hers and cleared his throat. "Well, before you decide anything, why don't I list out these materials, price them, then figure out my time and get back to you with numbers on Monday. Also, I'll get in touch with an electrician I know, Sammy Regis, and have him check the fuse box and wiring."

He began to go, but she grabbed onto his arm, stopping him. "No you don't, you can't leave. Not yet. You still haven't seen our most important project—the playroom."

Part way down the flight of stairs, he noticed a nightstick hanging from a wall nail. When he reached the bottom landing, he stopped. To the left, down several more stairs was what looked to Rusty like a storage vault.

"A wine cellar," Victoria explained. "Apparently one of the former owners made his own wine, then stored it there."

"Interesting. Did they leave you any samples?"

"Nope . . . I'll have to start my own collection."

Rusty stepped through a doorway to his right, then glanced around the dark, dank cellar, noting the one paneled wall already up. The furniture looked about to collapse. Suddenly he turned to Victoria. "Now I remember. Sure I was in this house before, and, in fact, I was right down here. I came to a party here when I was a kid."

Her eyes took on that smokey color that he first remembered. "Oh . . . was it a good party?"

"As I recall, not very."

"Oh, why not?"

He thought about it a moment, then his mouth tightened into a thin line. "Oh, you know how it is, some parties take off, some don't." Then, "What did you have in mind for this room?"

She looked around. "Well, for one thing, I want the two little windows removed."

"Why do that? You're just going to close off all your natural light."

"They don't give that much anyway. Besides, I don't like the looks of them."

He shrugged, then jotted it down on his pad. "We can fill them with cement blocks and sheetrock over them. What else?"

"I want a wet bar, a big one with lots of shelving surrounding it. And a bathroom with stall shower."

"Go on."

"I want the room to be completely soundproof."

He smiled. "Sounds to me like you plan to raise hell down here."

She flipped her head back, her dark hair swung onto her back. "I guess you could say that. Mostly, I don't want to disturb anyone. In New York, most of the time I felt like I was living in my neighbors' apartment. And I'm sure they felt the same."

"You don't really have to worry about that, the cement down here will be a good enough sound barrier. The neighbors won't hear a thing."

"Fine. What about upstairs?"

"What about it?"

"Well, will you be able to hear the noise up there?"

"What difference will that make? I assume you'll be down here, too busy to notice."

"Oh sure, but it's just the way I want it: completely sound-proof. Are you saying it can't be done?"

He shook his head. "No, no, I'm not saying that. What I can do is use a lot of insulation in the ceilings, then lay sound board between the overhead floor joists. After that, we sheetrock it."

"And that will block out every bit of noise?"

He grazed the door with his knuckles. "I'll replace this door, too. Put something more solid in. That ought to do it."

"What about a strong lock? I want one that locks from either side. With a key."

"A key's really not necessary, especially from the inside," then seeing the set look on her face, "whatever you want. What kind of walls did you have in mind?"

"Well, I really don't know. What would you suggest?"

"There's a number of things you might want to use. I'd rather you chose something yourself. After all, you're the one who's going to be living here."

"But I'd like you to pick something. Something you'd like."

He stared at her, studying her. "Why?" he asked finally.

"Because you know about wood . . . how things look once they're up."

Rusty looked around the room again. "Well, I guess if it were up to me, I'd want to keep with the period of the house. Wainscotting might be nice."

She nodded.

"The boards come in about two- to three-inch strips and have a bead, like a ridge going through the center. We could run it halfway up the wall over the sheetrock, and put a chair rail—that's a strip of molding—about here." He leaned over and pointed to the spot. "And the top area could be papered . . . maybe a colonial print. A crown moulding would go nice." Then not giving her a chance to respond, "Look, why don't you go to the lumberyard yourself and take a look at their selection. That way you could be sure—"

"No, no, that won't be necessary. What you described sounds great. Really. I trust your judgment completely."

"Maybe you shouldn't. My taste may not be yours. It *is* your room."

She stared at him for a few seconds, then ignoring what he'd just said, "Tell me what the girl was like?"

"What girl?"

"The one who had the party?"

Rusty hesitated. "Did I say it was a girl?"

"Didn't you, I thought you did. Maybe not, perhaps I just assumed so. After all, aren't they usually the ones who throw parties?"

"I don't know, I never thought about it."

"Well, tell me about her."

"There's nothing to tell, just a girl from school. In fact, I can't even remember her name. Why so interested?"

"It's all part of the house's background. Who knows, this house may have picked up some traits from the girl."

"You really *were* serious about that theory . . ."

Victoria frowned. "I just want to learn about the house's past. What's so strange about that?"

"Well, let me put your mind at ease," Rusty said. "If you're worried about an ax murderer living under this roof before you, forget it right now. As I recall, this girl we're talking about was pretty shy, in fact, meek. Definitely not a threat."

The moment Victoria entered her bedroom, she reached for the book, now in the nightstand drawer. She opened it, studying the photograph till she found the bush of dark hair framing the full face of Sam Regis.

Rusty had volunteered to contact him all on his own. That would just save her the trouble . . . How neatly everything was working out.

Victoria pulled down the doll from the shelf and held it close as she stared again at the picture. She remembered Sammy well, particularly the sound of that coarse, cruel laughter, that just wouldn't quit . . . "Even after you started to cry, Rosalie," she said to the doll.

CHAPTER FOUR

I T wasn't until Rusty got to the curtain department in K-mart
that he spotted the pile of red hair and purple clip. He went
over, tapped her shoulder, and she turned. "Hi there," he said.
"Just wanted to let you know I'd be walking around this area."
He looked at her nearly full carriage, then back to her. "So if
you could kind of keep an eye open . . ."

Her dark eyes met his, then, "You'll find the best defense is
to wheel your own carriage."

"I've tried that—it doesn't pay. I always get the one with the
lopsided wheel."

"I think the Complaint section is in the rear of the store."
And she began to push her carriage.

"Hey wait," he said clamping his hand over the edge of the
basket.

She looked up at him.

"You always shop like this . . . you know, so much? This
morning . . . now. By the looks of your baskets I'd say you're a
pretty serious shopper. Someone who knows what she's doing."

She tilted her head, studying him. "Is this one of those trick
questions where no matter what I answer, I lose?"

He took his hand from her cart. "Not exactly," he said, smiling. "You see, I need a pair of curtains for my apartment. The
only ones I've got there now are the parlor ones, and they were
there when I moved in."

"So you're saying you don't know how to pick out curtains?"

A hesitation. "Well, the thing is, I've never done it before."

"It's really very easy. You look around, see what you like,
then buy them."

Rusty picked up a cellophane-wrapped pair off the counter,
then looked at her. "How am I doing?"

"Not good;" then with a sigh, "Okay . . . what room are these for?"

"The kitchen."

Rae led Rusty to the next aisle, then, "What size?"

"Let me see . . . it's a pretty big window. I'd say seventy-two inches."

"Now we're getting somewhere." Rae looked around the displays, then reached over and fingered one set. "How about these?"

"They look fine to me."

"What color?"

He shrugged. "Any color will do."

She pressed her lips together and shook her head.

"Okay, how about red?"

"What color are your walls?"

"White."

"How about the appliances, the counter?"

"The appliances are white and the counter's yellow."

"And the floor?"

"Let me see . . . sort of speckled, I guess. Dark brown, tan, yellow . . ."

"Well . . . either brown or yellow would go nice. It's up to you."

He grabbed a brown pair of seventy-two inchers, then looked at Rae's expression. "Yellow's better, huh?"

"It's really up to you."

Rusty put down the brown curtains and picked up a yellow pair, then turned to Rae. "Listen, thanks a lot."

"No problem. I expect next time you'll know just how to go about this."

Rusty studied her expression, not quite sure if she was serious or just poking fun at him. Finally, "Put together that cabinet yet?"

"Come on, give me a chance. I just bought it."

"Sure you don't need some help on it?"

"Oh, I'm sure."

"Okay. But if I can help out another way." He held up the curtains. "You know, repayment for your advice."

A sudden frown, then, "You know, Rusty, there is something . . ."

"Go ahead, name it."

"I called my Aunt Sara a while ago, trying to find out where Bobby is . . . And it's kind of strange. I mean, it's not like he checks in with his mother every day, anything like that. But she's been trying to reach him, too."

"Maybe he went away a couple days, took a vacation. Wasn't he seeing some girl in Connecticut?"

"Yes, but it seems unlike him not to tell anyone where he's going."

"I think you're making too much of it, but I'll ask around, see if anyone else has seen him or knows where he's gone."

"Thanks, I'd appreciate that. If you find anything out, call me. My number's listed." She put her hands on the bar of her carriage, wheeled it down the aisle, then stopped and turned. "Have you got a curtain rod?"

He shook his head.

She pointed to the aisle running the back of the store. "Over there, next to Complaints."

Rusty tossed the bag on the seat beside him and started up the truck, thinking about the Louise job. He still didn't know what to make of her odd specifications for the playroom— bricking the windows, soundproofing, and the rest—but even in his short building career, he had fulfilled stranger requests than that. One old Indian lady had him close off her picture window and front door so she could have a jacuzzi built into her parlor.

If Victoria wanted everything she had mentioned done, he'd have at least a good three month's worth of work. Not including cost of materials, he couldn't see it coming to less than twenty-two grand. Just the kind of house he liked to work on, too. And the best part was that the job was coming at a good time, the winter, when contracting work was at a minimum.

He wasn't quite sure what to make of Victoria, though. He'd have to have been blind not to notice the way she was coming on to him. Certainly it wasn't the first time—one of the benefits or hazards of the job, depending on how you looked at it. Women who routinely iced up in bed with their white-color husbands, salivated the next morning over a guy in a T-shirt swinging a hammer. He usually handled it by pretending he was too dense to read the invitation, and eventually, they gave up trying. Not that he wasn't tempted at times to pick up on an offer, but the last thing he needed was to involve himself in a no-win relationship.

Of course this girl wasn't exactly the typical . . . She was unmarried, at least it seemed so . . . probably his age, and he would be an ass to deny that she was attractive. But there was definitely something strange about her, almost calculating. Maybe it was the way she pressed him about the girl who had lived in the house before . . . Rosalie, that was her name. Or maybe he was just reacting to the way she had spoken to that woman, Mrs. Mills. It wasn't anything she said really. It looked to him like Victoria was really squeezing hard on her hand, but she hadn't reacted at all. It must have been his imagination.

His mind then went to Rae. For that matter, he really didn't know what to make of her either: pretty—even prettier than he remembered . . . Bright and more than a little outspoken. *Not to worry though Rusty . . . she definitely was not coming on to you.*

"I'm impressed, Rusty. Really I am. The yellow goes great with the counter, and it really brightens the kitchen. Somehow I would have expected you to pick out something gaudy . . . like red."

He gave a look of mock indignation, then having hung the curtains to his satisfaction, jumped off the stool. "Sometimes I think you just don't give me any credit."

"Well, let's face it, normally you have zero taste."

"Thanks." He opened up what served as the junk drawer, fished out a yellow lined pad, and tossed it on the kitchen table, then with a wave of his hand toward the living room, said, "I've got work to do, so how about it?"

"Okay, but before I go," she went over to the telephone and picked up the sheet of paper beside it, "you've got two messages here."

He looked up. "Business?"

"Nope." Carol raised her sweetness level two octaves and dragged on the words. "One from Elaine. Wanted to know when you'd be home. I told her I had no idea."

"Good. Who's the other from?"

"Gena. She and Mac are having a get-together tonight. They want you to come. It's at eight o'clock." Rusty picked up a pen and began to list the materials he would need for the job. "You going to go?" Carol asked.

"I don't know, I'll see. All depends on how far I get with this." He looked up. "What are your plans for tonight?"

"I'm going over to Franny's now. Later we'll probably be going to Gary Schuler's house, he's invited a bunch of kids."

"His parents going to be home?"

Silence.

"Could you speak up a bit, I couldn't catch your answer."

"Quit it, Rusty. You know as well as I do that if his parents were home, there wouldn't be a party."

"I don't want you drinking."

She tossed her head, her thick golden braid landing over one shoulder. "Not to worry. I detest the taste of beer."

"You like wine coolers though, don't you?"

"How'd you know that?"

A sly smile. "I know these things, Carol. One of the advantages brothers have over parents."

"You listened in on one of my phone conversations, right?"

"Wrong. And to go back to the beginning of this conversation—no drinking."

"Okay, okay."

"What time you plan to be home?"

"I don't know . . . about one, I guess."

"About one exactly, no later. Listen, I don't want you taking a ride with anyone who's sloshed, so if you need a lift, you call me. If I'm not here, try Mac's."

"All right." She picked up a sleeveless blue parka, put it on, then picked up her purse. "You know, Rusty, you really ought to go."

He was jotting down figures. "Where?"

A sigh. "To Mac and Gena's, of course. You're so wrapped up in work, you never seem to have fun anymore." She smiled coyly, "I know one or two senior girls I could fix you up with if you're interested. They told me they thought you had a great bod."

"Two minutes, Carol. If you're not out of here by then—" He looked up, but all he could see was the top of her braid disappearing around the corner.

Mac, who had surpassed six-feet-five by the age of fifteen, answered the door. His wide shoulders thrust forward—a habit he'd picked up years ago—as though he had never resigned himself to his height. He pushed open the storm door with one meaty hand: the fingers of his other hand were wrapped around a sweating can of Budweiser. If not for a knee injury sustained while playing basketball in his second year at Boston College, he might have made it to the pros. As it was, he settled for a business degree and a high seat in his father's Honda dealership. He greeted Russ with his usual unsmiling, sleepy-eyed stare. "Well, sonofabitch, how did we get so lucky? We were beginning to think you had become a hermit or something."

Rusty walked in, reached up, and hung an arm over Mac's shoulder. "No such luck. How's Gena doing?"

"Swell, she hasn't stopped shopping since she got pregnant. The kid's room is already equipped with everything but a hot tub. I'm afraid some encyclopedia salesman is going to get hold of her name and make a pitch."

Rusty smiled. "I noticed a basketball net over the garage. I don't suppose—"

Mac raised his hand. "For me, I swear, strictly for me."

Rusty looked out into the parlor. "So who's here?"

"I don't know, who do you want?"

"How about Bobby?"

"Nope, sorry. Gena called him a dozen times, but couldn't reach him."

Of the twenty or so people there, Rusty counted out nine from the gang he'd hung out with in high school. In fact, the group was almost intact save for three or four that had implanted themselves elsewhere since graduation. Only three had married—Mac and Gena to each other, and Brad Kagan, fresh out of law school and working for his uncle's firm, to a New Hampshire girl. In the past year Rusty had missed a number of parties, so for a while he roamed around, catching up on news and asking if anyone had seen Bobby. None had, at least not lately.

He was heading back to the bar when he heard the boisterous laugh, then spotted the bushy black mustache of Sam Regis. Rusty maneuvered through the crowd, then held out his hand. "Sammy, why is it I always hear you before I see you?"

Sam Regis laughed again as he grabbed Rusty's hand in a clinch. "Hey, rust-man. How's it hangin', guy?"

Same old Sammy. "Not bad," Rusty said. "Say, you still doing residential electrical work?"

"Sure am. Why?"

"I have a job I need done, you interested?"

Sam swept a hand over his mustache. "I'm always hustling. Whereabouts?"

"In town. The lady just moved in, one of those big old houses, and she wants it restored. It looks to me like some of the wiring is frayed. It could use circuit breakers and a new service."

"No problem. Just give me the lady's name and number, and I'll give her a call Monday."

Rusty pulled a business card and pen from his pocket, jotted down the information, and handed him the card. "Funny thing is, she bought the old Queen Anne over on Valley. You might know it—between Patterson and Greene. A girl named Rosalie lived there, she went to school with us."

"I don't remember. What did she look like?"

One arm swung out of nowhere over Sam's shoulder, another arm over Russ's. "What girl?"

"Hi, Elaine," Sam said, "how you doing?"

"Just fine," she said, staring daggers at Rusty. "Of course I would be doing much better if Rusty saw fit to return his calls." She swept her blonde curls, widened her pale blue eyes and wrinkled her nose. Just like high school, Rusty thought, only the voice seemed to have gotten shrill. Then to him she said, "What girl?"

Rusty drained his can of Bud.

"Come on, who?"

"Rosalie. Can't remember her last name. We went to a party there once." Elaine waited for more. "On the quiet side. She kept pretty much to herself."

"Oh . . . yeah, now I remember," she said. "Rosalie Salino. She was really fat, not very good looking. She didn't say much, but when she did, it sounded like a fingernail scraping a blackboard. A really sad case. So what about her?"

"Nothing. Just that I'm doing a job at the house she used to live in." A slight pause then, "Say Elaine, have you seen Bobby around?"

"No, why?"

"No reason, just trying to get in touch with him." Then, "If you'll excuse me . . ." He ducked away to the bar where Mac was mixing a drink. Mac looked at him and shrugged. "Sorry, I know the girl bugs you, but Gena insists on inviting her."

"No big deal." He took another can of Bud and tore off the tin seal, then glanced at Gena's sizable belly as she made her way to the kitchen. "I don't know, Mac, I'd say it looks like twins."

"Can't afford 'em. I'm hoping it's one solid center. Like his old man."

"Ruuusty!" He turned toward the kitchen where Gena was pointing toward the telephone receiver slung over her shoulder. "For you," she mouthed.

Rusty glanced at his watch—not twelve yet—as he went to retrieve the phone.

"Why don't you give Elaine a chance, Rusty," Gena said, covering the mouthpiece with her hand. "She's still wild about you. And you always made such a cute couple. Everyone always expected—"

He held out his hand. "Please Gena . . . the phone."

She sighed. "You guys . . ." She handed him the receiver and walked away, closing the kitchen door behind her.

He put the phone to his ear. "Yeah?"

Hesitantly, "That you, Rusty?"

"Carol, what's the matter?"

"Nothing."

"Where are you?"

"Home."

"Did something happen?"

"No, nothing. The party was lousy so Franny and I left early."

"Okay. Then what's wrong, you sound funny."

"Franny's here with me. I wanted to ask you if she could stay the night."

"No."

"Oh, please, Rusty. We'll be quiet, I promise. You won't even hear us."

"Forget it. I told you before, I don't want to wake up in the morning and have to deal with giggling girls."

Silence.

"Are you still there, Carol?"

"I'm scared to stay here by myself, Rusty."

"Scared . . . what are you talking about?"

"Well, I didn't want to say anything about it." Rusty waited. "But when I left here earlier, there was a blue car out front. I didn't think much of it then."

"Go on."

"Well, when Franny was driving me home, I saw the same car again, at least I thought it was the same car. It was blue anyway. Franny and I thought it might be following us." She swallowed hard. "When Franny stopped to let me off, it stopped, too. Not right in front of our house, further up the street. So she came in with me."

"Look and see if the car's still there."

"Just a sec," then away from the receiver, "see if it's there now, Franny." A few moments passed . . .

"Carol, you there?"

Finally back to the phone, "She doesn't see it, Rusty. It must have left. Well, can she stay?"

A sigh. "Okay, but tell her to call her parents first. I'll be home in a while."

"You don't have to leave on my account. With Franny here, I'll be fine."

"Are you sure?"

"Yeah . . . don't worry."

He put down the phone. It was probably just their imaginations, a couple of girls scaring the wits out of each other, each playing on the other's fears. Even so, something didn't feel right. First he and Carol had gotten those weird phone calls and now this . . .

He went to the foyer, grabbed his jacket from the closet and headed out the front door.

"Rusty . . . wait!" Elaine caught up to him on the front lawn. "Where're you going?"

"Home."

She slid her arms up his chest and around his neck. "Come on, stay a while. The night's still young, we'll have some fun."

He freed her hands from his neck. "Sorry, I've gotta go."

Her hands slid around him again. "Take me with you then."

He stared at her for a minute, then held her, his hands sliding down to her waist. "Can I ask you something?"

She rubbed her body up close to him and nuzzled her nose in his neck. "Sure, Rusty, anything."

"And you'll give me a straight answer?"

"Of course."

"Have you been making phone calls to my house, hanging up when my kid sister answers?"

Her hands dropped away. "Fuck you, Rusty!"

CHAPTER FIVE

VICTORIA laid across her bed, the doll at her side, staring at the picture in front of her. Then she closed her eyes and relied only on her memory . . . Always Elaine's face came first to mind . . . it was for her that she reserved her deepest hate.

It was understandable that mama would think of inviting them to the birthday party. Rosalie had talked about the crowd so much, pretended so much, that mama had been convinced that they *were* really Rosalie's friends . . . And because Rosalie had expected only mama, Mrs. Mills and a few of mama's cronies to show up—just like her every other birthday party—she had worn the silly, pink, lacy dress mama had bought her special for the occasion.

The first face she saw when she entered the basement was Elaine's . . . then the others . . . And they were all yelling, "Surprise!"

"So say something," Mama said finally, searching Rosalie's face for an appropriate response.

"I don't understand," she said quietly to mama.

"What is not to understand?" Then pushing her toward the others who were all dressed in tight jeans and fashionable sweaters, she said, "Go to your friends, have fun. I'll be upstairs getting the pizza ready."

And then mama was gone, and she was facing Elaine. "Hey I like that dress, Rosalie," Elaine said fingering the lace on the sleeves. "Did your mama make it for you?"

Silence.

"Say something, Rosalie. What is this—we come here to party with you and you can't even talk to us?"

A big swallow. "I didn't mean . . . Thank you." The minute

she said the words she realized how dumb they sounded, but she couldn't take them back.

"What are you thanking me for?"

She could feel her face getting hotter. She shrugged. "You know . . . for coming here."

Elaine turned to the others, giggling. "Hear that, you guys— Rosalie wants to thank us for coming here." Then turning back to her. "No problem at all. Hey, you have any records?"

She nodded.

"Good . . . go get them. We need to put some life into this party."

Rosalie headed toward the back of the cellar to get the records, but not before she heard Roxanne say to Elaine, "I still don't know what we're doing here."

"Trust me, it'll be a lot of laughs."

"When're we gonna give her the presents."

"Later . . . First let's loosen her up some."

"Where's Rusty?"

"Some kind of recital for his sister. Don't worry, he'll be here."

Elaine turned to the other kids. "Hey, let's have a drink. Mac just added a secret ingredient to that fruit punch."

Rusty . . . he would be coming here too. Was it possible that they really did want to be her friends?

Victoria opened her eyes and stared at Elaine's face pushed right up against Rusty's in the photograph. Elaine still liked him, but it was clear, his feelings were no longer the same. Victoria had seen it herself from the car . . . She had followed Rusty to Mac's, left, then got back in time to see them together. She looked at the doll. "I wonder how Elaine handles rejection? By the expression on her face tonight, I don't suppose too well."

She thought then of the girl who was living with Rusty . . . she had gotten a good look at her, too. She was blonde . . . nice features, just like Elaine's. And young, too—in fact, much too young for Rusty. She was just going to have to do something to convince that girl how wrong the situation between them was.

Rusty belonged to her . . . She had waited patiently, and now it was her turn.

Victoria stood up, took off her clothes and slipped into a nightgown, then got into bed, pulling the covers up over her and the doll. She ran her fingers through its hair, trying to unsnarl it. "I'm totally exhausted, Rosalie," Victoria said to the doll. "What with all the things I had to do today, then getting Bobby ready . . ."

Bobby had been more trouble than she'd expected. She had guessed his thrashing about was just a simple matter of boredom, him being the first guest to arrive. No one liked to be first, but unfortunately someone had to be. To stop his complaining, though, she'd had to stuff the sockball back into his mouth. It apparently worked because he looked calmer when she left him.

"Ouch! Damnit, now I've done it!" She leaned over and drew a tissue from the box on her nightstand and pressed it against her lip, then pulled it away, examining it. Blood, she had drawn blood. She stared at the red blotch on the tissue, then switched off the lamp and snuggled up against the doll. She'd have to watch herself. The last thing she needed before the party was a bunch of sores and bruises messing up her lip.

Suddenly Victoria's mind directed itself to the old woman she had met on the bus. Why was she thinking about *her* now? When her thoughts flitted like that, it frightened her.

Mrs. Mills crept away from the door. Who could she have been talking to? Just a sentence or two, only enough to make the woman stop and notice on her way upstairs. But now it had quieted and the light had been turned off.

Agnes grabbed onto the banister and started up the next flight of stairs. She supposed it wasn't all that unusual. After all, people did occasionally talk to themselves, especially when they were lonely. But Victoria just didn't seem the type to her. What would a girl that good-looking and that at ease with people know about loneliness?

Agnes had suffered it when she was young, and so had

Rosalie. But no matter how much Agnes had tried to give the girl the benefit of her experience, to convince her that someday if she stopped trying so hard to win friends, her time would come, it never worked. Rosalie was persistent and impatient—she was determined to fit in right then.

The woman stopped on the landing, and looked down again at the closed door, then turned and climbed the remaining stairs to her room . . . She looked around at the photographs still covering the walls. Somehow she hadn't been able to bring herself to take them down yet. But time was running out . . . tomorrow she was leaving. She went over to the large photograph of Alex Salino in full police lieutenant regalia hanging over her bed and pulled out the tack fastening it. Then she went along the room, scooping up all the others. Of Rosalie and her father.

Rusty could tell his friends were wasted the moment he entered the room. That is, all except the girl named Rosalie, sitting silently and stiffly in the center of the circle opening the presents. A forced smile stretched her mouth into a tight line. The others were laughing . . . Sammy wriggling on the floor clutching his stomach as though it was about to roll off; Mac tossing jump-shots with the crumpled balls of wrapping paper. Rusty had known they were to bring joke gifts, but apparently they had gone overboard.

He looked down at the gifts now littering the cement floor around Rosalie: a giant-size panty girdle, a T-shirt with a picture of Porky Pig, a Halloween makeup kit, a king-size lunch box, a package of Odor-Eaters, a rubber cockroach . . . And the picture now unrolled like a scroll in her hands—clearly Bobby's handiwork: a caricature of Rosalie, exaggerating her beak nose and shapeless body.

"Rusty you're finally here! Hey you guys," Elaine called out over the laughter, "Rusty's here!"

"Where the hell you been?" Mac slurred.

All eyes focused on him, including Rosalie's. He quickly slid

*the tiny package of skunk perfume into his jeans pocket, then
nodded to Rosalie.*

No response.

*"Come look at the pisser presents Rosalie's got here," Millie
yelled out. Elaine picked up the girdle and leaned over, holding
it to Rosalie's waist. "How do you think this will do?" she asked
him.*

Rosalie swatted Elaine's hand away from her.

*"Hey, watch it there . . . what are you doing? Don't yu like
my present? I think it's real foxy." Elaine held the girdle up to
herself and began to swing her hips. "A teensie weensie big for
me maybe . . ." Someone turned up the music and Elaine
danced a circle around Rosalie, the panties flapping against her
thighs.*

*"Quit it!" Rusty called out, but by then it was too late. The
others joined into the bizarre dance, some stumbling over their
own feet, toppling onto the floor in fits of drunken laughter.*

*Suddenly Rosalie stood up. "Get out of here!" she screamed,
tears falling from beneath the rims of her glasses. "I hate you
all! Do you hear me . . . I hate you! Do you hear me?"*

Rusty's hand shot up, coming in contact with the lamp on
the end table. It toppled over, onto the floor. He got out of bed,
picked it up and switched it on, then ran his arm over his wet
brow.

A whisper. "Rusty?"

He turned around. "Yeah, Carol?"

"I heard the noise. What happened?"

"I was thinking, dreaming . . . I knocked the lamp over acci-
dently. Hope I didn't wake up your friend, too."

She came over to the sofa bed and sat down. "Don't worry,
she's still snoring away. Are you okay?"

"I'm fine. Go back to bed."

"What was the dream about, Rusty?"

"Nothing important. You know how those things are, you
forget them the minute you wake up. Come on now, get back
to bed."

Carol lingered a moment, then turned and went back to her room. Rusty switched off the lamp and laid back down. When he had gotten home last night, the girls had been braiding each other's hair—a million and one braids jutting out in all directions from their heads. He had questioned them about the mystery car, but both girls insisted it was probably just their imaginations. They had seen *Friday the Thirteenth,* sequel ninety-nine, only a week ago, "And maybe thinking about that. Besides, the car is gone now, so what's the big deal?"

A couple of crank phone calls, a blue car seen twice, a buddy who probably went off on an unplanned vacation, and a strange girl living in a house he'd once been to. And here he was having nightmares about some stupid incident out of the past . . . What the hell was the matter with him?

Rae Lemkin had awakened at about two o'clock and hadn't been able to fall back to sleep. Before she had gone to bed, she'd hung the new bookshelves, arranged the books on them, and drank a gallon of coffee. She had also tried Bobby's number at least five more times.

Actually Aunt Sara hadn't seemed all that worried. Maybe it was because Bobby was the youngest child of eight . . . Having that many children did it to you, Rae supposed. You either stayed loose or turned into a full-blown neurotic by the age of forty. And after all, a twenty-four-year old, a fully grown adult, missing for a few days was not exactly cause for alarm.

Sara's sister Rochelle, Rae's mother, had been totally the opposite.Quick, imaginative, and fun, but always wary of the dangers that might be lurking out there for little girls. As fearless as mom was for herself, when it came to Rae, it was different. She believed in the buddy system all the way: you didn't go up the street alone after dark, and you never dared swim— even in an above-ground swimming pool at the age of thirteen—without her being close by. But to be fair to mom, she was a single parent doing her best to bring up an only child. That is, until she was struck with leukemia and died a year later at age thirty-eight, and Rae had come to live with Aunt Sara.

Rae wondered if she'd be able to be as mellow a mother as her aunt, or would she tend to be strict, suspicious and super-cautious? She sighed. Already the signs weren't too encouraging. Maybe the solution was to have eight children. My god . . . what *was* she thinking? She didn't even have a relationship yet, let alone marriage prospects.

All through college she had dated very little—always too busy with studies or trying to support herself, waitressing as many hours as she could squeeze into her schedule. And when she was out of school, she was too "into" her new career to care much about dating. But she did get asked out, and occasionally she did go . . . But not once did any of those dates amount to any real involvement: either her initial interest in the guy would dwindle quickly or she'd manage to scare him away by saying something that would have been better left unsaid. Diplomacy was not her strong suit.

She stood up, went into the bedroom, and tore open the cardboard box containing the stereo cabinet. She had about four hours to go until her shift at the hospital began. And she wasn't about to waste that time worrying needlessly while her cousin Bobby was probably living it up somewhere with that girl from Connecticut.

CHAPTER SIX

ICTORIA leafed through the pages of the black book till she came to a page entitled Elaine Gray. It was a page she had reviewed many times. Some of the notations were crossed out, only to be replaced with new information. Like a running resumé.

The Bradley *Sun* held little resemblance to the pages of the New York *Times*. In fact, the *Sun* wasn't really much of anything, that is, if you were interested in hard news. But that wasn't why Victoria had continued to subscribe to the paper all these years—even when she was in New York. It was the type of weekly that concentrated on local stories: who'd been accepted to college; what new businesses had been established in town; results of beauty pageants. Seldom a week would go by that Victoria hadn't found at least one tidbit of information to keep her updated on the lives of her classmates.

Only six months ago, Elaine had opened her own boutique in a shopping plaza in Cranston, less than five miles from Bradley and right over the New Hampshire boarder. Elaine—of the girls, chosen best dressed and best partier of the senior class—had been ruler of fashion and fun at Bradley High. So her opening a boutique came as no surprise to Victoria.

Victoria closed the book and slid it away into her nightstand drawer. There were no Sunday blue laws in New Hampshire—today would be a good day to visit *Lanees*. She went into the shower and turned on the faucets: the hot water flowed full force, followed by a trickle of cold. There was nothing like a scalding shower to rub the bad feelings away. Not that she had those feelings often—she prided herself on positive thinking—but last night, dredging up all those memories had made it seem like she was Rosalie all over again . . .

A sudden realization brightened her mood. Today Mrs. Mills was finally leaving. She mustn't forget to say goodbye.

Rusty had just hung up the phone when Carol came in. "Who you trying to call?"

"No one you know. Besides she's not in."

"A she?"

Rusty went to the refrigerator, took out some ham, onions, tomatoes, zucchini, cheese, eggs, and butter and set them on the counter. "What you see here is the beginning of a new Erlich super omelet," he said. "Want some? If you do, tell me now."

"The combination looks gross. Come on, Rusty, who were you calling?"

"Rae Lemkin. You happy now that you know?"

"Hmmm. I didn't know there was a woman in your life. In fact, when I spoke to daddy, I told him just the opposite."

Rusty took down a bowl and cracked three eggs into it. "There isn't. And when did you speak to mom and dad?"

"Yesterday. Who's Rae Lemkin and why're you calling her?"

"She's trying to find Bobby, he's her cousin. Okay? Now what did mom and dad have to say?"

"Nothing much. Daddy wanted to know if you were behaving yourself, if you were hanging out in bars, that kind of thing."

"Sounds like one of dad's questions."

"Don't be so sensitive, Rusty."

Rusty dropped pieces of ham, cheese and the vegetables into the eggs, then poured it all into a buttered frying pan. "What else did he want to know?"

"Oh, how your business was coming along."

"What did you tell him?"

"That it was coming along fine. I'm a good liar."

Rusty smiled at her. "Well, if you're a good liar, you must have convinced him that you're behaving yourself here."

Carol nodded. "Certainly. How could he think otherwise."

Franny walked into the kitchen—her short brown straight hair, pug nose and pudgy smiling face reminiscent of Buster Brown. "Yum . . . what is that fantastic thing I smell?" she said. "It woke me out of a sound sleep."

Rusty looked at Franny, then at his omelet. "Forget it, this is taken. There're supplies in the refrigerator if you want to make one." With that, he poured the omelet onto the plate and carried it into the living room, where he settled into an easy chair.

Carol called to him from the kitchen, "Rusty, why is Rae looking for Bobby?"

"Why not?"

"I mean, why can't she find him . . . is he missing or something?"

Silence, then, "Carol, have you had any more of those crank calls?"

"Why?"

"I just want to know."

"I don't see why it's such—"

"Dammit Carol, it's a simple question. Just answer it."

"No I haven't. God—no need to go into a fit."

A bell sounded when the door opened, and Elaine looked up, smiled, then walked to the front of the store to greet Victoria. "Good morning," she said.

Ignoring Elaine, Victoria studied the outfitted mannequin near the entrance. "Nice," she said finally. "Though I think pearls would go better with that black silk than rhinestones. Don't you agree?"

Elaine stood there, her head turning from Victoria to the mannequin, and back. Finally she laughed. "Well, yeah. You might have a point." Then, "Can I help you?"

"I hope so. I'm looking for something special, but I'm not quite sure what."

"Day or evening wear?"

"Evening. Something elegant but casual. Something that will get noticed, if you know what I mean."

Elaine shook her curls and her smile grew fuller. "I think I have just the thing." She studied her a moment, appraising her. "I'd guess a size nine . . . am I right?"

Victoria nearly said size twenty-four but caught herself in time. She nodded.

"Come here, I'll show you. Elaine led Victoria to a rack and began to slide hangers across it, then plucked a vivid blue silk jumpsuit off and held it up. "Take a look at this, it just arrived. The color is perfect for you, and it's so chic." It had winged long sleeves, no waistline, but a matching rope belt that separated the top from the flowing pants. "What's the occasion?" Elaine asked.

"I'm hosting a party."

"Oh how nice. Come on, try it on, I'm dying to see how it looks. I have a knack for picking out just the right thing . . . you know, to play up a woman's good points. Of course, you're easy. Some gals . . ." She groaned and gazed at the ceiling. "Well, you know what I'm saying."

"What you really mean is, some people look a mess no matter what they put on. You and I, on the other hand, are a designer's dream."

Elaine's mouth dropped open. "You certainly are direct, aren't you? I don't know if I'd go that far, but it is a problem trying to fit some women." Then with a nod at the garment, "Go on, try it on."

It did look great—Elaine oohed and aahed over her. Finally Victoria changed back into the clothes she wore in and carried the outfit up to the register. "You really have been helpful, this will be perfect."

"Well I'm so glad. Trust me, your guests won't be able to take their eyes off you. Especially the gentlemen."

"Do you really think so?"

"Absolutely. Now will this be cash or charge?"

"Check." Victoria opened her purse and took out the few loose checks she had gotten from the bank. "The problem is I just recently moved to the area, and my checks aren't properly printed yet. I do have a new Massachusetts driver's license though for identification. One of those perfectly gruesome pictures, of course." She pulled out her pictured license and placed it on the counter.

Elaine looked at it. "Not so bad, mine's even worse. Bradley, huh? That's where I'm from." Then, "You say you just moved there?"

Victoria nodded. "From New York."

"Wow, quite a change. Well, how do you like living in the sticks?"

"Actually I like it. The city can be exciting, but eventually it gets to you. Too much filth and crime mixed in with the glamour."

"I can imagine. Tell me, do you have any family here?"

"No, and not many friends either. Oh, I've managed to meet a few people, mostly neighbors and business acquaintances. I figure this party I'm throwing will get me into the swing of things. If there's one thing I know how to do, it's throw a good party."

"It sounds to me like you're just what Bradley needs. Someone to get people off their duffs."

"Really?"

"Small-town people have a tendency to have small-town parties. Basically boring."

Victoria laughed. "You know, I just had an idea."

"What is it?"

"First of all, why don't you tell me your name?"

"Oh, of course." She put out her hand. "Forgive me. The name's Elaine Gray."

"Forgiven. Listen Elaine Gray, how does a little partying sound to you? You're just the type of person I delight in squeezing onto my guest list."

Mrs. Mills had carted every one of the twelve boxes down the street herself . . . in just as many trips. Although Victoria had been kind enough to carry the boxes downstairs for her, she hadn't offered to transport them any farther. And Agnes had far too much pride to ask.

She had left the bedroom furniture at the house; she wasn't about to be accused of taking what wasn't hers to take. Now she looked around at the tiny apartment that consisted of little more than a single bed, two floor lamps, three red plastic-covered chairs, a formica-topped table and a wood dresser minus knobs. It wouldn't be easy getting used to, not after the spacious, familiar house she just left behind.

First things first. She pushed the photograph box to the wall, then one of the chairs. She scooped out a handfull of pictures and tacks, then climbed onto the chair, pressing one hand against the wall for balance. Once these were up it would look more like home.

Rusty parked the truck in front of the triple story. Bobby lived on the top floor, one large attic room that served also as his studio. He looked up the long driveway—two cars were there, one a 1979 Chevy, Bobby's car. Quickly he went up the two flights and knocked. Nothing.

"Bobby . . . it's me, Rusty," he called out.

Still nothing.

He banged louder. "If you're there Bobby, open up."

Finally he walked down a flight and knocked on the door. A skinny, greasy-faced kid with dark vacant eyes opened it. "Yeah?"

"I'm looking for the manager. Do you know where I can find him?"

"Pop!" the kid called out.

Aside from a stubble of beard and striped suspenders that hiked up his loose-fitting jeans, the father was a replica of the son. "What's the matter?" he said.

"You the manager?"

He nodded.

"I'm Russ Erlich, a friend of Bob Cole's."

The man didn't blink an eye.

"You know, the guy who lives upstairs. The studio apartment."

"Sure I know. Whatdaya think I'm stupid, I don't know who lives here?"

"Well, I'm looking for him. Some friends of his have been trying to reach him."

"So what do you want from me?"

"Well, I noticed his car's outside, the 79 Chevy. It seems to me, if his car's here, he ought to be here too."

"So go knock on his door."

"I did that, and there's no answer. I'd like you to use your master key, let me take a look inside."

"Listen, don't bother me. The guy pays his rent, so I don't nose into his business. You come back another time, maybe he'll be home then." He began to close the door, but Rusty caught it and pushed it back open.

"Look I didn't want to cause you any grief, so I came here first by myself."

The guy stared at him.

"The next time, I don't come alone. I bring the police along with me."

"What're you looking for—drugs?"

Rusty shook his head. "I just want to see if anyone's in there. That's it. I take a look, then leave."

There was a moment of hesitation, then the man scooped up a key ring from a hook near the door and led the way upstairs. He slipped a key ring in the lock, then glanced at Rusty. "I don't want you touching nothin', you hear?"

Rusty nodded.

The door opened, the manager switched on the light and they both looked around: no signs of Bobby. The muscles that had tightened in Rusty's stomach now relaxed. He wasn't quite sure what he had expected to find . . . signs of a fight, his friend on the floor unconscious . . . Whatever his mind had conjured up, thank god, it was wrong.

"Okay, you saw," the guy said. "Now you leave."

Rusty walked over to the desk near the front windows. The phone sat in a pile of crumpled papers, doodling and cartoon characters at the edgings. One paper was set aside from the pile. It read, 10/22 . . . portrait.

CHAPTER SEVEN

WHEN Rusty rang Victoria's doorbell at eight Monday morning, she came to the door in a pink nightgown. He handed her a four-page stapled estimate, the top sheet headed: R&E Construction. "Listen, I'm sorry, I didn't mean to get you up. Why don't I just leave this for you to look over, then I'll get back to you this evening so we can talk about it."

She opened the storm door wider. "Oh, that's not necessary. Now's fine."

Rusty stepped in. The short-sleeved gown was even more sheer than he had thought at first glance. His eyes were drawn immediately to dark nipples showing through the filmy material.

"Why don't we go sit down," she said gesturing to the parlor.

He looked into her eyes, then cleared his throat, heading for the parlor. "I think you'll find that the prices are right in line. If you'd like, you can get a second estimate to compare it to. Some people do that."

Victoria sat, skimming through the pages, then looked up. Rusty was pacing in front of the bay window. "You're not much of a salesman, are you?" she said.

He stopped and turned. "I guess not. But I do like my customers to know that they're getting a fair price."

"Oh, I trust you. I did the moment I saw you."

"Yeah . . . why?"

"Instincts. I usually go with them."

He crossed his arms at his chest and stared at her. "People have been known to get burnt that way. Maybe you ought to try a more scientific method. Check the prices out."

She laid down the sheets on her lap. "Uh-uh. I'll stick to this method. When can you get started?"

"Did you take a look at the payment schedule?"

She nodded. "I'll write the first check for you now."

He shrugged. "Okay, fine. What about Wednesday? I'm just finishing off a porch. I ought to be done tomorrow morning."

"Then what about the afternoon?"

"All right, Tuesday it is. I thought I'd start with the outside, get some things done before the real cold weather hits."

"No, I want the playroom done first."

"If I could have just a week outside, I'd be able to—"

"No . . . the playroom. When can it be ready?"

He thought about it a minute. "Three weeks."

"That's too long, I want it sooner."

"The only way I could get it done sooner is to get a helper in. But that'll jack up the price."

"I don't want strangers here. What about working overtime? I'm willing to pay the extra cost."

Silence, staring, then, "With overtime it'll be done in less than two weeks. Does that satisfy you?"

She smiled. "I don't mean to give you a hard time, but the playroom is really important to me. And I'm counting on you to make it perfect." She stood up, took a check out of her purse, and made it out to R&E Construction, then handed it to Rusty.

Subtlely definitely wasn't her strong suit. He hoped she didn't plan to traipse around the house clothed like that every day or he wouldn't have a chance in hell of getting that playroom done on schedule. The strange thing was, as seductive as she looked, there was something almost treacherous about her . . . And what did that remark mean, not wanting strangers in the house . . . what the hell was he?

Rusty stopped at Dunkin Donuts. He got a crueller and coffee and headed toward the phone booth, then dropping change in the slot, dialed Rae's number. She picked up on the second ring."

"Rae, this is Rusty."

"Hi, I'm kind of glad you called."

"I did try to get you yesterday."

"Sundays I work till three. After my shift, I rode over to Bobby's apartment. He wasn't there, but his car was. I went home, then I began to imagine all sorts of things, that maybe he was stuck in the apartment, sick or hurt and couldn't get to the phone. I was up half the night worrying."

"Well, you can stop. I had the manager open Bobby's apartment for me, and he wasn't there. Everything looked normal enough. The only thing I can think of is that he *did* take a vacation and maybe flew."

"But wouldn't he have taken his car to the airport?"

"Unless he got a ride so he could save parking costs."

"Yeah, I suppose."

"You don't sound convinced."

"I'm not."

A pause, then, "Listen, if you're not busy tonight, why don't I stop by. Maybe if we put our heads together, we could come up with some answers."

Silence, then, "Okay, but you're not going to ask to put together that stereo cabinet, are you?"

Rusty smiled. "Stereo cabinet . . . what stereo cabinet?"

Victoria took the bottle of Noctec from her drawer, the sleeping pills the doctor had prescribed after her surgery. She had gotten two refills plus the one she had never used, making three in all. It had taken only three pills and ten minutes to put Bobby under, but Sammy was bigger . . .

She unscrewed the cap and poured out five green capsules. With a pin, she punctured the gelatinous covering and squeezed the clear liquid into a cup, then set it on the nightstand. Finally she slid the cardboard box from her closet floor and pulled up the flaps, her eyes going immediately to her father's favorite pistol—the one he had been issued when he became a police officer. No, she was sure she wouldn't need that—at least, not now. She picked up a pair of handcuffs from her father's collection and several yards of rope, then brought it all downstairs. Guest number two would be arriving shortly . . .

Sam Regis stopped his van in front of the Queen Anne on Seventeen Valley. He glanced into the rear-view mirror, running his thick fingers through his mustache, then his bush of curly hair. Though he had always hated having all that hair—even so thick on his body that the girls had secretly nicknamed him "Gorilla"—nowadays he was beginning to appreciate it. A lot of young guys—Bobby for one—were beginning to run short on hair. He slid out of the front seat, aware of the few extra pounds on his body. Only six, seven years ago, he was in top shape, one of the best high school wrestlers in the state. Now look at him . . . only twenty-four, and he was letting his muscles turn to mush. Maybe he'd start working out in one of those spas . . .

He went up to the porch and rang the bell. He did remember this house. And the party Rusty had mentioned to Elaine . . . As he recalled, it was a real bad scene . . . the whole bunch of them had acted like animals, making the girl feel like shit . . . The door opened and the memories of the party passed immediately. He sucked in his breath—a great-looking lady . . . in a nightgown.

"You must be Sam Regis, the electrician," she said.

That sonofabitch Russ, he didn't warn him. "Yes, ma'am," he said, staring at her.

"Come in." She pushed the door open. "Victoria will do just fine."

He crammed his finger between his neck and shirt collar, then stretching his neck and clearing his throat. "As I said on the phone, Russ Erlich asked me to check over the fuse box and wiring."

"Come this way." She led the way to the kitchen. "I was just having some coffee. You'll join me, won't you?"

"Well, uh, I don't know. I—"

She laughed softly, turning toward the counter—the soft

material of her nightie fanning around her thighs. She picked up the cup, poured the coffee in, then brushing up close to him, put it into his hand. "Come on, sit a minute and talk to me."

He took the cup, set it on the table, then laid his hands on her shoulders. Jesus shit, he was sweating like a pig. "You know, you are some beautiful lady. Maybe we can," he began, but she laid a finger against his lips, smiling.

"There's a sofa downstairs. Old but comfortable. But first things first—I want to get to know you. Besides, rumor has it, these things are even better when you have to wait a little."

It was like some fuckin' fantasy, she must be one of those nymphos—the kind he heard about and read about, but never actually had the good fortune to meet. "Sure . . . of course, whatever you say," he said, then sat across from her and picked up his coffee cup. "What'll we talk about?"

Mondays were slow for the boutique. Elaine had fussed around, sprucing up the showcases and windows for the past hour, even exchanging the rhinestones for the pearls on the mannequin. As much as she loved the opportunity to be working with fashion, she hated the boredom that set in when there was no one around to chat with.

Her thoughts turned to Rusty. Damn him . . . he was being so stubborn. No matter what she did, he refused to see her. Male pride. When they had broken up shortly after high school it was mostly her doing—after all, she did need the freedom to know other guys. She remembered how often her father tried to drum that into her head, but how she ignored his advice right through high school. The fact was that Elaine had snagged the best-looking guy in the school—where does one go from there? Except for one indiscretion in high school, it wasn't until she graduated and experienced that intense feeling of power—the sky was the limit—that she decided to fool around with other men.

As soon as she got a taste of what was out there, she came running back to Rusty. But by then it was too late. Not that she had much competition . . . as far as she knew, aside for an occasional date, he saw no one. He spent most of his time building his business and now worrying about his kid sister. Well, Elaine wasn't about to give up on him. Sooner or later, he'd come to his senses and come back to her.

In the meantime, what she needed was some excitement. Now. She went to the Rolodex where she kept the names, addresses and phone numbers of her customers. She turned the cards till she came to Louise, then dialed. What the hell . . . Victoria Louise seemed to have more style then all her friends put together. And she *had* asked her to the party . . .

The phone had rung seven times before Victoria got to it. "Hello," she said, her heart pounding and her voice breathless.

"Where were you, I was just about to hang up."

Silence.

"Victoria, it's me, Elaine. You remember . . . from the boutique."

"Of course, of course . . . How are you?"

"A little bored, but fine. You sound out of breath . . . did I take you away from something?"

"No, I was finished."

"With what?"

"Oh, it was nothing important. You surprised me, that's all. I didn't expect to hear from you."

"Why not? After all, one good turn deserves another. You invited me to a party so I thought the least I could do is invite you out for a drink, show you the town. Such as it is."

Silence.

"Victoria . . . are you there?"

"Sure, I'm here."

"Well, what do you say?"

A pause, then, "Sure . . . why not? It sounds great."

"Good. For a minute there, I thought I had the wrong number."

"Not at all. In fact, I'm looking forward to seeing you. It's not often I find someone I connect with so easily. Most people find me a bit bizarre."

Elaine laughed. "I'll bet. What about the Ninety-Nine Club, it's a pretty decent nightspot. About sevenish. It's right up on route 208, next to—"

"Never mind, if it's there, I'll find it."

Victoria put down the receiver. What horrible timing. She hadn't even had a second to think about it. Did she really want to go out with Elaine? It certainly hadn't been in her plan. But no matter what Victoria thought about the girl, there was no denying the fact that they had something in common. After all, they both loved Rusty.

She looked at her hands . . . there was blood on them—she hadn't meant to hit Sammy *that* hard. She'd just wanted to find a way to knock him out when the doctored coffee had failed to do its job. Suddenly, as if in a dream, her hand had reached for the nightstick and, the next moment, it was coming down on Sammy's head.

Mrs. Mills had been gazing out the window, watching the passersby, when she saw Victoria coming out and get into the van parked in front. It wasn't Victoria's, she was sure of that. Why the girl had gotten a new blue Honda no more than a week ago. But still, she must have been given a key to the van because she started it right up. Maybe she had borrowed it from a friend.

When the girl drove off, Agnes came downstairs and crossed the street. She walked to the house and looked up at her old bedroom window, then down to Victoria's window. What was that sitting on the windowsill? She squinted . . . No, her eyes surely weren't getting any younger. No matter how hard she tried, she couldn't make out what it was . . .

CHAPTER EIGHT

VICTORIA slipped on a red knit pullover, then standing in front of the full-length mirror, hooked black hoops into her ears. She glanced at the doll. "Elaine wants to be friends, Rosalie. Can you imagine that?" Victoria began to remember times Elaine ignored Rosalie, never betraying a sign she even existed. There was that one particular time when Elaine and Rusty had passed down the corridor . . .

As it always did, Rosalie's heart had seemed to skip a beat. She had stopped, staring at Rusty, not even noticing that she was standing right in their path. Not until his foot had smashed into her leg and she had fallen back onto the polished hardwood floor, her books flying out of her arms, papers sailing from her looseleaf. "I'm sorry," he had said.

Elaine had sighed, and as if Rosalie weren't even there or just deaf and dumb, said, "It was her own fault, Rusty. She was just standing there like a klutz, waiting to be knocked over."

Rosalie hadn't known what to say and even if she had, her throat was so locked, she knew the words would never come out.

"Here . . . let me help you," Rusty had said. He'd taken hold of her hands and began to pull her up.

"Watch it—you'll pull a muscle for Saturday's game, Rusty," Elaine had put in.

But Rusty had lifted her with ease and then crouched down on his knees and begun to retrieve her papers.

"Rusty, would you leave it. The bell's going to ring, we're going to be late for class," Elaine had warned.

But Rusty had continued picking up the papers long after Elaine had left . . . Rosalie would always remember that.

* * *

Rusty pressed the bell.

"Who's there?"

"Me, Rusty."

"Hold on." He waited a moment, heard the buzz, then opened the door and went up the stairwell. She was wearing jeans, a baggy sweater and her hair was tied in a pony tail. "Come on in," Rae said, leading him inside.

He looked around the room, and noticing the bookshelves, leaned over to inspect the wall bracket. "Nice job," he said, smiling.

"Thanks," she said. "I think so, too. Can I get you something, a drink maybe?"

He shook his head, then glanced into the bedroom at the pile of wood, screws, nuts and caps littering the floor.

Rae rushed over and closed the bedroom door. "I haven't been in the right frame of mind yet."

Rusty shrugged. "Did I ask?"

"No, I guess not," then, "come on, sit down."

Rae sat and Rusty followed suit. "I asked around about Bobby," he began, "but no one has seen him. I assume you've talked to your family?"

"Today I called most of my cousins, Bobby's brothers and sisters. Jack, his oldest brother, told me something interesting."

"What's that?"

She hesitated, then, "Well, according to Jack, Bobby pulled this once before. It seems a few years ago while I was in nursing school he took off for a few weeks without mentioning a word to anyone. He needed some time to be alone. The creative spirit needing space . . . something like that."

"Where'd he go?"

"He drove up to Vermont."

Rusty pressed his lips together.

"I know what you're thinking."

"Yeah, what's that?"

"Why didn't he drive this time?"

"You said it, not me. I really don't know if that means any-thing. After all, he might have decided to see another part of the country. Maybe even Mexico. In fact, I remember him once talking about doing a painting of a bullfight."

Suddenly she smiled. "You know something, now that I think of it, after graduation from high school he talked a lot about traveling. But of course, he didn't have much money. Unless, he went the hobo route . . ."

"How close were you with him, Rae? I knew you lived with his family, but I seldom saw you around."

"Well, until we graduated, not very. In fact, we did our best to stay out of each other's way."

"Why was that?"

Rae shrugged. "We were different types."

"What does that mean?"

"Look Rusty, I don't see the point of going into this. It's history."

"No tell me, I'm curious. After all, I was Bobby's closest friend in high school. What type are we talking about here?"

"Oh, I don't know . . . I guess, well, the type of person who acts and thinks as part of a unit. If it's not the group philosophy, it doesn't exist."

"I see. Then we're not just talking about Bobby here, are we?"

"I guess not."

"I take it you've always prided yourself on being a free thinker. March to your own drummer—that sort of thing."

"That probably overstates the case, but . . . yeah, I like to think so."

"Sounds to me like you missed out on some fun."

"You're probably right. But at least I didn't feel I had license to go around thinking I was better than everyone else."

"See, that's where you read it all wrong. Simply signs of insecurity. A camouflage to protect an undeveloped ego."

"Thank you, Dr. Freud, for that explanation, but ego problems or not, the fact is that a lot of kids are made to feel like shit."

"Kids are bastards . . . it's every man for himself."

"And you think that's okay?"

Rusty sighed and shook his head. "No, not okay, not at all. But unfortunately that's how it is. And most of us—both dumpers and dumpees—seem to come out of it feet first, learning something from the painful process."

"Was it painful for you?"

"We are talking about growing up, aren't we?"

Rae bit down on her lip, then shrugged. "Maybe you're not so bad, Rusty. Still, I'm sure I was right to think you, Bobby and your friends were a bunch of asses in high school."

"No problem. You notice, I didn't look at you twice. I detested pompous, know-it-all redheads."

A fake smile. "No, as I recall, it was empty-headed blonds. Am I right?"

"Then you *were* taking notice of me. Tell me, what did Rae Lemkin do when she wasn't busy putting down the rest of us?"

"That's not how it was at all. Actually I was into a lot of things. I loved roughing it in the outdoors. Bobby thought I was strange, of course, but Jack didn't. We used to go camping in the White Mountains. And I loved to mess around with cars. Actually I was pretty good at it. Once Aunt Sara made Bobby cart me all over town looking for junk car parts. I had this wild idea that I'd build a race car from scratch . . ."

"And did you?"

"Nope. It all ended up in one big heap in the backyard and—" She stopped. "Why am I telling all this?"

Victoria did not remember ever being in the Ninety-Nine Club, but it was just as she expected: dim lights, clouds of smoke and a mishmash of loud music and voices. She spotted Elaine in a corner booth: a tall guy with remains of acne stood at her table making conversation. Victoria went over and slid into the booth across from Elaine.

"Oh, am I glad to see you." She looked up at the guy. "If you'll excuse us, please?"

"Whatsamatter, honey," he said, gesturing toward Victoria, "this your week for girls?"

"Actually I like men. When you see one, send him over."

He muttered what Victoria suspected was a profanity and strutted away. Elaine waved to a waitress. "Another beer here." Then to Victoria, "Is that okay?"

She nodded. "He certainly was loathsome."

"Each guy seems creepier than the one before. It's like a disease around here lately."

"You come to this place often?"

"Often enough." She shrugged. "You need to do something to pass time."

"Sounds dismal. No special guy?"

"Oh, there used to be one. Maybe again soon."

A mug of beer sailed into place in front of her, along with a basket of pretzels. Victoria lifted the mug. "Sounds like you've got him hand-picked already."

Elaine smiled. "You're very perceptive. And actually, I do. Someone I should have never let go. And once I get him to see things my way again, I never will."

"Why did you to begin with?"

"Don't *you* ever make mistakes?"

Victoria shook her head. "Never."

Elaine paused, then burst out laughing. "God—you are something else, Victoria. You sounded so serious, I damned near believed that you meant it."

"Oh I did." She looked at her watch. "Excuse me, I have to make a phone call."

Rusty had stayed far later than he had intended to. There was something unique about Rae. She was spunky, straightforward. She didn't pull any punches—and Rusty appreciated that. Maybe that showed how much he'd changed since his teen years. The fact is, that dig he had given her wasn't completely untrue—back in high school he wouldn't have given two glances at a girl like her.

Though their conversation hadn't faltered once, they hadn't gotten very far in figuring out where Bobby was. Jack's story about Bobby's secret exodus last year seemed to satisfy Rae for the time being. And Rusty had embellished on it himself, talking about the painting of the bullfight Bobby had once mentioned. Well, it was possible. Maybe he did go on a trip . . .

Rusty banged the steering wheel with his fist. Dammit—he didn't like it, not one bit. For one thing, why would he leave now, just after getting a painting of his hung in a well-known gallery—you'd think he'd want to stick around, if for nothing else than to see how it did. For another, Jack's story didn't satisfy him at all. The truth was, Bobby hadn't gone to Vermont without telling anyone . . .

He had told Rusty.

Carol sat on the sofa bed with her knees drawn up to her chest. She turned and glanced again at the clock: eleven-thirty. Where was Rusty? She knew he had gone to Bobby's cousin Rae's house after dinner, but on work nights he seldom stayed out past ten. And tomorrow he was starting on that big, important job, the one where he'd be doing all that overtime.

God . . . she felt sick to her stomach, mostly, she guessed, because of the lie she'd told. She didn't lie very often, and she felt particularly bad about lying to Rusty. Ever since she was little, she had been able to tell him anything—no matter how outrageous—and never be afraid he'd laugh, or worse still, let slip what she'd said.

But here the situation was different. Daddy hadn't been at all sure that he was doing the right thing by leaving her behind in Massachusetts with Rusty. And to make matters worse, now Rusty was getting frazzled over the responsibility of having to watch out for her: she had already seen how much those crank calls had worried him. If he got worried enough, he would insist on watching her every move, and that would be unbearable. There was always the possibility, too, that he might say something to their parents. Then where would she be? Sitting at some stupid desert, graduating high school with a bunch of strangers.

But the phone call she had just gotten was worse than the others, much worse. This time there wasn't just an empty line, there was a message. And it was uttered in a voice that seemed at once like a woman's and like a little girl's.

If Carol heard what she thought she heard, the message was: *Get the fuck out of that house.* Now she couldn't very well tell her brother that . . .

CHAPTER NINE

A quick stop for a McDonald's Big Mac, then straight on to Seventeen Valley Road. Russ backed his truck in the driveway, stopping it just before he reached the garage, then unloaded a jack, a tool box, eight cinder blocks, two two-by-fours, a bag of mortar and an eight-foot round steel column. First he'd fill in the windows, then jack-up the living room floor.

He lugged the materials inside, into the cellar. Victoria followed behind. Luckily, she was dressed more appropriately today: tightfitting jeans and a baggy blue sweater. "Can I watch?" she said.

"Suit yourself."

She leaned against a wall, folding her arms at her chest. "Can I interest you in a cup of coffee or a danish? It'd be no trouble."

He shook his head. "Where's that lady who was here last time, Mrs. Mills? I remember her from way back. When Rosalie Salino lived here."

"I thought you forgot the girl's name."

He shrugged. "It came back to me."

There were a few seconds of silence. "Do you live alone, Rusty?"

He looked up at her, staring . . . "No . . . why?"

"No reason. Just wondering."

He slid a chisel in at the edge of one window, then hammered it in, moving it along the edge. "Oh by the way, what day will Sam be coming?"

"Who's Sam?"

"Sam Regis, the electrician. He *did* contact you, didn't he?"

"Oh that's right, you did mention that you'd have him call. Well, he didn't, at least not yet."

"Hmmm, that's strange." Rusty pulled out the window—frame and all—and set it down on the floor, then went to the next one. That *was* strange. Sammy had his weak points, to be sure, but forgetting things was not one of them. And when he said he'd be somewhere, you could usually lay bets on it. Maybe something came up . . . he'd give Sammy a call tonight.

Carol plunked her milk carton and tuna sandwich across from Franny, and looked up and down the table. "Where is everyone?"

"Sherr, Lin, Chug, and Denny had work to do in the *Observer*—some last minute copy. Peter is running the cameras for one of McDougal's history classes, and Mona's absent."

Carol nodded and undid the sandwich wrapping. "What's wrong with Mona?"

"A cold, I think. At least that's what she said last night. Personally, I think she just wants to watch today's episode of 'General Hospital.'"

"She should tape it on her VCR."

"Usually she does. But the other day it went on the fritz. So now she's stuck."

"Well, she'd better show tomorrow, we have a council meeting. I've got an excellent agenda of senior activities to present for discussion. I've got the list in my locker, remind me to show it to you."

Franny nodded with her mouth full, then pushed aside her bangs. "Oh, yeah, I almost forgot: some kids are going skating tonight, want to go?"

"I'd like to, but Rusty's working overtime. And I can't just go off like that. At least not without asking him."

"Geez, Carol, you're a senior in high school. Why don't you ask your brother to cut you some slack?"

"Oh, Rusty's all right. He just feels responsible—that's all."

"Well, *call* him then. We're going early—five-thirty till nine-thirty. We'll be home by ten."

Silence.

"What's the matter?"

"Nothing."

"It's me, Carol . . . Franny. Talk to me."

Carol put down her sandwich. "You know those crank calls I told you about?"

Franny moved in closer. "Yeah?"

"Well, I'm still getting them. Only now they're worse. Someone—a girl, I think—is threatening me, telling me to get the fuck out of the house."

Franny shrugged. "Do you think it's someone from school?"

"I don't know. The voice was weird, unnatural. She could be younger than me or older."

"Did you tell Rusty about it?"

"No."

"Why not?"

"First of all, he'd want to know why I lied to begin with, when I said they *had* stopped. Then he'd probably double up security—he'd watch every move I made. I'd for sure never get to go skating tonight."

Franny sighed. "Well, if it happens again just hang up."

"I do, but—"

"But what?"

"I'm scared, Franny. I know it's dumb . . . but it's starting to scare me."

"Millie Carton, please."

"Speaking." The voice was deep, sharp, well defined.

"Ms. Carton, your school was one of five nursery schools picked in the Merrimack Valley."

"I don't understand, for what?"

"I represent Amco Educational Toys, Inc., a St. Louis-based operation."

"Oh yes, I'm familiar with Amco. In fact, we use some of your items."

"I'm not surprised. Why I'm calling, Ms. Carton, is, Amco is in the process of putting out a Tiny-Tot physical fitness line.

It's not yet in the marketplace, actually it's still in the experimental stages."

Silence.

"What we're looking for is some feedback from our professional educators out in the field. Those that actually work with the youngsters and are aware of what best would suit their physical needs."

"And you mean, you want me?" She laughed. "That's nice of you, really, but I don't think I'm qualified to give you what you're looking for. My school is only a year old. Right now it's a one-woman operation. I employ only two part-time helpers and have fifteen youngsters. Maybe you ought to ask someone more experienced."

"No, not at all. All we want is your immediate reaction to the products and, of course, any suggestions you might like to offer. We understand that this is an imposition on your time."

"Well, no, it's not that."

A soft laugh, then, "Of course it is. But we're willing to compensate for that. Each of the nursery schools taking part in the study—which by the way will take only one hour of your time—will receive a three-hundred-dollar gift certificate to be used for any Amco items of their choice."

A pause. "Well, where is this study taking place?" she asked finally. "And when?"

"Tomorrow evening at nine. Right here in Bradley—Seventeen Valley Road."

Victoria scanned the rest of the information about Millie, noted in her black book: single, a topnotch athlete, graduated Salem State two years ago, opened a playschool shortly thereafter. More interested in women than men. The last notation was written in red—that meant Victoria had nothing really to base it on, just a sneaking suspicion about the girl . . .

She remembered it all now—Millie was always a leader of a team in gym, and of course, the honor that everyone coveted was to be a member of Millie's super hand-picked team . . . Victoria stooped down to chair level and looked at the doll on the windowsill, staring at its chipped blue eyes. "But no matter how hard you tried to be her friend—always volunteering to go drag the equipment to and from the storage bins—she never chose you, Rosalie. Not once."

Now Victoria lifted Rosalie and cradled her in her arms, rocking her. "Poor, baby. Poor, poor baby."

Carol squeezed the receiver to her ear. "Oh, come on, answer, will you?" Finally on the eighth ring, Victoria picked up. "Hello."

"Hi. Is Rusty Erlich there?"

"Sorry, he took a short dinner break. He said he'd be right back. Can I have him call you back?"

"Oh." A few moments' hesitation, then, "Can you give him a message for me?"

"Sure."

"Tell him Carol called. I'm going skating tonight at Zoee's, so if he comes home and I'm not there, he's not to worry. I'll be home about ten."

"All right, no problem."

As Victoria put down the phone, a thread of heat wired down her throat. How eerie . . . an opportunity presenting itself like this. Was it possible that the girl was actually asking to be warned?

Rusty stood at the pay phone, waiting. Finally, "Regis Electrical, can I help you?"

"Is Sammy around?"

"No, everyone's gone for the day. This is the answering service."

"Oh . . . well, ask him to call Russ Erlich please . . . about the Louise job. The number's 555-9280."

"Will do, Mr. Erlich."

He put the phone down, dialed Sam's home number. Nothing. Then he dialed Carol. No answer there either. Where was *she* at this hour? Finally he dialed Rae. He let it ring ten times before he finally slammed it down. Dammit—where was everyone?

He had grabbed a chocolate milkshake and headed back to the job. He was gone only twenty minutes—it was almost six. As he'd told Victoria, he'd stay till eight, eight-thirty tops. Any later than that and his work would start to get sloppy . . .

The door was ajar when he came in. Scotch-taped to the inside door was an envelope with his name printed across it. He pulled it off, tore it open, and took out the sheet of paper: "Something came up, had to leave. If I miss you before I get back, see you in the morning . . . And I do appreciate you putting in all this overtime. Maybe some day you'll let me thank you properly. Victoria. PS—by the way, Carol called . . . she won't be home till ten. And, oh yes, you're not to worry— whatever that means."

Rusty folded the note into his pocket and went downstairs. As he passed the nightstick, he tapped it lightly with his hand, leaving it swinging from the nail. Well, at least he knew Carol was okay, but he didn't really like her out on a school night . . . And, of course, she could have mentioned where she was going.

Rusty rubbed his hand across his chest as he looked at the cinder blocks filling what once were windows. The mortar was already dry. The lolli column was in place, and he had already framed in some of the cellar. He was making steady progress . . .

He thought of the note in his pocket. All the proper thanks he'd need from Victoria was the payment of the time and a half overtime he'd charge in his bill . . .

He lifted a stud onto the saw horses, and marked it off, then rubbed his fingers together. Now what the hell was this sticky crap on his fingers?

Victoria laced up the dirty white shoeskates, then clumsily tied them. Her hands were actually trembling . . . She hadn't been on roller skates in years, since her father had taken her . . . And even then, she never was any good at it. She stood up, looking around—she spotted Carol's long thick gold braid, like a flag, waving to get her attention . . . Victoria took one step . . . another, then just as her feet began to slip from under her, wrapped her arms around a pole and hung on. This might not be as easy as she thought . . .

Victoria waited till the braid came around again, then forced herself to let go of the pole. She pushed herself out into the rotating circle, behind Carol. There were lots of people, some Victoria supposed were Carol's friends . . .

Finally she began to move her feet ahead, first merely shuffles, then working up her nerve, lifting her feet a little off the floor, taking steps in time to the music. And slowly, the knots inside her dissolving, she stood straighter, and she could see Carol way out in front of her, the gap between them closing.

A curve came up, and she took it. Like a pro. Suddenly she burst out laughing—a few people passed her, noticing and staring as if she were nuts—and she raised her hand over her mouth, trying to muffle her outburst. One quick lesson in skating and here she was, nearly ready for a roller derby. If only daddy could see his little princess now!

CHAPTER TEN

AE could hear the commotion even before she peered into the emergency waiting room: there were, at a minimum, seven teenagers out there. She turned to the nurse on desk duty, an excruciatingly thin girl, who never failed to have a snack at hand. Right now, a stack of peanut-butter crackers sat on her desk. "What's going on out there, Meg?"

Meg hung up the phone. "It's not really as bad as it looks . . . or sounds. Only one's waiting treatment. The rest are moral support for the accident in number three."

"Car crash?"

"Would you believe, roller crash? The girl skated smack into a brick wall. We've applied ice, stopped the bleeding and managed to bring down some of the swelling. But the girl will definitely need stitches."

"So what's the hold up?"

"She's underage, and we don't do anything here without authorization. Seems a brother's in charge and the girl doesn't know where he is. I've been trying to reach him for an hour, since her friends brought her in."

Rae shook her head. "The poor kid, anyone in there with her?"

"We've limited it to one friend, we just let her go in. I've told the others that they might as well go home, but as you can see," she pointed a long, thin finger out to the waiting room, "I might as well have been talking to myself."

A man with a short wiry beard rounded the corner. "Any luck reaching the brother of that Erlich girl, Meg?"

"None yet, Dr. Cantowitz. Still trying."

Cantowitz looked at Rae. "Why don't you work up the next one. I'll be right in."

Rae glanced at the pad in front of Meg: Robert Sinclair, stomach distress. "Please come into the examining room, Mr. Sinclair."

Erlich . . . did Russ have a sister?

"It's going to be okay, Carol, honest. Rusty will be here any minute, you'll see." Franny took the damp, crumpled tissue and brushed away the tear that slid down the side of Carol's swollen face.

"Boy, aren't I the big, brave one?"

"Don't be dumb, anyone would cry."

"What do they do when they stitch you, Franny?"

"I don't know, I guess they just take a needle and start sewing."

"Oh, my god! I'm going to start screaming. I just know it."

"Stop it, Carol. They'll probably give you something so it won't hurt so much." Then, "How does it feel now . . . does it kill?"

"Not so much." She lifted the ice pack off her forehead. "How does it look? No, forget it, forget it, don't tell me."

"I'd like to get my hands on the klutz who did this to you."

"Did you see who it was, Franny?"

"No, I didn't see a thing. One minute you were out there skating and the next minute you were sprawled out on the floor. I mean, you'd think that whoever it was would have come back to help or something. What kind of person just crashes into someone, then leaves?"

Carol swallowed hard and laid her hand on Franny's arm. "The kind that doesn't want to get caught."

"What do you mean?"

"You have to promise not to breathe a word of this to anyone. Especially not to Rusty."

"Your hand is shaking, Carol, what is it?"

"First promise me."

"Of course, I promise. What?"

"I don't know who it was, I didn't see anyone. But I felt the hands on my back, shoving me, really hard so I couldn't even turn. It wasn't an accident, Franny. Whoever did this to me, did it on purpose."

Rusty had left Victoria's at eight-thirty and driven past Bobby's apartment. The studio was pitch dark, but the car was still there, in the same place, untouched. He then swung past Rae's place, but she was still out. Finally he stopped for a burger. By the time he got home, it was nearly ten and the telephone was ringing. He raced inside and grabbed the receiver, noticing the message leaning against the lamp. "Went skating. Be home at ten. Carol." "Hello," he said.

"Rusty, this is Rae."

"I just went past your house. Where are you?"

"I'm working the three to eleven shift tonight. Emergency room."

"Oh. What's the matter, not enough work to keep you busy?"

"Listen, I don't want you to get upset at what I'm about to tell you. Everything's okay."

Rusty sucked in his breath. "You found Bobby?"

"No. Rusty, it's your sister, Carol. She's here."

He could feel his body stiffen.

"She skated into a wall. She's bruised up, but she'll be okay. She *is* going to need a few stitches in her forehead though, and you're going to have to give authorization."

"I'm on my way."

Victoria was worn out when she got home. Muscles that she hadn't even known existed till now, ached. She showered, then slipped into her nightgown and sat on the chair near the window, looking at the doll. "The skating part was fun, really it was. You should have seen me gliding along . . . I was something else."

Well, it was done . . . The girl had been warned. Now it was up to Victoria to move on . . . For instance, there was tomorrow and Millie. How long had it been since she'd seen her? Victoria thought back. Yes, it had been more than six years—Millie had been out the whole last semester of her senior year with mono.

Victoria picked up the doll and kissed her. What would she ever do without Rosalie? If not for her jogging Victoria's memory just when she needed it, she'd be lost. Victoria knew there was still more to remember. But she had complete confidence that when she was ready to know whatever it was, Rosalie would tell her . . .

Agnes Mills stood behind the bushes outside the Queen Anne, looking up at the window. This time she had worn her glasses purposely. But now her glasses were off, lying on the ground, and she was wiping tears from her eyes with the hemline of her dress . . .

Never once did she believe, or even suspect. But she should have—the biting on the lip when she was angry or upset, the other similarities . . . Her instincts had told her that Rosalie would never sell the house. Why hadn't she listened to those instincts? Still, she didn't understand how it could be possible . . . how had her Rosalie turned into this girl?

But she had, of this Agnes was certain. And her certainty was based on a simple observation. She had finally recognized what it was sitting on the second-story bedroom windowsill: Rosalie's doll . . . the one Agnes had sewn for the child even before she'd been born. And yes—the one the child had called Victoria!

But the biggest question was, why had she sent Agnes away? Had the girl thought she would tell others her secret . . . who she really was? Why would she think that—hadn't Agnes always kept Rosalie's secrets?

Carol was so shaken, Rae had asked that the doctor prescribe a mild tranquilizer. Rae gave it to her, then slipped out when Rusty came into the room. Now Dr. Cantowitz tapped her shoulder and gestured into Carol's room. "Are we ready for the suturing in there?"

"Everything's set."

"Okay then, get the brother out of there."

Rae opened the door and went in. "Well, if I can break this up for ten minutes, Dr. Cantowitz is ready."

Carol squeezed Rusty's arm. "The stitches?"

"It won't hurt, Carol, it's nothing." Then to Rae, "Tell her."

"The truth?" Rae asked Carol.

She nodded.

"The stitches are a breeze, it's the needle the doctor uses to numb the area that hurts. However, that's over before you know it." She turned to Rusty. "Big brother will have to wait outside, I'm afraid."

Rusty smiled. "Okay, if the doctor doesn't want my expert advice . . ." He stood up and grabbed his jacket, then leaned down and gave Carol a mock punch on the shoulder. "Show them that Erlich toughness, okay?"

Carol nodded.

After Rusty left the room Rae wheeled the suturing tray over to the examining table. She saw a question forming on Carol's lips. "Yes?" Rae said.

Carol gave an embarrassed smile. "It's just that I noticed your name tag: R. Lemkin. You know my brother, right?"

"Uh huh."

"Have you found your cousin yet? Rusty told me he was helping you look for him."

Silence, then, "No, Carol, I haven't. But I'm sure he'll turn up soon." Rae averted her eyes.

"I'm sure, too," Carol said hopefully, and then the doctor entered the room.

Rusty sent Franny and the other kids home, then waited in the empty room. He jumped up when Rae came out. "It's over," Rae said, "and she's fine. The doctor will talk to you in a minute."

Rusty put his hands on her arm. "Thanks for helping her out."

"No problem. Tell me, what *did* happen to her at that rink?"

"According to what you told me, she skated into a wall. Carol verified that. Why, is there something I ought to know?"

Rae sighed. "I don't know, she was pretty shaken up when I first spoke to her. She seemed frightened. I had the doctor prescribe a tranquilizer to calm her."

"Well, this whole thing has been traumatic. I can see why she'd be upset."

"I'm sure that was some of it, but . . . I don't know, it just seemed like there was more . . ." She put her hand on the front of his sweatshirt and examined it. "What's this?"

He looked down at his shirt. "Just a dirt stain . . . why?"

"It looks like blood."

Suddenly he remembered his sticky fingers. He looked down at his hand—a brown stain was still there. Had he cut himself on the job and not felt it?

"Hungry?" Rusty asked Carol the moment he got her inside.

"No, but I'm so dry, I can barely swallow."

"Sit down. A glass of milk?"

"How about a Seven-Up?"

Rusty went into the kitchen, poured a glass of Seven-Up, came back and handed it to her, then inspected her bruised face and bandaged forehead, shaking his head as he did. "Jesus . . . do you look like shit."

"Gee thanks. I may not look so hot, but I feel pretty loose from that pill they gave me. I'm beginning to see what druggies see in this stuff."

"Don't even joke about it, Carol." He sank down on the sofa, across from her, leaning forward. "I don't understand, how did it happen? You're a pretty decent skater. Not many people, even the worst of skaters, go into walls."

"I told you, it was crowded, you know how people crash into one another. Someone or other is always getting knocked over."

"Did the kid who ran into you get hurt?"

She shrugged. "I don't know, I wasn't really paying much attention."

He sat a few moments, staring at her as she sipped her soda. "Listen, maybe we ought to call mom and dad and tell them about this."

"Don't you dare, Rusty. Can you picture us calling them at this hour, they'd think I was half-dead or something."

"You're right, you can give them a call tomorrow."

"Even then, what's the point? They'll just worry, especially daddy . . . and for nothing. You can see I'm fine now."

"Does it hurt at all? Let me get you a cold pack." He began to get up.

Carol grabbed onto his sweatshirt, bringing him back down. "Would you stop worrying about me, Rusty. Please."

He raised his hands, palms forward. "Okay, okay, I'll ease up."

"Good. Now you can tell me about that nurse."

"What nurse?"

"Rae, of course. She is *so* pretty. I love her hair, I wish I saw it down."

"What do you want to know?"

"How did you meet her, through Bobby?"

"Not really. She ran over me with a shopping cart in Line Lumber."

"I love it—just like in the movies."

Rusty shook his head. "You're sick, you do know that, don't you?"

"Well, do you like her?"

Rusty stood, took the almost empty glass out of Carol's hands and set it on the table. "End of conversation. It's late, and I want you to get some rest. In fact, maybe you ought to stay home tomorrow. Laze around, it won't hurt."

"I can't, I have a student council meeting. I'm presenting senior activities."

"So miss it. Call Franny tomorrow morning, give her your agenda and let *her* present it. I'll even come home and have lunch with you. Tacos or subs?"

"Pizza. Pepperoni."

As soon as Carol got to bed, Rusty turned on the hot water faucet and with a bar of soap cleansed his hands. He looked for a cut, but found nothing . . . Finally he dried his hands, went to the refrigerator and took out a cold beer—he needed something to calm himself.

It was only an accident, and the bottom line was, it was over and the doctor had assured him that Carol would be fine. Then why was there a voice whispering to him, saying that it wasn't over yet at all?

CHAPTER ELEVEN

IT was close to noon when Rusty came up from the basement. Victoria was in the kitchen preparing food. "Do you mind if I use the phone?" Rusty asked.

"Help yourself."

He dialed Sam's office, and a voice sang into the phone, "Regis Electric."

"Hi, Russ Erlich here. Is Sammy in?"

"This is his answering service."

"Oh. When's he getting back?"

"I couldn't tell you, Mr. Erlich."

"I called yesterday, did you give him my message?"

"Just a moment please."

Rusty leaned back against the kitchen wall, watching Victoria cut up chunks of chicken, mushrooms and peppers.

Finally the voice was back, "You called at 5:33 P.M. Tuesday. Yesterday."

He sighed. "Yes."

"Well, he hasn't received that message yet."

"Why not?"

"Because he hasn't called in to get it."

"Since when?"

"Excuse me?"

"How long *has* it been since he's called in?"

Irritation now in her voice. "Just a moment please."

Then she was back. "Since Monday."

"You mean to tell me it's been two days since he called in for his messages?"

"That's right, sir. We just take them, from there on, it's the responsibility of the client to pick them up."

Rusty put down the phone, called another local electrical company and made arrangements for them to do the work.

"Sounds like your buddy Sam isn't too responsible," Victoria said, as she slid the Corning casserole dish into the oven.

"It isn't like him at all." He looked at her, "Well, whatever. As you heard, Sardo Electric will be here tomorrow."

"Fine. Oh, by the way," she said pointing to the oven, "lunch will be ready in forty minutes. I've prepared a very special dish . . . You will join me, won't you?"

"Sorry, I can't . . . I have other plans."

"Well, break them."

"I can't do that." A pause, then, "Listen, maybe another time." He picked up the receiver again, dialed, then waited. "Can you have a pepperoni pizza ready in twenty minutes? To go, and the name's Erlich."

Victoria pulled the kitchen curtain aside, watching as Rusty pulled his truck out of the driveway, then down the street. After she had gone to all that trouble preparing a special lunch, he picked a pepperoni pizza instead. Did that mean he was sharing it with Carol . . . that she was still living with him even after that warning? She went to the phone and dialed the number she had long ago memorized.

"Hello." The voice was Carol's, but now much meeker than before.

Victoria didn't answer. One, two, three, four, five, six, she counted to herself, then the phone clicked in her ear.

She went to the oven and pulled out the casserole. The chicken really hadn't had a chance to sop up the sauce yet, but what did it matter—she'd give it to Sammy and Bobby. They'd probably be happy to get some fancy food.

She tossed some plastic utensils and paper plates on a tray with the casserole and headed downstairs. When she got to the bottom, she turned left and went down the remaining stairs. With one hand, she slid the key in the lock, then with all the force she could muster, pushed open the four-inch-thick door.

"Hi, there. Sammy, Bobby, stay right where you are. I've brought you a special lunch today."

Actually the "stay right where you are" part was meant to be funny . . . but neither of them laughed. They just sat there, staring at her. Both were in handcuffs, their feet tied with rope and secured to one of the thick pipes overhead. No, they definitely weren't about to go anywhere. Come to think of it, she wasn't even sure they could laugh. That was an interesting question—could a person laugh with a sockball stuffed in his mouth?

Rusty was about to take another slice of pizza when he noticed Carol playing with the pepperoni on her first slice. "Something wrong with it?"

She jumped, then forced a smile. "No, it's great. I'm just not so hungry."

They sat in silence, staring at each other. Rusty glanced at the clock. "I've still got thirty-five minutes to go yet. How about a short game of Scrabble?"

"You hate to play Scrabble."

"Says who?"

"You never want to play when *I* ask."

"I just hate to destroy your ego on a regular basis. I know how badly you lose. Remember that time you wouldn't talk to me for two days after I totally crushed you?"

"Give me a break. As I recall, I was eight and you were sixteen. Not exactly an even match."

"Listen, are you going to give me excuses, or do we play?"

Carol set down the word "cables," attaching the "s" onto "rug." "Fifteen," she said.

Rusty marked down her score, then looked at her. "Okay, you going to tell me what's going on now?"

"What do you mean?"

"You're throwing this game, right?"

She pressed her lips together and folded her arms over her chest.

He pointed to the word abutting the orange square. "Why didn't you hang your 's' here. Triple word score both ways."

She sighed. "So I missed it."

"I've never known you to waste an 's' on a meager fifteen points."

"So sue me," she said.

Rusty pushed back his chair . . . "I'm only teasing. Come on, what's bugging you, Carol. Since I got here, you've been in a pissass mood. You do feel okay, don't you?"

"Yeah, I'm okay. I guess I'm just in a funk—that's all. Sitting around the house isn't much fun."

"I've never known you to mind taking a day off from school."

She fiddled with the wooden tile holder. "I guess I don't really."

"Then what is it? Are you worried about being left with a scar on your forehead?"

Carol looked up at him, then shrugged. "Maybe."

"You heard what the doctor said. Once it heals, it won't be more than a thin line, if that. Not even noticeble."

"You think he's telling the truth?"

"You don't think he's going to risk his reputation just to make you feel good, do you?"

"No, I guess not." A half smile, then pointing to the board. "Go ahead, it's your turn."

"You're sure now?"

"Of course I'm sure."

"Well, if you really want to play . . ." One by one he picked up his letters, all seven of them, and formed "daggers," hanging the "s" on the word "back." "And if you'll notice," he said, "right on the triple letter space that you so nicely left for me. Let me see . . ." He counted out his score. "Seventy-two plus fifty for the seven letter word . . . is one hundred twenty-two."

Carol looked at the weird combination of words.

"Well, what do you think? Impressive?"

Silence.

"Yoo-hoo, Carol?" He waved his hand in front of her face. She looked up. "Big deal."

"Not a very sportsmanlike reaction, I—" Suddenly the phone rang. "Grab it will you," Rusty said as he marked down his score.

She jumped up. "I've got a stomachache. You get it." She ran out of the room, and Rusty picked it up.

Carol listened at the bathroom door . . . then she heard her brother talking. There had been an ache in her stomach, there really had been, but now it was lessening. She went over to the medicine chest and leaned her arms on the chipped porcelain sink underneath. At least it wasn't another one of those crank calls.

She looked up, studying her reflection in the mirror—she did look a mess: her lip was puffy and the black and blue marks on her cheek were starting to take on a sickening yellow tinge. And then the gash on her forehead, still covered by a large square gauze. It would heal, she hadn't even thought to be concerned that it wouldn't until Rusty had brought it up. Besides, even if the gash didn't heal all the way, she could always throw a few more strands of hair down over her forehead . . .

But even though that hadn't really worried her, she *had* let Rusty think it had. Now that she was caught up in these lies, what else could she have said? But the tranquilizer the doctor had given her last night had worn off, and all she could think about was those heavy hands pressing on her back at the roller rink.

She went to the door and opened it. Rusty put down the receiver and glanced at her. "You okay?"

She nodded.

"Well, are you coming back here or are you conceding this game? I've got ten minutes yet before I have to leave."

"You know better than that. I never give up." She took the seat across from her brother and studied her tiles, then looked up. "Who was that on the phone?"

"Rae."

"What did she want?"

"She asked me to stop by after work. Actually I was going to call her and suggest the same thing. I want to talk to her about Bobby."

"I mentioned him to Rae at the hospital. She tried to hide it, but I had the feeling she was really worried about him."

Rusty nodded. "I ought to be home early, around ten, ten-thirty. You don't mind me going, do you?"

"No, why should I mind? Do what you want. I don't need you here to hold my hand. I—"

"Hey, easy. You don't have to snap my head off."

Rusty speeded, driving back to Victoria's. He had taken a longer lunch than intended. But he didn't like the idea of leaving Carol, not in the mood she was in. No matter how hard he tried, he was barely able to squeeze a smile out of her. Maybe Rae was right . . . maybe there was something more to that accident than Carol was letting on . . .

He parked the truck, then went in the house by the opened side door. He headed downstairs, pleased that he had avoided Victoria. She wasn't too thrilled that he had turned down the lunch invitation—that was clear from her face when he left the house. It wasn't like he had an obligation to eat lunch with her or to do anything with her for that matter. But some women had the ability to apply pressure, make you feel like a first-class louse just for saying "no" to them. Elaine was one of those women—for a lot of years he was barely able to refuse her anything.

Victoria was like that, too . . . definitely not an easy woman to say "no" to.

CHAPTER TWELVE

IT was 8:30 by the time Rusty got to Rae's apartment. "You look awful," she said, taking his jacket.

"I just got out of work."

"Why so late?"

"The lady's in a hurry for a playroom."

Rae went into the kitchen, opened the breadbox and pulled out a bag of rolls. "Then I assume you haven't eaten?"

He followed her in. "Don't bother, I'm not hungry."

She opened the refrigerator. "Tuna, ham, cheese, take your pick."

"Tuna, cheese, tomato, cucumber and mayonnaise."

A quizzical glance, then she picked through the shelves, coming up with an armload.

"You ought to try it," he said. "It's good."

"I'll take your word. Milk, beer, diet Coke?"

He leaned over, pulled out a can of beer, then pushed the door closed. He flipped open the tab and took a swallow.

"How's Carol?" she asked.

He shrugged. "Okay, I guess."

"That didn't sound too reassuring."

"She's all right, at least physically I think she is. Everything seems to be healing. But she's acting strange . . . not talking about what's bugging her."

"Sometimes it's hard to talk to a brother."

"Yeah. That reminds me . . . mind if I use your phone?"

She shook her head.

He lifted the receiver, got the number of Zoee's skating rink and dialed it. "Let me speak to the manager please." He waited a moment.

"Donato speaking."

"My name's Rusty Erlich, my sister was the girl who got hurt last night."

"Oh yeah, listen, that wasn't our fault. I checked the floor out for grooves, something that might of tripped her up, but there was nothing. I swear, I even took pictures, you could come look for yourself."

"I'm not looking for a lawsuit, I just want to know what happened."

"What do you mean, what happened?"

"I mean, was there a fight, a scuffle, anything like that?"

"No, nothing. One minute the kid was skating, the next she was plastered into the wall. I figured somebody must of rammed into her by accident."

"Did you see who it was who rammed into her?"

"You've got to be kidding. There's a hundred-fifty, two hundred kids out there and at night we keep the lights pretty dim. All the rinks do that. You know, the kids like the romance."

"So it was just an accident, neat and simple?"

"Yeah, right, you said it. The minute it happened we gave her first aid, then her friends took her to the hospital. I mean, sure we would have taken her, but they took right over."

"Listen, Donato, I figure you're one of those silent worriers, the kind who only pretends he doesn't give a shit . . . But my sister doesn't need your ulcer on her conscience so try to ease up about this whole thing." He hung up and stared down at the counter, then looked at Rae: she was grinning. "What's so funny?" he said.

She tilted her head. "You have incredible style, Erlich."

"Why is it no woman told me that before?"

She shrugged. "Well wait . . . maybe I was too quick to form that opinion. I'll withdraw it for further observation."

Rusty drank some more beer, then set the can down. "Rae, I was thinking, maybe Jack or one of the other family members has Bobby's studio key. It wouldn't hurt to get it and nose around some."

Rae picked up a key off the kitchen windowsill and tossed it on the table, smiling. "I picked it up from Aunt Sara this afternoon." Then she put the sandwich on a plate. "First eat."

Millie Carton loved the smell of leather, still strong in her sleek '88 Dodge stationwagon. She would really have preferred a smaller car, a sportier one, but with a bunch of preschoolers to transport everyday, the wagon was more practical. Actually she couldn't afford either car, but that's why bank loans were invented, she supposed.

She pulled up to number Seventeen Valley, turned off the ignition, then took off her glasses. During the day she wore contacts, but at night the reflection from the oncoming headlights was irritating. She looked in the rearview mirror. Her hair was short and dark, almost boyish in style. Though she had never been considered a beauty—her features were too sharp— she was cute, and to her amusement, she was still carded at bars.

She got out of the car and squinted up at the house. An odd place to conduct a study, an odd time, too, though she supposed since all of the participants worked, it made some sense . . . Actually she never would have accepted the invitation if not for the three hundred dollar's worth of toys for the school. After a long day with the kiddies, what she really had in mind was an ice cold Bloody Mary in a tall glass with salted rim.

She walked up the stairs, closer to the house. There was something definitely familiar about this place . . . Yes, the kids had once been to a birthday party here. Wasn't that the one where they really dumped on that girl?

Rusty switched on the overhead light. "Come on," he said to Rae. They both entered the studio, then he closed the door behind them. Rae walked around the room, looking for something that might strike her as odd.

Rusty went to the desk—first things first. He turned on the answering machine, then sat down. About eight messages from him and Rae, one from Jack, two from Gena, and two from Bobby's mother.

Then, "Bobby, this is Edgar from Raneers. I've got some good news on your "Marathon Man." Not a lot of dough, but it's respectable. Give me a call right away, I want to see some more slides of your work. Maybe we can talk about giving you a corner section in the gallery, four or five paintings. How's that sound?"

"That's wonderful!" Rae said.

Rusty stopped the machine. "Bobby's got one of those gizmos to pick up his messages, doesn't he?"

"He does. Which means he would definitely hear this and contact Edgar right away."

"Give the gallery a call first thing tomorrow," Russ said as he pressed start again.

Fifteen seconds of silence, then, "Bobby, it's Maxine," the tape began. "Where've you been? God—you know how I hate to talk on these machines so I'm going to cut out. Give me a call, will you?"

Silence, then two more messages from Rae and that was it. Rusty turned the machine off. "Maxine's the girl from Connecticut. Do you know her last name?"

"Renneck, Rellick, something like that."

Rusty snapped his fingers. "Resnick." He drew the Rolodex to him and ran through the R's. Finally . . . Maxine Resnick. "What's the area code there?"

"203."

He dialed the number. It rang a dozen times. Finally he hung up.

Rae opened her purse, pulled out a pad and pen and copied the number. "I'm off duty tomorrow, I'll call both of them."

Rusty leaned his head back against the tall chair back, squeezed his eyes shut, rubbing them with his fists, then sat forward. "Mail . . . what about mail?"

"Yeah, I should have thought of that. We'll check the box on the way out."

Rusty stood up and looked over the papers on the desk, still seeing nothing that looked significant. "Do you know anyone who wanted Bobby to do a portrait?" he asked Rae.

"No, why?"

"One paper here says, 10/22 . . . portrait. No name, no address, I don't even know if it means anything. October 22nd—about ten days ago." He looked around at all the paintings hanging on the wall, then the one on the easel, partially done: a cage full of chimpanzees. "I wonder if he ever did that portrait."

In the front hallway, they picked up the mail: about eighteen envelopes jammed into the box, some sticking out the edges. Rusty handed the bunch to Rae. "You go through this." She took the stack, not saying aloud what both of them were thinking: Bobby would never go off without asking someone to pick up his mail.

It was 9:20 and Millie was getting restless. Victoria could tell by the way the girl continually changed positions and checked her watch. "Listen," Millie said finally, "I really can't stay and wait for the others. You led me to believe this would be quick and painless."

"Why don't you relax and have more of that drink."

"Look, not to be rude or anything. But punch is not really my thing."

Victoria stood up. "You should have told me. Let me get you something stronger."

Millie put up her hands and sat forward in her chair. "Don't bother. I'd really rather get this over with. If the others aren't coming, maybe we'd better forget it."

"No wait, we can't do that." Victoria cleared her throat, forcing a calmer tone. "What I mean is, suppose I have you do the study yourself?"

"Could I? I was under the impression it couldn't be done without the entire group."

"I'm not supposed to do it that way, of course. But I don't really see why not. I'm sure you wouldn't base your opinion on what any of the others would say anyway."

Millie smiled. "I definitely have a mind of my own."

"Good." Victoria stood up. "Then let's get this done. Now, you won't tell anyone that we bent the rules, will you?"

Millie stood up—a head shorter than Victoria—raising her right hand as she did. "You have my solemn oath."

Victoria led her to the basement door and turned on the light, then, "Why don't you go first."

Millie looked down the stairs. "Where're we going?"

"The equipment is all assembled downstairs. You'll see it when you round the corner."

Millie wrinkled her nose. "It's your house, you'd better lead the way."

Victoria felt like a wire had come loose in her chest and was dancing wildly around. Nothing was going right . . . not the doctored drink and not this. She put her hand over her chest, hoping the pressure would secure the wire back into place.

"Well?" Millie said.

Victoria started down the stairs—she passed the nightstick hanging on the wall. When she reached the landing, she turned right and Millie came up in back of her. "Hey, what's going on? Where the hell is the exercise equipment?"

Victoria pointed off to the side with one hand. With the other, she lifted Rusty's hammer off of the sawhorse.

Millie squinted her eyes, then turned back quickly. "I can't—" The hammer grazed her head, throwing her momentarily off balance. "What the?" Hands that had immediately gone to the pain, now went toward Victoria. Millie's fists beat at Victoria's face.

Victoria tried to lift the hammer again, but with a quick hand chop, Millie knocked it to the floor. Victoria tried to reach the girl's throat, but she couldn't . . . She reached her ear, folding it into her fist, and twisted it, ripping . . .

Millie screamed, her hands shooting to her ear to ply away the hands, but Victoria held on. Millie sank to the floor, writhing and sobbing. Victoria came down on top of her, stretching one arm for the hammer, then brought the hammer back, driving it into Millie's head. Finally Millie was quiet.

Victoria dropped the hammer, then took her hand from the

girl's ear: the top cartilage, now bloody and torn away, collapsed, drooping over the earlobe. God—she had never meant to hurt her like this. Once she got Millie secured in the wine cellar with the others, she'd apply cold compresses to her head and ear. Millie was tough, she'd recuperate just fine—she had to. In time for the party.

Rusty had dropped off Rae and was heading home. Before they had left Bobby's, they had checked his car. That was another thing, he never would have left it unlocked had he gone on a trip. But Rusty hadn't said that to Rae . . . Like the accumulated mail, he didn't have to say a word about it. She knew it as well as he did.

Maybe, just maybe Rae would learn that Bobby did contact either Maxine or Edgar. Or both. But for some reason, he wasn't too optimistic about either possibility. And if his instincts *were* right, what then? Rusty sighed, wondering if Rae was thinking the same thing he was . . .

Then it was time to involve the police.

CHAPTER THIRTEEN

CAROL was crouched on the floor, a few feet from the telephone, watching the dial as if she expected a face to appear and leap out at her. When she heard the noise in the hallway, she sucked in her breath, and her eyes darted toward the door. "Who's there?" she asked, her voice no louder than a whisper.

The door flew open, and she scrambled to her feet. "Who is it?" she cried out, before she recognized Rusty.

He raised his hands. "Carol. Take it easy, it's only me."

She stared at him, breathing heavily.

"What's going on here, what's the matter?"

"Nothing. You scared me, that's all."

"It's late. What are you doing up?"

Carol turned, glanced at the kitchen clock—eleven-forty-five—then glared at Rusty, her hands rolled into fists at her sides. "Suppose you explain what *you're* doing coming home at this hour on a work night." Rusty didn't answer, she didn't give him a chance. "You said you'd be home no later than ten."

Rusty went up to her and laid his hands on her shoulders. "Okay, what's going on?"

She tried to squirm away, but he held her. She hung her head, looking down at the worn carpeting. "I told you, I expected you earlier. You said you'd be home earlier."

Rusty opened his mouth to say something: instead he laughed.

Carol's head snapped up, her eyes meeting his. "Don't you dare laugh at me!" Then suddenly there were tears down her cheeks—dammit—and she couldn't even stop them.

Rusty led her to the sofa and sat her down, then kneeled in front of her. He pulled the quilt hanging over the sofa back toward him, and with the corner of it, clumsily wiped her tears. More fell. "You keep this up, and we go for your blanket."

She sniffled, then smiled. "I'm okay now."

He dropped the quilt on the floor. "Good, but I'm not. Now suppose you tell me what's going on."

"It was nothing . . . really."

"Dammit, Carol, it was something, and I want to know what!" He glanced at the telephone on the floor, went over, picked it up and set it on the table, then came back to her. "Who were you talking to?"

"No one." She began to stand up. "I'm tired, if it's okay with you, I'm going to bed."

He put his hand at her shoulder, shoving her back down. "Well, it's not okay. You're not going anywhere till I find out what you're hiding from me. And if that means we sit up the whole damned night to do it, then that's how it is."

Silence, then, "It was getting late, and you weren't home yet, and I started to think some awful things and—"

"What kind of things?"

She shrugged and looked at the floor. "Just things."

"Not good enough, try again."

She swallowed hard, then her eyes met his. "Okay, okay, it's the calls, Rusty, the crank calls."

"I thought you told me they stopped."

"I lied, I didn't want to worry you."

He nodded his head, studying her. "Looking out for me, huh? Pretty noble of you, I'd say. I would have guessed your reasons might be more self-serving. Like afraid I might clamp down on you, cramp your social life?"

"Well, I guess I thought of that, too. And maybe mom or daddy getting wind of this and insisting I go out to Arizona with them."

He rubbed his palms over his eyes, then looked down at her. "How often have you been getting these calls?"

"Not that often, Rusty. Honest."

"But you got one tonight?"

She nodded.

"Did the person say anything?"

"No, not this time."

"I take that to mean the caller has talked to you on other occasions."

"Once, but not really talked. It was a female voice. The girl—I guess it was a girl—said, 'Get the fuck out of that house.'"

Silence, then, "Have you had any fights in school?"

"None."

"Maybe over some guy?"

"No, I told you, no."

"What about last night?"

"What about it, I told you what happened."

"Tell me again."

"Someone smashed into me and I went into the wall."

"And you didn't see who it was?"

"I swear, Rusty, I didn't."

"Was it done purposely or was it an accident?"

Should she tell him the rest? But she didn't even know if there really was more. Maybe it *was* just her imagination at the roller rink. It's not as if she saw someone push her. Besides . . . could a young girl have pushed so hard, with so much strength? "How would I know," she said finally. "When someone bangs into you, you can't really tell—" She stopped, tears again coming to her eyes.

He sighed, his features softening, then laid his hand on her shoulder. "Okay stop. Some girl is apparently trying to put a scare into you, Carol. And it looks like she's succeeding. Let's put this in perspective . . . we're talking here about a lousy phone call by some frustrated girl who has no other way to get her kicks."

"But—"

"What?"

"Nothing. You're right, Rusty." She leaned back in the sofa and ran her fingers through her damp hair. "You're right, you're right, you're right. I'm acting like a total cry baby about this whole thing. You must think I'm a wimp."

Rusty smiled. "You? Never. You forget, I'm the same one you punched in the eye when I used your silly putty to plug up a hole in my carburetor."

"You remember that, so long ago?"

"A guy doesn't easily forget those kinds of things. I mean, a sixteen-year-old ego doesn't deal too well with humiliation. How do you think I felt having to tell my friends my kid sister gave me the black eye?"

"Rusty, you never told me how much that affected you before. You're making me feel almost guilty about punching you."

"*Almost* guilty?"

Carol tilted her head and smiled. "Well, you did deserve it. As I remember, what was left of my silly putty was so covered with grease and gunk, I had to trash it."

Rusty took her by the elbow and stood her up. "Come on, get to bed. As you pointed out, it's past my bedtime. And don't worry any more about the calls. They're going to stop."

"What will you do?"

"Get us a new phone number. An unlisted one."

"What about if my friends want to call?"

"You'll give them the number."

"What about other people. Suppose some guy wants to ask me out?"

"He'll ask you in school."

"But what if he doesn't go to my school?"

His eyes narrowed . . .

She reached up quickly and kissed his cheek. "Good night, Rusty."

Before Victoria delivered the car back to the vacant private school lot attached to Millie's house, she had called Carol. Now she walked the two miles back home from the school. She could have taken a bus—they ran till one—but she was too rattled to do that. Besides, she wanted the time to think . . .

Until now, she prided herself on being organized, everything planned, replanned, then acted on. But tonight had been different—Millie had disrupted the proper chain of events. And the entire party, relying on those events, might have been ruined. Of course, it wasn't—but that didn't excuse her stupidity. How would she ever face—

"Rosalie."

Victoria stopped, listened. She was half a block away from her house.

Again the thin voice seeming to come from nowhere.

"Rosalie, it's me."

Victoria looked around her, at the trees, the bushes lining the sidewalk, the open window of a parked car. Suddenly she saw the figure sitting on the porch. She moved closer, and Mrs. Mills stood up.

"What do *you* want?"

The woman put her hand on the girl's arm. "I don't want to hurt you, only to talk."

Victoria pulled back. "We have nothing to say."

"But I know, Rosalie. You don't have to pretend with me now that I know."

"You must be insane."

"You can trust me, I won't tell your secret." Then she took a tissue from her dress pocket and lifted it to the girl's face. "Your lip, it's bleeding. And you've got a cut on your face. Why, you look like you've been in a boxing match. Here, dear, let me fix it."

"My name's Victoria," she cried, pushing her away . . . then ran down the street into the house.

It was after midnight and Rusty still felt weighed down with questions. Who the hell would be bothering Carol this way? Sure, she was pretty and popular, but not cruel or stuck on herself like so many other girls her age. Was it really possible some girl at school was carrying out a vendetta against her?

He thought about whether the calls might be linked to the skating incident? Carol would have known if it was done maliciously, wouldn't she? He blew out a stream of air—sexist or not, he was glad it was a female harassing her. A guy making those kinds of strange calls would have painted a far more threatening picture.

Luckily he had named the construction company R&E, not Erlich. He'd be able to instruct the phone company to give out the number just for R&E. Of course, the money he had sunk into the quarter-page advertisement in the yellow pages would be useless . . .

He rolled over . . . What about Bobby? And for that matter, what the fuck had happened to Sammy? Why was it, nothing, no matter how many times he turned it over in his mind, was making any sense?

Victoria promised herself it would never happen again. Never again would she put herself in such a compromising situation. She went to the closet, bent over and dragged the cardboard box out into the room, then sat down next to it. First she pulled out a couple of sets of handcuffs, the keys tied neatly to each set. Her father had been so proud of his unique collection—he must have had twenty-five pairs of handcuffs in all, each one a little different from the next, and some chain and ankle cuffs dating back to the 1800s. Rosalie had insisted on taking the collection when she left home—it was a cumbersome memento, but no less meaningful. Finally she reached deep into the box and pulled out the gun. She ran her finger along it, feeling its smoothness. Not that she planned to use it—the truth was, she was scared to death of the thing—even holding it made her nervous. But it wouldn't hurt to keep it handy. Just as an option.

She painstakingly went over all the events in her mind. She had washed off the hammer and placed it back on the sawhorse where Rusty had left it. She had applied cold packs to Millie's head and ear, and she had gotten the station wagon back where it belonged without anyone seeing. Now what she had to do was relax.

Victoria shoved the box back into the closet, put the gun in her nightstand drawer, then lifted the doll from the windowsill to her bed, climbing in beside her. "Oh, yes, I almost forgot, Rosalie. Mrs. Mills stopped me outside and you'll never guess what . . . She thinks I'm you!"

Victoria started to laugh, softly into the covers.

CHAPTER FOURTEEN

VICTORIA used make-up that morning, but still Rusty noticed the facial bruise she had gotten as a result of her fight with Millie. "What happened to you?" he asked when she let him in.

She gestured to the stairwell, leading to the second floor. "Nothing too terrible. I tripped on one of those warped stairs."

"Which one?" he asked, heading for the stairs. "Maybe I ought to see about fixing it now."

"Oh, no, don't bother. Really. It can wait till the playroom's done. I'll just be more careful."

"All right, if you say so." Then he headed for the kitchen.

"Wait!"

He turned to her.

"Could I ask a favor?"

"Go ahead, ask."

"I have a sticky window upstairs. I've been trying to get it open to air out the room, but—"

"Sure, where is it?"

"Well, it's in my bedroom. But if you could come up maybe in a half hour . . . I want to shower and dress first."

"No problem."

Victoria went to the stairs, then stopped. "The front bedroom on your right. Just go in, I'll probably be gone by then. I've got some errands to run."

But nearly an hour had passed before he remembered the sticky window. He laid down the electric saw he was using and went upstairs . . .

Rae had been biding her time, waiting for a decent hour to make the calls. She had gone through Bobby's mail—nothing unusual, mostly bills and advertisements. At 8:30 she picked up the receiver and dialed Maxine.

She recognized the voice immediately from the tape. "Maxine, this is Rae Lemkin," she said. "I'm Bobby Cole's cousin. From Massachusetts."

Silence, then, "Hi, how you doing?"

"Well, not great. The reason I'm calling is, I've been trying to locate Bobby."

"I don't understand."

"No one seems to know where he is. I thought maybe he had been in touch with you."

"I haven't talked to him in . . . let's see, maybe two weeks. Usually he calls a couple of times during the week, then we get together most weekends. I thought it was strange, I tried to reach him . . . But then I thought maybe it's his way of saying, 'see you later.' Pretty insecure of me, huh? Listen is there something I can do?"

"No, not really. Just be sure to give me a call if you do hear from him."

"Hold it . . . what's your number?"

"555-7483. Area code 617."

"Right. Listen Rae, would you let me know what's up? I mean, no matter what, even if he's off with some girl, I want to hear that he's okay."

Rae agreed to get back to Maxine, then pressed the disconnect button, and dialed the gallery. "Let me speak to Edgar please."

"Speaking."

"This is Rae Lemkin, Bobby Cole's cousin."

Silence.

"The Marathon Man."

"Oh yeah, okay. So where's he been hiding out?"

Rae sighed. "Then you haven't heard from him?"

"No, why? I left a message on his machine last week, and I've been waiting to hear a response. I don't get it, any other artist would have jumped at—"

"Listen, I don't mean to cut you short, but I've got to get off."

Rae put down the phone and closed her eyes. Her hands were trembling. Dammit—where could Bobby be?

Rusty opened the door, then stopped. He inhaled deeply. "I'm sorry, I didn't mean . . . I thought you'd be gone."

"It's okay." Victoria stood up from the bed, her black see-through negligee sashed at the waist, fell to her thighs. "Don't be embarrassed, I'm not. I mean, we *are* adults."

"Uh . . . the window?"

"Here, let me show you." She walked slowly to the other side of her bed to the window and made an attempt at opening it, then turned to him. "See?"

Rusty walked over, staring at her, then forced his eyes to the stuck window. He put his hands beneath the wood strip and pushed. Nothing. Then again.

"It really is stuck, isn't it?" she said, moving in closer to him.

He looked down at her, into her smoky eyes and she undid the tie at her waist, letting the filmy garment fall open. He lifted his hands from the window, one hand caressing her breast, the other moving around her waist and coming to rest on the curve of her buttocks.

"Oh, Rusty," she sighed.

He kissed her, pulling her down with him to the bed.

"Yes, yes," she whispered.

He laid her down, kissing her throat, burying his lips in her breasts, then sliding his hand down . . . Then from only partially opened eyes, he saw it, the image halting him as abruptly as if he had doused by a pail of water. A doll, a beat-up rag doll was clutched in her hand by her side. Two blue chipped eyes staring up at him . . . He looked at Victoria: her eyes were squeezed shut.

He ran his hand across the back of his neck and sat up.

Victoria looked at him. "What, Rusty?"

He moved to the door. "I'm sorry, Victoria. Really, I am. But this is a mistake . . . For both of us."

*   *   *

She didn't open her eyes again until the door closed behind him, then she looked at the doll. "Don't worry, Rosalie. He loves us, I know he does."

Victoria guessed it was Rusty's sense of chivalry that had prevented him from going further. He probably thought he was taking advantage of her, of the situation . . . He didn't want to rush things, only knowing her such a short time. Or so he thought.

But the way he had kissed her before he came back to his senses . . . Oh, he'd come around, she knew he would. And just so he wouldn't start feeling awkward around her—he had to stay and finish the playroom—she'd apologize for getting so carried away. She thought about it more: was she misleading herself, thinking he cared when he didn't really? Because if that was the case . . . well, then he'd have to be treated like all the others. She'd be forced to include Rusty in the party, too . . .

He stood at the bottom of the basement stairs, staring in at the unfinished room and wondering how he could have been so stupid not to see it coming. And then not to leave once he did.

He hadn't wanted to get involved with her. Not at all. But in spite of that, it had taken the silly doll to bring him to his senses. So what should he do, thank *it* for stopping him? He thought of the ratty doll staring at him and felt a chill snake up his spine, then grabbed his jacket off the sawhorse. He needed some time away from here, away from Victoria. He was to meet Rae for lunch at the Oak Tavern at noon. Right now, he really didn't feel much like seeing *her* either. But he had at least an hour to kill. Maybe by then he could conceal his anger.

Victoria sat at the upstairs telephone with the black book opened in front of her. "This *is* Roxanne Miller, isn't it?"

"Yes."

"Then I *do* have the right number."

The woman giggled. "But a dating service, I'm hardly in need of one of those."

"We're not merely a dating service. *Select Matches* is an entirely different concept. We're statewide. Let's face it, an attractive girl like yourself is stifled by limiting herself to one small town. Think of the potential mates out there, men that due to your narrow contact, you would never meet."

"Wait a second . . . how do *you* know I'm attractive?"

"Simple. All our members are referred, hand-picked by our scouts."

"What scouts?"

"People that we employ to pick out appropriate singles. By that I mean attractive, intelligent, charming, personable and successful."

She laughed again. "That sort of limits your membership I would think."

"If you mean, do we just take the cream of the crop, you're right. But considering that cream is skimmed off the entire state, we do have a considerable membership."

"You make it sound like a beauty contest."

"In a way it is. In fact, we refuse to advertise. Once we throw our services out to the general public, we're caught in the trap of having to accept just anyone."

"Suppose I did agree, what would this membership cost me?"

"I'm not allowed to talk figures over the phone. But I guarantee you, it's within your means. In any event, you'll have the opportunity to see videos of the membership and look over the vital statistics before making your final decision."

"How do you know what's within my means?"

Victoria laughed. "Our scouts do their work well."

Roxanne hesitated. "Tell me, do I get to meet my mystery patron?"

"Sorry . . . against the rules."

"I see. Would I be alone at this meeting?"

"Actually no. Two other women were picked from Bradley. I expect both of them will be here, too."

She giggled again. "Both I assume are as attractive, charming, personable and intelligent as I?"

Victoria checked off Roxanne's name. Still two more to call, and she suspected they'd be even easier than Roxanne. Although in high school Roxanne had had the reputation of being adventurous, even reckless, she wasn't stupid.

Hmmm . . . three together. Maybe she'd get some of those little Italian pastries to go with the fruit punch.

Rusty's grim mood hadn't changed by lunchtime. It wasn't just the charade he had just played out with Victoria, it was everything . . . When he had walked into the Oak Tavern, he had gone directly to the phone booth to call the telephone company. They assured him the new number would be hooked up by Monday. Then he sat at a table, sipping a Heineken, thinking . . .

"Been here long?" Rae said, sliding into the booth across from him.

He looked up. "Just a few minutes."

"You look like you already know what I'm about to tell you."

"I take it that means neither Maxine nor the gallery had anything on Bobby."

"That's right. And I'm getting frightened, Rusty. Where could he be?"

"I don't know, but I think it's time we let the police in on this. We could go down the station tonight, after I get off work."

A hesitation, then a nod. "I'll call the family and tell them what we're doing. Aunt Sara will probably think I'm going overboard, but I don't care. It seems to me, we should have had some answers by now."

Silence.

"There's something else, isn't there?" Rae asked.

"No, not really. At least not one thing in particular. Tell me, did it ever seem to you like everything was falling in on you?"

"A couple of times."

He looked at her for a few moments, waiting. "That's it, that's all you're going to say?"

She sighed. "Well, the first time was when I was eight. My father picked up one morning, without saying a word, and took off. Disappeared. Two months later, my mother and I got a brief letter from somewhere in Texas, just to let us know he was fine. You know, one of those 'don't worry, all's well' notes. No 'wish you were here's' though." She shrugged. "Well, at least we stopped worrying."

He shook his head. "Were you two close?"

"I thought so then . . . But I guess I was wrong."

He shook his head. "And the second time?"

"That's when my mother died."

A pause, then, "When was that?"

"Just before my senior year. That was why I came to live with Bobby. Dad was gone, so when mom went, I had no one."

"What happened to her?"

"Well, at first I was told she had anemia. Later, of course, when she had to be hospitalized, I learned it was leukemia. By then, she was pretty weak. I used to go to the hospital every day after school and sit with her till they threw me out at eight o'clock."

"You were only sixteen, Carol's age. God, it must have been rough."

"It was. The worst part was, there were none of those medical miracles I had heard so much about. They tried chemotherapy, but they couldn't get her into remission. I hated the whole lot of them at the hospital—doctors, nurses, everyone involved. In fact, once mom died, I swore I'd never walk through the doors of a hospital again."

"Yet you became a nurse?"

Rae looked down at the place setting in front of her, then back at Rusty. "Later I remembered things, things I hadn't thought much about at the time. Like how a nurse saved a man in the next room when he went into cardiac arrest. How another nurse saved a young woman from choking . . ." She sighed. "So maybe they couldn't save my mother, but they did save somebody else's mother. Or father or son or daughter . . . as the case may be."

"So you decided to get in on that, huh?"

"Something like that. Or if not that dramatic a role, give the best care I could. Make the patient comfortable. The nurses did give my mother good care . . . she commented about that a lot."

Rusty put his hand over hers and squeezed it. "So when you came to Bobby's, you must have been pretty lonely."

She pulled her hand away and pushed back a fallen strand of hair. "For a while. But it's not easy being lonely, thrown into a family of ten. I was used to a fairly sedate environment, it being just my mother and me. But the noise and confusion turned out to be therapeutic. In an odd sense, I found it comforting."

Rusty shook his head.

"What?"

"I don't know, I'm just having a hard time figuring you out. The other day when you put down groups, I said to myself, well, I guess she's more self-reliant than the rest of us. Now, in spite of what you said, I get the picture that as a kid you might have wanted to be a part of a group."

Rae smiled. "I guess you're right on both counts."

"What does that mean?"

"It means there was a part of me that was envious of 'the group,' so to speak. The fun, the recklessness, the antics. But it just wasn't me. Maybe I was just too independent for my own good." She tilted her head. "So now you know my secret, Rusty Erlich. Now what?"

Rusty shook his head. "Who are you . . . and why didn't I see you before?"

"I think we should get back to the subject."

"What subject is that?"

"This all started off by you asking, did I ever feel as if everything were falling in. Now what was it *you* had in mind?"

He leaned back and sighed. "Can this wait till tonight?"

"If you want it to."

"Good. First we'll go to the police about Bobby, then we'll talk. Now let's eat lunch."

*   *   *

Agnes Mills had walked around her parlor all morning, looking at and touching the pictures of Rosalie. Different ages, different steps of her growth . . . Now she walked out of the supermarket, her arms full of bundles, heading home, but still thinking of the girl.

Mrs. Salino never should have let the girl go traipsing off to New York like that. Of course, at the time, Agnes' protests went unheeded. If only Alex had been alive . . . He never would have agreed to let Rosalie go off on her own. He would have seen that she wasn't competent to care for herself. But then again, if Alex had been alive, Rosalie's childhood might not have been riddled with confusion and suffering . . .

But what good did that kind of thinking do? The fact was, the girl did go off, and she did have her face transformed. And now she not only didn't look like Rosalie or act much like her, she didn't even believe she was . . .

"Want a lift?"

Mrs. Mills looked up, squinting through the sun at the blue truck stopped in front of her.

The young man leaned out the window. "Remember me . . . Rusty Erlich, I met you at Victoria Louise's."

She nodded. "Why, yes."

"Can I give you and those bundles a lift home?"

"Well, I wouldn't want to take you out of your way."

"No problem. Hop in." He opened the door, took the bundles from her, then gave her a hand up the step into the cab. "Where to?"

She pointed up the street. "Not far from . . . from Victoria's."

Rusty shifted gears, and went up the street. Agnes studied his profile, then asked, "How old are you, young man?"

"Twenty-four."

"I suspect you went to the high school here. Bradley High."

"That's right, why do you ask?"

"Just that it seems that I've seen you before."

"Actually, you have. I recognized you when I saw you last week at Victoria's. You lived in that house way back, when Rosalie Salino was there, didn't you?"

"You knew Rosalie?"

"Not really well. I went to a party there once."

Suddenly Agnes remembered the party, and she knew why the boy's face and name stood out so to her. He was the latecomer, the one she herself had showed downstairs. And he was the one Rosalie had talked about since she'd been a very young child. Oh, not confiding many of her secrets to Agnes or Mrs. Salino, of course . . . rather, to the doll.

Rosalie had kept up the pretense of having friends for so long that Mrs. Salino actually believed it. Agnes hadn't believed it though, not for a moment. And she had tried to dissuade Mrs. Salino from throwing that surprise party for Rosalie, but she wouldn't listen. The strange part was, all the youngsters showed up, even Rusty, the one Rosalie cared about most. But still it ended in disaster.

CHAPTER FIFTEEN

"I'M ready to go," Rae said, standing in the doorway, slipping on her jacket.

Rusty went past her into the apartment to the phone. "Let me make a call first." He dialed his home number, and Carol answered. "Hi, it's me."

"Oh, hi, Rusty. When you getting off work?"

"I am off, but I've got some things to do. Are you going to be okay?"

"I'm fine, really. The talk we had last night helped me see things better. I realize how silly I was being. And then once I went to school, saw my friends and everything, well, the world seemed a lot brighter."

"Good. We'll be getting the new number hooked in Monday."

"I've been thinking about that. Maybe it's not really necessary. I mean, I didn't get one crank call today."

"It's done, Carol. The end of it."

Silence, then, "You with Rae?"

"Yeah, but we'll be going out."

"All right. Say hello to Rae for me and have fun. If you want, you can even stay out past ten."

"Real generous of you. Listen, Carol, don't go opening the door for just anyone . . ."

"Oh great. Is that supposed to make me feel better?"

"No, that's supposed to make you smart."

Rae studied Rusty as he put down the phone. "What was all that about, what's going on with Carol?"

"Nothing."

"That's not true, tell me."

"Later. First let's take care of Bobby." He took her by the

elbow and led her back toward the door, glancing in her bedroom as they went: the stereo cabinet was still in pieces on the floor.

Victoria squeezed the Noctec liquid into the pitcher of fruit and vodka punch. She laid out the pastries on a plate, put the plate, napkins, punch and glasses on the parlor table, then rubbed her hands together. She looked at the screen and projector—the film of the cosmetic surgeon's success stories was wound in place. She was ready . . .

Although Victoria had planned to have the girls come tomorrow night, Roxanne had pleaded plans for Friday. So on impulse, she set it up for tonight. And neither Barbara nor Penelope objected to such late notice. In fact, they both sounded rather eager . . .

Within ten minutes, the bell rang. Victoria ran to answer it. "Well, here I am," the young woman said, her full rosy cheeks pumped up, "attractive, intelligent, personable and available."

Victoria laughed. "Roxanne, right?"

"How'd you guess?"

"Come on in. The other girls should be here any time now. Let me pour you some punch."

Victoria poured a drink and gave it to Roxanne.

"Okay, bring out the screen and projector," Roxanne said as she took a sip of her drink. "I want to see what the Commonwealth has to offer."

"I want to report a missing person," Rusty said to the officer on desk duty.

"Hold on," he said, "I'll get you someone to talk to." He ran a finger under his thin, beak nose. "Crandall, how about taking this one."

"Sorry, Hawk, I'm off duty. Get Spanski."

Hawk gestured to a door. "Go in there," he told Rusty, then picked up a phone and pressed a button. "Spanski, I'm sending you one."

Rusty and Rae walked into the office. A thick-chested officer with a white face and short, stiff straight brown hair stood up. "My name's Spanski—lieutenant. What can I do you for?"

Rusty introduced Rae and himself. "We're here to report a missing person." They both sat.

Spanski stuck a large hand in his drawer and pulled out a sheet of paper, then lifted a pen in his left hand. "Name and address of this person?"

"Robert Cole, 27 Caradin Ave. Everyone calls him Bobby." Rae said.

"Age?"

"Twenty-five."

"What's he to you?"

"My cousin."

He looked at Rusty. "And you?"

"A friend."

"Any signs of foul play?"

"No, nothing we could see—we looked around his apartment," Rusty said. "We've both been trying to reach him for ten days, two weeks. He's not answered his messages, his mail's been piling up. His car's parked in the driveway, unlocked. We spoke to his friends, his girl, his family, his business acquaintances, and no one knows where he's gone."

"What's he do for a living?"

"He's an artist."

Spanski dropped the pen on the paper and folded his hands together. "One of those creative fellas, huh? I once knew an artist who dropped out of sight, went off into the world to do his thing . . . For two years, no one saw hide or hair of him, the family were beside themselves. When he came back home, he settled right down, went into selling used cars."

Rusty and Rae looked at each other. It was Rae who spoke first. "I'm sorry, Lieutenant, but I don't see the relevance."

The lieutenant shrugged. "Those creative types need space, know what I mean? It doesn't mean your guy won't come walking home some day."

"Bobby's not like that."

"But he is a grown man. He doesn't have to report his whereabouts to anyone. So long as he doesn't commit a crime, it's a free country."

"So you're saying, you won't do anything?" Rusty said.

"Hey listen, from where I sit, it sounds to me like there's no crime been committed here. You show me some evidence that there was one, and I'll more than gladly investigate it."

"Come on," Rusty said to Rae, standing up. "This is a waste of time."

"Now, don't get me wrong, I'll be more than happy to file this report for you people, but . . ." He spread his arms, shrugging.

Rusty leaned over, took the paper with it's few notations, and tossed it in the box marked, "for file." "Don't put yourself out, lieutenant."

Barbara and Penny came to the door together, both giggling. Victoria led them into the parlor; they looked at Roxanne and laughed louder. "I don't believe this," Barbara said catching her breath, "I just don't believe this. Of all people to come to a dating service, you, Roxy?"

Roxanne stood up, her face crimson. "Well, after all, they *were* looking for the best in town . . . and I had nothing else to do tonight. Besides, what kind of garbage is this? Why am I the one making excuses? What are you two doing here?"

"Same thing you are, I guess. I saw Penny walking from the bus stop," Barbara said.

"My brother took my car so I'm bussing it," Penny interjected.

"So I picked her up," Barbara went on. "When she finally told me where she was heading, I thought I'd die. Then to find you here. It's too much."

Roxanne shrugged. "Well, here we are—the cream of Bradley. The way I see it, none of us have a thing to be embarrassed about."

"True," Barbara said. "Just wait till we tell Elaine about this. Can you just see her face when she learns she wasn't one of the chosen few?"

"What do you say we go out later?" Penny said.

"Okay," Roxanne said plopping down into a chair. "That is, if I hold up through these home movies. I am *so* tired, I can just about keep my eyes open now."

Barbara and Penny sat on the sofa. Victoria refilled Roxanne's punch glass, then handed glasses to the other two. "Low cal," she said, noticing Penny's thick hips. Victoria moved the screen into place, then went to the doorway . . .

Barbara turned to Roxanne. "Penny and I were saying when we came up, that this place looks familiar. Then we remembered: this is the place where that strange girl lived. Remember that awful party, how we razzed her so much, she actually threw us out of the house? God, when I think back on that one, we *were* real shits, weren't we?"

Silence.

"Roxy!"

Roxanne jumped and her eyes opened. "See what I mean, I'm dead. What did you say?"

Barbara flipped her hand, smiling. "Forget it, go to sleep. I'm going to watch these films and find me a guy."

"Okay, everyone ready?" Victoria said. "Lights out."

Rusty stopped by first to check on Carol, then he and Rae went to a coffeehouse called Morgan's.

"Let's forget about Bobby for a few minutes. You're worried about Carol, too, and I want to know why."

He sat there, staring into his coffee.

"Rusty?"

He picked up his spoon and tapped it on the saucer. "For a week or so, she's been getting crank calls. Usually nothing's said, one time there was a girl's voice saying, 'Get the fuck out of the house.' Then with this thing happening at the skating rink . . . I don't know. I just don't like it."

"Does Carol think it's connected."

He shrugged. "She doesn't know, at least that's what she says. According to her, someone rammed into her and she couldn't tell if it was done purposely or not."

"But you do think it was connected?"

"I don't know. Maybe I'm just over-reacting, reading too much into it. I do have a tendency to get that way when it comes to Carol."

Rae put down her coffee cup. "But I like that about you."

"You like your men a little neurotic, do you?"

"You care about people, you're willing to step in and do something. That's what I like."

"Yeah . . . well, I don't know if that was always so true about me. I've let things pass that maybe shouldn't have. You *do* remember, I wasn't one of those free thinkers like yourself."

"Me and my big mouth, huh?"

"No, you said it like it was. There were definitely some minuses in belonging. It made it easy for you, delaying the moment when you had to get out there and make your own decisions."

"So what kind of things are you talking about?"

Rusty sat back, folding his arms at his chest. "I'm doing some work on a house in town. Way back when I was in school, a girl named Rosalie Salino lived in that house. Did you know her?"

Rae shook her head. "I don't think so."

"Well, she was kind of a sad case. Fat, not at all pretty or sure of herself. The kind other kids like to pick on."

"And you picked on her?"

"No, not me. But I stood and watched others do it. Which doesn't say much for me, of course."

Rae sighed. "I don't suppose it's easy for a kid to buck his friends—it takes more guts than most have. Of course if you don't belong anyway, you don't have to worry about ruffling any feathers."

"High school wasn't really so long ago, but sometimes I wonder who that kid back there was—he seems so foreign to me now. I was really into that whole scene: the football quarterback eating up all that hero worship . . ."

"Oh, I don't know . . . you seemed to like it then."

"Sure I did, but I knew it was fake. When you're a kid, though, you don't always care. You just sit back and let it feed your ego, let kids kiss up to you without even knowing who you are. You become some kind of symbol."

"But you did have real friends."

"Oh sure. Most of the kids I hung around with. Not to say we all didn't pull a lot of juvenile stunts, sometimes even some we regret—at least, I know I do. But on the whole, we've turned into pretty decent people."

"And what about that blonde you went with?"

"Elaine? To her, I was only a symbol and who knows, maybe she was that for me, too. The only difference is, she'd like nothing better than to go back to how it was."

"But you're not interested?"

He shook his head. "I'm not interested in going backward. Besides, my tastes have changed from high school."

"How so?"

A half smile, then, "Well, when I was a kid I always took a frankfurter at a barbecue. Now it's a burger."

Rae repressed a smile. "I *am* impressed."

Then he frowned. "However, once or twice, I find my hand going straight for that hot dog."

Rae studied Rusty's expression, then, "Well, maybe your tastes haven't changed as much as you think."

Rusty leaned forward, putting his hands over hers. "They have. Trust me."

Rae licked her lips and pulled her hands back to her coffee cup. "I think we should get back to the subject of Carol. What will you do?"

Rusty stared at her a moment, then sat back in his seat. "Well, as you've heard, I already had my phone number changed," he said. "Hopefully that will solve the problem. If not—" Suddenly he looked up, past Rae, and his features tightened.

"What's wrong?" she asked, turning and following his stare to the table nearest the entrance. An attractive girl with dark hair was sitting there. Staring back at her. "Who is she, Rusty?"

He sighed. "That's Victoria Louise. The Salino house I'm working on now . . ."

"Yes."

"Well, now it's *her* house."

*   *   *

The first time back with Barbara's car, Victoria had taken a bus. This time—after returning Roxanne's car—she had walked. When she passed Morgan's and saw Rusty's truck, she walked in.

If it had been Carol he was with, she wouldn't have been nearly so stunned. But it wasn't—it was another girl, one that she recognized from high school. And the worst part was, it was a girl who had been as much on the fringe as Rosalie had been.

And he was holding her hand . . .

CHAPTER SIXTEEN

VICTORIA was waiting in the basement when Rusty came to work the next day. "It's coming out wonderfully, Rusty. Exactly as I pictured it."

"Good, I'm glad you like it."

"When do you think it'll all be done?"

"The electricians will be here today. I'll be working most of the weekend, and by Monday, the plumber will be able to put in the bathroom fixtures and hook up the heating. I'd say next Wednesday, it should be ready for wallpapering and carpeting."

"And that's it?"

"Right, then on to the upstairs work." Rusty picked up a piece of paneling and laid it in.

A few moments of silence. "Then you're not still upset, angry with me. You know, about what happened yesterday."

A deep sigh, then, "Look if I acted angry, I'm sorry, I didn't mean to put any blame anywhere. It was just one of those things that wouldn't have worked out. But hey, who cares, the thing is, nothing did really happen. Let's just forget it."

"Of course if we knew each other better . . . I mean, I know you keep pretty busy, but still it might be fun. Getting to know one another, that is."

Rusty put a nail in place, hammered it in, then turned to her. "Look, why don't we leave it just like it is? Business relationship, friends . . ."

"But I don't see why—"

"Because that's how I want it!"

He turned back to his work, and Victoria felt a sudden emptiness in her stomach as though pieces had been ripped out. She took a deep breath, then turned toward the stairs. "Sure, of

125

course," she said in the lightest voice she could manage. "I understand."

She walked up the stairs. *Oh sure, she understood all right—he couldn't have made it much clearer. But would Rosalie understand that he was no better than the rest of them? God, what would this do to her?*

Rusty rubbed his forehead with the palm of his hand . . . finally she was gone. He hadn't meant to shout at her like that—after all, he *was* working for the lady—but what do you do with someone that persistent? Soon he'd be done with the playroom, but still there was the other work to do on the house. Would he be able to deal with her on a long-term basis without them having a major blow-up?

What the fuck did she want with him anyway . . . why didn't she give up? He had enough on his mind—Bobby out there somewhere and the cops not giving a shit, and then the business with Carol—without having to worry about Victoria's hurt feelings . . .

Victoria clasped the phone tightly with both hands.

"Is this Gena McDermott?"

"Yes it is."

"I represent Broadgay, the publisher of children's educational books and magazines."

"Oh yes, of course, I've heard of you. I saw your name in a magazine at my obstetrician's office."

"Fine. I'm calling because we have a campaign going on this month to get prospective parents familiar with our numerous publications. Your and your husband's name were picked from our list of expectants."

"Really . . . for what?"

"To come to our presentation. We're offering special prices this month on most of our books and magazines, but naturally there's no obligation to buy."

"Well . . ." Gena seemed to be mulling over the offer. "The baby isn't even born yet. I'm not due for a few more weeks."

"You'd be surprised at how many parents, at least those that think ahead, begin their child's library right at birth. You see, they realize the necessity of a quality education. Unless you prepare your child for the competition he's going to meet out there, he'll be already behind by the time he starts school."

"But such a young child, what would he do with a magazine?"

"Naturally nothing alone. But our early childhood education material is geared for parents to use *with* their child. For instance, one of our very popular publications is directed to the child's first year only. With the help of his parents, that child will be ready to read by his second year."

"A two year old reading . . you're kidding?"

"Not at all. And I'm sure you want that to be *your* child, not your neighbor's child."

"Well yes, of course."

"And you've heard of the *Answer Me Now* series?"

"Oh, yes, one of my nephews has those books. They're very good."

"Well then you'll appreciate it when I tell you that the complete twelve-book series will be given free to you and your husband just for showing up at our presentation."

"Just a second." Then coming back to the phone. "When is it and where?"

Rusty worked straight through lunch, then dinner, trying to give his frustration a legitimate outlet. At 8:15 he knocked off and went home. "Hi, Rusty," Carol called out when he came in. Then she came into the parlor carrying her jacket.

"Where do you think you're going?" he asked.

"Out. It is Friday night, you know. There's some fried chicken in the fridge. Heat it up if you're hungry."

He tossed a pillow on the sofa and laid down. "Why don't you stay in tonight?"

"I don't want to," then, "why should I?"

A sigh. "No reason, I guess. So where are you going?"

"Bowling. Merrimack Lanes."

"Who with?"

"Let me see . . . Franny, Mona, Lin, Peter, Chug, and Denny."

"Who's driving?"

"Peter. And I'll be home at twelve. No later. Peter's got to get the car back early."

Silence.

"Well, say something, Rusty don't just lay there and stare through me."

Rusty rubbed his eyes, then shut them. "I'm tired, Carol."

"Where's Rae?"

"Working, why do you ask?"

Carl shrugged. "I don't know, it seems as if you and her have been a twosome lately."

"We're together so much because we're trying to find Bobby. That's it."

She rolled her eyes. "Okay, if you say so. Well, have you come up with anything yet?"

More silence.

She waited a moment, then said, "Rusty . . . ?" Realizing he was asleep, she grabbed the comforter off the chair and carefully laid it over him.

Weekend nights were full house in the emergency room, and tonight was no exception at Valley. Two car accidents, a drug overdose, a heart attack and an assortment of strep throats and ear infections. And still two hours until Rae's shift was over at eleven.

If nothing else though, it had kept her busy, too busy to think about all the things that were cluttering her mind—that is, until now. Rae walked into the nearly deserted cafeteria, got a styrofoam container of coffee and brought it over to one of the empty tables.

Last night the lieutenant's attitude had made her so angry she wanted to strangle him. But she tried to conceal her anger from Rusty when they got to Morgan's. In addition to his concern over Bobby, he was upset over Carol. She remembered the way Rusty had held her hands and then the way she had pulled her hands away, even though she didn't really want to ... Why had she done it, then?

Rusty had looked at her oddly, but he hadn't said anything. Then, right after, he had spotted that woman so it had gone forgotten. Victoria Louise—she had been staring at both of them. Rusty said he was working for her ... Was it possible that there was more to it than that? She was immediately annoyed at herself. And so if there was ... what business was it of hers? Here *she* was, not even willing to let him touch her.

She pushed the thought aside, exchanging it for another: Was she right in thinking that a bright blue Honda had followed her to work that afternoon—that is, until she pulled into the hospital parking lot, and it kept on going? She had only noticed it because she had a Honda herself, not such a late model, of course. But it *was* true, every single time she glanced into her rearview mirror, there it was ...

There you go again, Rae, reading dark implications into the simplest things. She downed the rest of her coffee, tossing the paper cup into the trash. She was better off working ...

Mac took off his coat, tossed it on a chair, then leaned over and patted Gena's belly. "How's my boy?"

"Would you stop that, Mac, I'm trying to paint this rocker, and if I spill paint on the carpet I'll strangle you."

He looked at the miniature rocking chair sitting on newspapers laid out on the floor. "Where'd you get that?"

"A garage sale in Merrimack. A little old man, he must have been 102, you should have seen some of the things he had to sell."

"How much?"

"What?"

"The chair naturally?"

"Thirty-five. It's worth twice that."

He studied the chair, then sat down. "The kid can't sit yet."

"He can't play basketball yet either."

"Where's the newspaper?" Then he pointed to the paper protecting the carpet. "There, right?"

Gena smiled. "But not the business or sports page." She pulled the two newspaper sections from the chair and tossed them over to him. "Oh, by the way, Mac, don't make plans for tomorrow night."

"Why not?"

"You know those *Answer Me Now* books my nephew Leon has?"

"What books?"

"Don't pretend you don't know what they are."

"Okay I know. What about them?"

"We're getting a set free. For the baby."

"He can't read."

"He can't play basketball either."

"Dammit, will you stop saying that. I put the goddamned hoop up for myself. If it bothers you, I'll take it down tomorrow."

She leaned over and patted his leg. "Come on, Mackipie . . . Why must you fight everything?"

"Because you, Gena, eat through money like a termite."

"The books are free. Honest."

"Nothing is free. What do we have to do?"

"Just go to a presentation on children's publications. Books, magazines, that type of thing. There's absolutely no obligation to buy."

"Tomorrow is Saturday. The Celtics are playing Saturday night."

"Don't you care at all about your son's education? Do you want him to be at the bottom of his class or would you rather have him doing better than the rest of the kids?" The white paint from the brush spattered onto the carpet. "Dammit, Mac, look what you made me do now?"

"Wait up," Meg called out to Rae. "I'll walk with you. Rae stopped till Meg caught up. "I hate walking out alone to these dark lots. It gives me the creeps."

Rae smiled. "Working tomorrow?"

"Yeah, another late shift." Meg pulled out a chocolate bar from her jacket pocket. "Want some?"

Rae shook her head. "I'm off till Sunday."

"Good, and if you're smart, you'll sleep in, try to relax some. Stop worrying about your cousin, he'll show up, you'll see."

"You really think so?"

"I'm sure so. People don't disappear, they take off. At least the smart ones do." She stopped short at her car. "Well, here I am. Have a safe ride home."

Rae went to her car, got in and started it up. She pulled out of the lot, stopped, then swung onto the road. Meg thought she was worrying needlessly, just like the rest of the family. Oh, Aunt Sara wasn't any too happy, but she was more annoyed at Bobby than anything. Only Rusty believed that there might be something wrong.

She stopped at the red light, waited for it to turn, then continued on, thinking about Rusty. She remembered the very first time she'd seen him. It was after a football game. He had looked so handsome, so unapproachable . . . And in a way he was—two dozen kids surrounding him, and Elaine like chief of secret service close at his side . . . He must be full of himself, she had decided without even talking to him. Then later when Bobby introduced them . . . He had nodded, even smiled, but hadn't said a word. First impression fully confirmed.

Of course, she hadn't said a word either . . . In fact, she hadn't even smiled at him.

Coming back to the present, Rae spotted a red light up ahead with a van stopped by it—she applied the brakes to slow the car. Then again. They weren't working!

Her mind froze, sweat beading instantly along her forehead. She pumped the brakes. Still nothing. Suddenly she remembered the downshift. She put it in second, then in first . . . The car slowed, but still she was going to smash the rear end of the van. She glanced to the right—a row of trees—then left to the field. She wrenched the steering wheel to the left, crossed the median strip, the road, over the curb and sidewalk, and plowed into the bushes. The car stopped.

She folded her arms across the wheel and laid her head on them. Her body was trembling . . . What would have happened if there had been traffic?

Victoria put the Honda driver's manual back into the dining room hutch, then went downstairs and replaced Rusty's tool. She didn't know the first thing about mechanics, but this had been easy. She had just popped a few holes into the plastic master cylinder and that was all there was to it.

She went upstairs, took the doll off the windowsill and laid her on the bed. "Don't worry, Rosalie," she said, "Rusty will be coming too—along with the others. Everyone will be at the party. I'll make sure."

Suddenly a memory came to her . . . a memory of all those parties she had almost missed. What would they have thought if they knew she was there?

"Where you going?" Mama asked as the girl put on her jacket.

"A party, mama. The kids asked me to a party."

"So where is the boy, he doesn't come call for you?"

"It's not like that, mama. I told you before—everyone meets, then we all go together."

"Where will you meet?"

"At the drugstore, mama."

"No, no, I don't like this."

"I'm going, mama. If you like it or not, I'm going." She opened the door. Mrs. Mills was standing there, blocking her way.

"Don't lie, Rosalie, there is no party."

"You shut up and mind your own business!" She pushed the woman aside, then ran out of the house, up the street. The party was to be at Millie's house. She liked when parties were held there. Millie had a cement incline outside the basement window where her father kept the hose. From there Rosalie could see everything . . .

Victoria's thoughts snapped back to the present, and she heard crying. She picked up Rosalie and hugged her. "Don't, please don't," she pleaded. Dammit ... what was ... what was going on? The tears were falling down her cheeks, not the dolls!

A timid voice. "Hello."

"Carol, this is Rae."

A sigh of relief.

"Oh, I'm sorry, Carol. I didn't mean to frighten you. Rusty told me about those calls you've been getting."

"It's okay, really. I just got in the house this second."

"I know it's late, but can I speak to Rusty?"

"Sure. He's sleeping, but I'll wake him."

"No, Carol, wait." Rae pondered a moment. "Don't do that. Let him sleep."

"Are you sure? He wouldn't be mad."

"I'm sure. It's no problem. I'll talk to him tomorrow."

Rae put down the telephone and closed her eyes. Someone had purposely let out the brake fluid. She had seen the punctures in the cylinder herself. And tomorrow she would have a mechanic confirm it. But she had to hold herself together—she couldn't panic.

Chapter Seventeen

"TELEPHONE for you, Rusty," Carol said, nudging his shoulder the next morning."
He sat up instantly. "What time is it, Carol, I overslept."
"Take it easy, it's only eight o'clock."
He stretched his arms and shoulders, yawning, then gestured to the phone receiver Carol was holding. "Who is it?"
"Mrs. Burns, Penny's mother."
Rusty's brow furrowed slightly as he took the receiver. "Hello."
"Rusty, this is Hazel Burns, Penelope's mother."
"Of course. How are you?"
"Not so good. Forgive me for bothering you at this hour on a weekend."
"No problem. I should have been up twenty minutes ago. What can I do for you?"
"I know you haven't been in touch much with Penelope lately, but I'm at my wits end. I called every one I could think of whom she might have been in contact with. Then I thought of you . . ."
"What's the problem, Mrs. Burns?"
"Well, Thursday night Penelope went to check into a computer dating service."
"Penny . . . at a dating service?"
"Yes, I agree, it's silly. But you know how girls get, they're out of college a year or two and unless they're wrapped up in a career, they start worrying. With all this talk about biological clocks, they think they're carrying around a time bomb."
Rusty smiled.

"In any event, she lent her car to her younger brother, and said she'd hop a bus. Well, the thing is, she never returned home."

Silence, then, "Where was this dating service, what was the name of it?"

"All I know is, it was in town."

"I know those things are pretty popular, but I can't say I've ever heard of one in Bradley. Tell me, did you call Elaine?"

"I did, but she didn't know of one either. The last she saw of Penelope was last week at Gena's house. Then I spoke to Gena, but of course, being married, she knew less about those things than Elaine. I tried some of the other girls, but couldn't reach them."

Rusty rubbed his hand over the back of his neck and leaned his elbows on his knees. "I really don't know what advice to give you, Mrs. Burns. Last Saturday was the last time I saw her myself. And before that, well, it was months."

"I know what you may be thinking, that she went off with some young man and didn't want to tell me. But I know the score, and Penelope is quite aware of that. I can't imagine her worrying me like this."

A pause, then, "Did you call the police and report this?"

"Yes, and they tried to pacify me by saying they'd look into it. But Columbo's they're not. I'm not exactly holding my breath."

Rusty couldn't help smiling. "Listen, I'll make a few calls and see what I can find out. I can't promise you much more, it seems like you've covered most of the ground."

"Do it, Rusty. Whatever you can do, please."

"Well?" Carol said when he put down the receiver.

"You heard. Penny's missing."

"Why didn't you tell Mrs. Burns about Bobby?"

Rusty stood up—he had slept in his clothes. He went to a hutch, opened it and pulled out some clean clothes, then headed for the bathroom. "Why . . . what good would that do?"

Carol followed after him. "Maybe it's connected."

"I actually thought about that for a second, but no, it's ridiculous. Other than for a party now and then, Bobby rarely sees Penny. Get me a towel."

Carol opened the linen closet, pulled out a bath towel and tossed it to Rusty. "But they used to be so close."

"Sure, but that was in high school, Carol. Then everyone was close." He shut the door and turned on the shower.

Rusty came out of the bathroom, running a comb through his hair. He went for his jacket.

"Wait, I've got breakfast. Waffles."

"Thanks, but I can't. I'm already a half hour behind schedule."

"I think it stinks you working all this overtime."

"I agree, but I've got to do it."

"Why?"

"Because the lady's paying for it, that's why. Besides she's having a lot of work done. She could have given it to a bigger outfit, but she didn't. She chose me."

"Why you?"

"What does that mean? Why not me?"

"I don't know. Just that if I were in her place and didn't know anyone in town, I think I would have chosen a big company. I would have felt that there was more chance that they knew what they were doing."

"Well, lucky for me, it wasn't you. What are you doing today?"

Carol shrugged. "Hanging around with Franny, I guess. Maybe we'll go into town and look through the stores."

"Okay, be home before dark."

"What time will you be back?"

"About four-thirty. I'll call around to see what I can find out about Penny when I get home."

Carol's hand went to her chest. "Uh-oh."

"What?"

Rae called last night. About twelve. She sounded kind of shaky. I don't knwo though, maybe it was my imagination."

"Why didn't you wake me?"

"Because she wouldn't let me, that's why. She said to let you sleep. Are you mad?"

He pulled her braid, then slipped on his jacket. "No. Go eat those waffles."

"Hi, Victoria, this is Elaine."

Silence.

"Victoria?"

"Yes, I'm here. How are you doing?"

"Okay, I guess. Actually I'm looking forward to next week, the party. I've got a big red circle around it on my calendar."

"Well, I'm sure you won't be disappointed."

"Good, but in the meantime, I was thinking. Since your social life isn't quite in full gear yet, maybe we could do something together tonight."

"No, I can't."

"Oh . . . you have a date?"

"No, I'm staying in."

"Then maybe I could come over. We could order out Chinese?"

"No, don't do that!"

Elaine sat up in her chair. "Take it easy, Victoria. I have no intention of barging in where I'm not wanted."

"It's not that, I didn't mean for it to come across that way. I'm tired, Elaine, I'm in the midst of having my house done over, and it's a bitch. I want everything to be so perfect for the party. You do understand, not one thing can go wrong."

"Sure, of course. Well, then I'll see you next Friday."

Elaine hung up. Victoria was okay, she guessed. At least she was more exciting than most of the regular crowd as they settled into early infirmity. But there was no doubt about it— the girl *was* moody.

Rusty didn't bother phoning, instead he picked up a dozen munchkins and two coffees and headed to Rae's. He'd give himself ten minutes—that's all he could spare.

He rang the doorbell several times, then saw her standing out in the hall, looking down through the plate glass before she finally rang the buzzer and let him in. "You getting nervous these days?" he said climbing the steps.

She gave a silent nod, then led him inside the apartment.

He put down the coffee and donuts, then sighed. "Okay, what's wrong now?"

"I'm really sorry to be such a bother to you, Rusty," she said, chips of ice spraying from her voice. "There was no need to put yourself out."

"What's gotten into you? That's not what I meant, and you know it."

"What did you mean?"

"Simply that every time I turn around there's a new disaster staring me in the face."

"Why, what happened?"

"A girl I used to hang around with, Penny Burns . . . she's missing. Her mother called me this morning to ask if I've seen her."

"And had you?"

"Last week at a party. But I know very little about what she's up to these days. I told her mother I'd ask around though."

"I'm sorry, I didn't mean to act so bitchy."

"Then why did you?"

A sigh. She looked at the coffee on the end table. "One of those for me?" she asked.

Rusty opened the container and handed her one, then opened the other for himself. "Come on, sit down," he said leading her to the sofa. "I want to hear what's wrong."

"On the way home from work last night, my brakes went out."

"Christ. What happened, were you hurt?"

"No. And nothing really happened. I downshifted, then when I couldn't stop completely, I went into some bushes across the road."

"What about your emergency?"

She shook her head. "I didn't think of that."

"Well, at least you found a soft spot to land. It must have been frightening, though."

"Yes, but it was more than that."

"What do you mean, more?"

"When I finally pulled myself together, I looked under the hood . . . You remember me telling you I used to fool around with cars?"

"I remember, so?"

"The master cylinder had several holes punctured in it. Someone did it purposely so that the brake fluid would drain out. I sent over a garage to tow it."

Rusty stared at her, then went over to the window, not saying anything, just looking out at the street.

She stood up and followed him to the window, and touched his arm. "What are you thinking, Rusty?"

"I'm thinking that normally these are things you read about in newspapers, that happen to other people. Single unrelated incidents. This time, we have a series of incidents—Bobby, Carol, Penny, you—and these things are happening to people I know. Every time."

"What are you saying, that there's a connection to all of this . . . and that you're it?"

He rolled his hands into fists and placed them on the window frame. "I am, but it doesn't make much sense, does it? Sure I know Penny, but I run into her now what—two, three times a year? And then only to say, 'Hello.'" Russ turned around and faced Rae. "What connection do I really have to her?"

Rae shook her head, and Russ reached out and touched her face, running his fingers down her cheek, then pulled his hand back. "I'm late, I've got to leave."

"Go ahead, I'm fine. Really."

"I assume your car won't get repaired today." Rae nodded. "I'll be off work about four. Can I pick you up? We'll go to my house, have some dinner . . . And talk more then."

Every nail Russ hammered into the paneling presented another unanswered question: Could it have something to do with the kids he had hung around with? But then, where did Carol and Rae fit in? And if so, why not the rest of them . . . for that matter, why not him?

Again he went back to theory number one—a connection to him, but still Penny's involvement made absolutely no sense. Unless whatever danger existed presented a threat to everyone he knew in Bradley. If that were true, things could only get worse.

CHAPTER EIGHTEEN

RUSTY opened the apartment door and let Rae in. "This is nice," Rae said looking around.

Rusty took her jacket, and tossed it, along with his, onto a chair. "Mostly second-hand furniture and blue light specials. Carol's responsible for the knickknacks and throw pillows. And of course, it was I who picked out those terrific kitchen curtains."

Rae smiled, then sat on the sofa, pulling a throw pillow onto her lap. "Can I ask you something, Russ? Not to do with your taste in curtains."

"Go ahead."

"Why did you get so uptight the other night when you saw that girl at Morgan's?"

"You're talking about Victoria?"

Rae nodded.

"It showed then?"

"Uh-huh."

A hesitation, then, "I'm not sure myself. Just something about her puts me on edge."

She screwed up her face, her eyes avoiding his and her fingers pulling at the tassles on the pillow. "Seems to me, she's got a thing for you."

He fell onto the couch beside her, taking the pillow from her and tossing it aside, then put his arm around her and ran his fingers into her hair. "You think so? Tell me, what about you?"

"Rusty . . . we're talking about Victoria."

"I'm not, I'm talking about you." He released the combs holding her hair up, and the sides swung forward, thick fiery red waves falling past her shoulders.

She swallowed hard. "Why did you do that?"

"I wanted to see it down . . . It's beautiful, you know." He took a deep breath, then let it out. "So are you."

Silence, then she went for the combs in his hand, a tense smile on her lips. "Not very practical though. If I wore it this way in work, they'd hang me."

He stretched out his arm and dropped the combs onto the floor. "You're not *at* work. Why are you so scared?"

"That's silly, scared of what?"

He shrugged. "I don't know . . . of me, of letting yourself go maybe."

She yanked herself back, her eyes darkening, challenging his. "Still carrying around that inflated ego from high school days, aren't you? A girl pulls away from you and you don't think for one minute it could be you, do you? Immediately i   he who has the problem!"

"Who hurt you, Rae, was it a guy?"

She began to get up. "You don't give up, do you? Not that's it's really any of your business, but it wasn't a guy. There's never been a guy!"

He grabbed a hold of her arm and pulled her back down next to him. "Why not?"

Her eyes filled up. She shrugged.

"Because every time you dared love someone—your dad, your mom—they deserted you?"

"How dare you say that? Maybe my dad . . . but not my mom. I mean, she died, it wasn't her fault. Surely you can't blame her for leaving me . . ." Suddenly two tears spilt over, down her cheeks, and she quickly brushed them away.

"Tell me about it," he said.

She took a deep breath, then looked up at him. "I did blame her," she said finally. "For such a long time, I hated her for leaving me . . . She had always been so strong, so independent. Even when my dad left—I never saw her break down once. In my eyes, there was nothing she couldn't do if she really wanted to do it bad enough. So if that were true, why couldn't she have lived?"

"Sounds like she was a special lady . . . maybe something like you."

Rae pressed her lips together, then relaxed them. "God, we were so close, Rusty, sometimes we talked and laughed way into the night. Like two kids. We were more like sisters than mother and daughter. When she died, the pain was so awful, I thought I was going to die, too."

"But of course you didn't—you came here to live with Bobby's family."

A half smile. "Not that easily did I come. Jack had to bodily drag me away from the apartment. Screaming, kicking, swearing—the works."

Rusty put his hand to her cheek and stroked it. "And then you decided, never again?"

She looked into Rusty's eyes, not answering. "I guess I did," she said finally. "Oh, you can care, that's allowed. But just don't let yourself get too involved."

"Then it wasn't worth it?"

"What?"

"The pain. In exchange for what you had with your mother for those years."

She closed her eyes for a moment, sighed, then opened them. "It was, of course it was. But why does there have to be a payoff?"

"There doesn't always. But then again you can't count on it. What a waste not to chance it though."

"I suppose now we're talking about us."

He nodded. "Take a chance on *me*, Rae. I won't rush you. Or pressure you."

Silence, staring.

He ran his hand along her shoulder. "Let me hold you, dammit, just let me hold you."

She moved closer, finally resting her head against his chest, then she looked up at him. "You know what the silliest part of all this is?"

"What's that?"

"I feel so involved already."

He leaned forward, gently putting his lips to hers. Slowly, her arms wrapped around his back, her fingers sliding up around his neck . . .

"I'm home, Rusty!" Carol called out as the door opened. Russ and Rae pulled apart. "Oops, scuse me," Carol said feigning embarrassment. "I didn't mean to interrupt, I mean, if you want, I could go out and—"

Rae's face flushed, and Rusty leaned his head back against the sofa for a moment. "Enough, Carol," he said, then sitting upright. "You remember Rae, don't you?"

"Of course I do. Hi."

"Hi yourself." Rae knelt down, picked up the two curved black combs from the floor and pulled her hair back, knotting it and securing it to her head with the combs. "When do you get those stitches out?"

"My appointment's Monday." Then making a face, "You had to remind me, huh?"

"Oh stop worrying. Trust me, it's nothing."

"Bet you think I'm a real coward."

Rae smiled. "Not at all. As I recall, once the doctor got down to business, you didn't make a sound."

Carol took off her coat and dropped it over one of the chairs, then looking at both of them, "Well, do I have something to tell you people."

"Is this going to be good or bad?" Rusty asked.

"Bad."

He sat forward. "What happened now . . . not another one of those telephone calls?"

"Not bad to me, Rusty. To Millie."

"Who's Millie?"

"You know, the one you used to hang around with. Millie . . . oh what's her name?"

"Carton."

"Right."

"What happened to her?"

"Well, nothing really that I know of. Just that she's not there. At the school."

Russ stood up. "Okay, take it slow and from the start. What school are we talking about?"

"Millie runs a nursery school in town, and Franny's little sister goes there. Well, a couple days ago, Friday, I think . . . Millie just didn't show up. All the kids were waiting, ready to be picked up, but no Millie. Franny's mother called and according to the two aides she has working for her, she wasn't at the school or home. She lives next door to the school, and her car was parked right in the driveway. And that's it."

"Have the police been notified?"

"Yup. Millie's parents called them, but as far as Franny knows they haven't done one single thing to find her."

Rusty looked at Rae. "Someone else from the group missing." Then he stood up, went to the bookshelf and slid out a book. He stared at the cover.

"What's that, Russ?" Rae asked.

"Our yearbook. 1981. Maybe it wouldn't be such a bad idea to go through this . . . Maybe pick out kids who had a grudge against the kids I hung out with."

"Why?" Carol said. "You think someone you knew in high school is *taking* people?"

"You promised me, Mac."

Mac turned on the TV, then eased his massive frame into the recliner. "I did no such thing, I simply stopped arguing."

"That's the same thing, and you know it."

"Look, Gena, have some compassion, you know how I look forward to seeing a Celtics Lakers game. How can you, in good conscience, ask me to give it up to go look at a pile of kid's magazines."

"But I want those books, Mac. And the lady specifically asked that we both be there."

Mac looked at his watch. "What time is it over?"

"Around nine-thirty."

"I'll tell you what. That's around half time. Suppose I drive you over, leave you off, then pick you up an hour and a half later. This way, she can't say I didn't show, and I can schlep the books in the car so you won't have to."

"Do you think that'll work?"

"Sure it'll work, why wouldn't it? When I come in, I'll even go through the motions of looking over the material. Maybe I'll even order a magazine for junior . . . now what more could the lady want?"

They had put aside the list and had been looking for ten minutes at the picture of the gang surrounding The Thinker before Rae spotted the tiny figure in the background of the photograph. "Who's that?" Rae asked, pointing to it.

Rusty held up the picture closer, squinting . . . "I'm not certain, but . . . It looks like that girl, Rosalie, I told you about. Just a second." He flipped through the pages till he came to the s's, to Salino, then opened it to Rosalie's class picture.

Rae took the book from Rusty's hands. "You know, I do remember her. I have to admit, I didn't like her very much."

"Why not?"

Rae tilted her head, thinking, then, "She was always sneaking around, listening to other people's conversations. Like she was taking notes on what they were saying. I never really spoke to her . . . Once or twice I said, 'hi,' but she never answered. She seemed only interested in the popular kids . . ."

"Our gang was asked to a birthday party of hers. We went—it was a pretty grim affair."

"I'm surprised you went."

Rusty shrugged. "To be honest, so am I. If it were up to me, I probably wouldn't have."

A half smile, "But of course, majority ruled out."

A glance. "Let's not get snide now." He sighed. "I guess the truth is, the consensus was, it might be fun. Somebody came up with the idea of bringing joke gifts. We had done it before, at other parties . . . no big deal. But this was different—some of the gifts were pretty nasty, really giving it to her, and since none of us were really her friends . . . Well, need I say more. The jokes were hardly jokes. I arrived late, just in time to know I'd better ditch my gift—a bottle of skunk perfume—in my pocket before she saw it."

"Why, what was going on when you got there?"

"Most of the kids were laughing, naturally they had snuck in liquor and had had plenty to drink. Rosalie was screaming, telling them all to get out, that she hated them. Then she was crying."

Rae shook her head. "God, I didn't like her but . . . That was such a lousy thing to do to anyone."

"I guess she took a lot of teasing, a lot of garbage from the kids, but that was probably the worst fiasco. Kids can be really cruel."

Rae put her hand on Rusty's arm. "But hopefully they grow out of it . . ."

Rusty frowned. "Yeah sure, right . . . look at me." He turned the page.

"What about putting her name on the list?"

He looked at the four names on the paper—guys who either had grudges against the crowd or were just all around troublemakers. "Why?" Rosalie doesn't fit what we're looking for at all. She was the one dumped on, not the other way around. In fact, aside for that one night where she told everyone where to get off, she was as meek as they come. Definitely no threat." He stopped—he had said those words not too long ago to someone . . . And about Rosalie.

"What is it, Rusty?"

"Nothing." Then, "Even if she did have a grievance with the crowd, what would it matter? She left town right after graduation. I read it myself in *The Bradley Sun.*"

Mac stretched over and pushed open the door for Gena. "Okay, out."

"You don't have to sound that desperate to get rid of me."

Mac looked at his watch. "Don't play cutsie, they're already into the second half."

Gena looked at the house. "You know, Mac, I've been here before. I could swear . . . Just looking at this place gives me a bad feeling. Why do you suppose—"

"Gena, please, I'll pick you up like I promised. Just let me get back to the game now."

She pushed herself over and clumsily exited the car. "Do you hear yourself lately, Mac? The only thing you care about these days is basketball."

"Not true." Then pointing to the house. "Watch your footing on those steps, they're in bad shape."

Gena raised her dark eyebrows. "Wait, did I hear correctly . . . you're worried about me?"

"Not you, I'm worried about that little basketball player you're carrying around with you."

"You fink!" Gena slammed the car door, and Mac with one of his rare smiles, waved, and took off.

Victoria had watched from the parlor window as Mac drove off and Gena waddled up the stairs alone . . . She looked at the punch, already prepared. No, she wouldn't use it, not for Gena alone. She waited for the bell, then went to the door and opened it.

"Hi, I'm Gena McDermott. I'm here for the book presentation."

Victoria let her inside, then took her coat. "I expected your husband to come, too. In fact, that was one of the requirements. That is, if you want the free books."

"Oh, he'll be here later. He had business to take care of—it just couldn't wait—but he's actually looking forward to seeing the books." Then peeking into the parlor, "I sort of expected to see some other couples here, too?"

"Oh, they're here. Downstairs."

"Great. Well, what are we waiting for?"

Victoria led her to the basement stairs, then moved aside. "You first."

Gena started slowly down the stairs. "You know, you really made a point the other day. I mean, nowadays, competition is fierce, and I'd hate to think of my child not being equipped to handle it. It's funny . . . you never really realize how awesome a responsibility parenthood is until—" She stopped at the landing and turned, then threw up her hands as Victoria lifted the nightstick. "I don't understand! What . . . why?" Then her hands going to her belly. "The baby, please . . . Oh please no, not the baby!"

"Go to the left, down the stairs," Victoria demanded.

Gena scurried down and Victoria unlocked the door. "Close your eyes, walk in and sit down."

Gena squeezed her eyes shut, then with her arms stretched out in front of her went in and sank down to the floor. "Please, I'll do anything you want," she pleaded, "just don't hurt my baby."

Victoria dragged Gena to the wall, secured the handcuffs, then tied her ankles with rope and secured them to the pipe overhead. She picked up a sockball and stuffed it into her mouth, then drew two strips of adhesive tape over it, to keep it in place. Finally Victoria walked out of the room, pulling the heavy door shut behind her. "Okay, Gena," she said, "now you can open your eyes."

Rae sat on the sofa, her bare feet up and her knees up to her chin, watching Russ. This was his seventh phone call. "Mac," Rusty said. "I'm glad you're in."

"Listen, Rusty, let me call you back. The Celtics are on."

"Don't worry, this won't take long."

A sigh. "Okay, what?"

"Something weird is going on, and I don't know what to make of it? For one thing, Bobby has been missing now about two weeks."

"What do you mean, missing?"

"What the hell does it sound like I mean? I mean, no one has been able to get in touch with him."

"So . . . maybe he went away."

"Why thank you, buddy, such an original thought. Why

didn't I think of that? Would I be fuckin around calling you if I didn't think this was serious?"

"Okay, okay."

"Since then, Mrs. Burns, Penny's mother, called to say Penny's missing. Then I hear that Millie Carton has disappeared."

"So what are you saying?"

"Don't you find any of this bizarre?"

"Only if they've really disappeared. But I don't think so. What I think is, there's too many people running around worrying about where everyone is. Shit . . . we're talking about adults here, not some sixteen-year-old runaways."

"Sammy was supposed to do a job for me Monday. He never showed up. I haven't been able to contact him since. Now you know how reliable Sammy is."

"I'm sure there's an explanation. What is this, Erlich, you make it sound like there's some kind of vendetta going on, directed at *our* bunch."

"Maybe there is."

"Well, I don't buy it."

"Suit yourself. I just wanted to let you know. Listen, put Gena on . . . I want to see if she can give me any clues to what's happening."

"I can't do that, she's not home. She went to a kids' book show. I'll tell her to call you later."

"Okay. In the meantime, Mac, do me a favor . . . watch yourself."

Rusty put down the phone, resting his head back against the chair.

"He didn't believe you?" Rae said.

"Nope. I don't know that I believe it myself. There's still Carol's incident . . . and yours, neither of which fits in with the rest of this 'get the crowd' theory."

"How many of them did you reach?"

"Only two . . . Elaine and Mac." Then looking at the four names listed on the paper. "Tomorrow, I'll see if I can find out what became of these characters we went to school with."

*　　*　　*

It was a real bitch—by the time he got off the phone with Rusty, Bird had scored three baskets, pulling the Celtics ahead 74 to 70. And Bird had done it without Mac watching. Come on, Rusty boy, what's gotten into you? A vendetta aimed at their high school crowd? No one would be quite so nuts. No matter what anyone thought of their bunch.

He pulled the car up to Seventeen Valley Road and threw it in park, then got out and took the stairs, two at a time. The game ended later than expected, so Gena was probably stewing already. He rang the bell, and Victoria came to the door.

"Mac McDermott, my wife Gena's here?"

"I'm Victoria Louise. Do come in."

He stepped in, following her to the parlor. "Where is she?"

She poured a red drink into a cup. "She's downstairs, still looking over our selection. Why don't you join me for a drink first."

He waved his hand. "Not me. I'm not a punch man." Then turning toward the kitchen, "Let's go get Gena."

"You know the way?"

He looked around the room, puzzled. "Yeah, for some reason, it seems I do."

Victoria swallowed hard. "Then why don't I follow you."

She rushed to keep up with him. Even down the stairs. When he reached the foot of the stairs and turned, she had the gun pointed straight at him . . . She ordered him to lay down, belly against the floor, then, when his head was turned away from her, she raised the nightstick she held in her other hand and whacked him as hard as she could.

Mac's last thought as he descended into unconsciousness was, *Fuckin shit, Rusty was right.*

CHAPTER NINETEEN

"WAKE up, Rusty, it's almost eight," Carol called from the kitchen. "There's Cheerios and bananas if you want it."

He sat up.

"What time did you bring Rae home?" she asked.

"About midnight, why?"

"Just wondered. I like her. She's right for you. Not the type that falls all over you, but still it's obvious how much she cares about you. She's tough, too. I even told daddy that."

He turned. "You talked to dad about Rae?"

"Uh-huh. Yesterday afternoon when he called, making his usual inquiries about you. He says you never call him."

"There's a reason for that."

"Aw, Rusty, give him a chance. I know he used to pick on you a lot, but fathers do that, at least to their sons. They can't always say what they mean. It wouldn't hurt to give him a call once in a while . . . tell him what you're doing."

Russ got some clean clothes and headed to the bath. "I will . . . when I get around to it." Then, "Did you tell him and mom about our telephone number being changed?"

"Yeah. I said something went screwy with the line so we had to get a new number."

Russ nodded. "You never told either of them about the skating accident, did you?"

"No."

"Somehow these little lies you pass by them don't seem to fit with the rest of your philosophy?"

"I don't see where it doesn't fit . . . after all, there's no need to get them worried for nothing, is there?"

*   *   *

Rusty arrived at Victoria's at nine, worked till three-thirty, then stopped by Rae's.

"Did you make any headway on that list?" she asked, as she handed him a beer.

He pulled the list from his pocket. "Paul Winger runs a topless bar in Philadelphia. Stanley Freemont is doing time in Walpole for drug dealing, and Malcolm Turner has a wife and four kids and lives with them on a dairy farm in Vermont."

She sighed. "Well, that eliminates them as suspects."

"And listen to this one: Nicholas Stillato is now Father Stillato. He runs a parish in some town south of Boston."

She smiled. "You're kidding?"

"Nope."

"Where in the world did you find all this out?"

"Brad Kagan. He practices law here in town. His uncle's firm represents half the criminal element in Merrimack Valley. And then some."

"So where does all this leave us now?"

"Back to the beginning, I guess. Nowhere."

Silence.

Rusty swallowed some beer, then put down the can. "What is it, Rae?"

"I know you don't agree with me on this."

"Say it anyway, we have little enough to go on."

"Rosalie Salino. I agree, she was shy, and she certainly never caused any trouble, at least that I know of. But she was hurt, Rusty, and some of that hurt was due to your friends. You admitted it yourself."

"People get over things like that."

"Sure . . . most people do."

Rusty stood up and began to pace around the room. "Picture her, Rae. What could *she* possibly do to someone like Bobby. Or for that matter someone as muscular as Sammy?" He shook his head. "No, the whole idea is crazy."

Silence.

Rusty stopped and looked at her. "Well, say something, will you."

"What can I say, you're probably right. Besides, you say she moved away. So if that's true, you're definitely right."

"I don't even know that Brad would know anything about the whereabouts of Rosalie Salino, we're not talking now about someone we'd expect to find mixed up in the rackets . . ."

Rae shrugged. "But he did know about Malcolm Turner and Father Stillato."

Rusty nodded.

Rae went to the phone, picked it up and brought it over to Rusty. "Here," she said handing him the receiver, "Go ahead."

"Brad, Rusty again. Listen, can I pick your brains one more time?"

"Sure, what I got left of them. The wife dragged me to one of those fleamarkets today after I talked to you. Those things should be outlawed. My head feels like the culmination of a fireworks exhibition."

"Then I'll make this as painless as possible. I'm trying to track another person."

"You still think there's something going on . . . something connected with Bobby, Sammy and the girls?"

"Unless you can come up with some better answers for me."

"I wish I could. Okay, who's your suspect now?"

"Well, I don't know that I'd go so far as to call her a suspect. The name's Rosalie Salino. She went to school with us. A heavy girl, not very well liked."

"I remember. We went to some kind of a party at her house once." He laughed. "C'mon, you don't think that she—"

"I don't think anything. I just want to know if you have any information as to where she is now."

"No idea at all, buddy, none. You realize that most of our work is criminal. We do take in some general work, but usually it's for a client we've represented in a prior criminal action. A courtesy to the client."

"How did you know about Stillato."

"Oh that. When he left school, he had some minor violations we represented him on. Nothing serious and apparently he learned his lesson. By the way, that information is off the record."

"Sure. What about Turner, how'd you know where he was?"

"Oh that one is public information. My mother belongs to the same garden club as his mother."

Rusty smiled. "Okay, that's it then. Go take some aspirins."

"I just wish—Wait . . . a second."

"What is it, Brad?"

"Is Rosalie any relation to the late Alexander and Theresa Salino?"

"I don't know, I suppose they could have been her parents."

"Well, if so, I just thought of someone who could maybe give you the information you're looking for."

"Who?"

"A lady named Agnes Mills. She gets a check every month through the Salino estate. From a trust fund. I've handled it myself a couple times." Then with frustration riding his voice, "I still do clerical shit, they don't let me near the big stuff yet."

"That must be them," Rusty said ignoring Brad's complaint. "I know who Agnes Mills is, and she lived with the Salino family for years. Your firm represented them?"

"No, just Agnes Mills. We handle the transfer of monies to her account."

"Why? I thought you people stuck mainly to criminal work."

Silence, then, "You got me, buddy, we usually do. Maybe she knows someone in the firm. When I go to the office tomorrow, I'll pull the file and check into that."

Rusty hung up the phone and slowly stroked his chin. Of course—Mrs. Mills would know where Rosalie was. Why hadn't he thought of that to begin with?

Elaine had closed the shop early and had been soaking in bubble bath for over an hour now. When Rusty called last night, her spirits had lifted dramatically. Maybe he hadn't called to chat or even to ask her out, but apparently he was worried about her. And that was a start, wasn't it?

Today she set aside a dress—red silk and smashing—to wear to Victoria's party next week. Not that she expected to meet anyone she cared about as much as Rusty, but one never knew. She could very well meet someone charming enough to foster some jealousy. That strategy had worked flawlessly in high school.

She still wasn't quite sure why Rusty had sounded so unstrung on the phone. So what—he couldn't reach Bobby and Sammy and the girls—what was the big deal? Elaine knew for a fact that aside from Bobby, Russ hardly ever saw any of them. Not that Elaine did either. Since the boutique opened, she hadn't had much time for daily or even weekly calls to the girls. It sure would have been nice if Victoria wasn't so odd. She might have made for an interesting friend.

She stood up and wrapped a towel around her, then examined her waterlogged hands. Ugh . . . they looked like snakeskin.

Agnes Mills hated Sundays. Not that she did much during the rest of the week, but Sundays always seemed to drag relentlessly. Of course, she did have her daily walks, but on weekdays, she had her trips to the market, too. Actually she spent a lot of her free time at the window, looking across the street at the house, hoping to spot Rosalie in her comings and goings. One of these days, the girl would need to put the bad memories to rest. And then she'd come across the street to see Agnes.

Suddenly the bell rang. Could it be her? She hurried to the door. "Who's there?" she asked.

"It's me, Rusty Erlich."

Silence.

"The fellow who drove you home in the truck."

A pause, then she cracked open the door. A pretty little redhead was standing at his side.

"I wonder if I could talk to you, Mrs. Mills." Then his hand going to the redhead's back. "This is Rae Lemkin, a friend of mine."

The girl smiled, and Agnes nodded, then opened the door. She looked around the room. "Why . . . the place is quite a bit of a mess. I don't often have company."

"We won't take long," Rusty said. "Just a couple of questions."

She led them to the worn sofa, and Agnes took the straight-backed chair across from them. "Now, what may I do for you?"

"I want to know a little about Rosalie Salino," Rusty said.

Agnes stared at him. "I don't understand."

"Just where she's living now. I remember a few years back reading that she left Bradley."

"Yes, that's certainly true. Right after graduation."

"Where did she go, Mrs. Mills?"

"New York. Manhattan, I believe."

"I see. And she's still there?"

She wrung her hands together. "I wouldn't know, I would imagine so. I mean, where else would she be?"

"I don't know," Russ said. "We just thought, since you knew the family so well, you might."

"Not that well at all. Besides children grow up and go off, and then whereas I was only a boarder . . . I can't really expect contact to keep up."

"You knew nothing of her plans, maybe to come home some day?"

Mrs. Mills took a deep breath. "As you know, young man, the property was sold. If Rosalie were planning to come back, surely she wouldn't have sold her home."

"No, I guess not."

"May I ask why you're asking me these questions?"

Rusty stood up. Rae followed, then walked over to the wall, staring up at it. "It's nothing really that important, Mrs. Mills," Rusty said. "We're planning a class reunion, and it's our job to hunt up missing classmates."

"Not an easy job, I'd say."

He headed toward the door. "No, it's not." He grabbed hold of Rae's arm and tugged her away from what she was staring at, "Come on, Rae."

＊　＊　＊

"Why didn't you tell Mrs. Mills the truth, Rusty?" Rae asked as soon as they got to the truck.

"Why worry her with something we don't know to be true. Something that's so far fetched."

"She's lying. Rusty, I know she's lying."

"Well, I don't. So she was nervous, but that's understandable —the woman hardly sees anybody. She's not used to having company."

"I don't believe she wasn't close to that family."

He shrugged. "She *was* only a boarder."

"Then why the monthly check?"

"Perhaps in payment of services. She lived with them a lot of years, and I assume did something to earn her keep."

"Didn't you see the pictures?"

Rusty shook his head.

"Well, I did. Some were of a little girl alone and some of a man alone. And some were of the two together. The little girl was Rosalie, and I assume that the man was Rosalie's father."

"So?"

"Rusty, there must have been fifty pictures hanging there. And I don't care what you tell me, no one wallpapers their apartment with pictures of people they don't care about."

CHAPTER TWENTY

USTY was at work early Monday morning. A couple more days of busting his butt, and the playroom would be done. The night before Rae and he had sat up until two in the morning, wracking their brains, trying to figure out what was going on, but they drew the same zeros as before.

They talked about Rosalie, too, but as far as he was concerned, her involvement in any of it was unlikely. Chances were that she'd made a new life for herself in New York and forgotten that Bradley even existed. Even if Mrs. Mills had been lying, what did it really prove? Only that the Salino family meant far more to Agnes Mills than she was willing to admit.

"Coffee, Rusty?"

He swung around: Victoria was holding out a mug. In her other hand was a brown paper bag. "Victoria . . . you surprised me."

"I'm sorry, I just thought—"

He smiled, then taking the mug from her hand. "Thanks."

Victoria moved back to the wall, leaning against it. "You seem jumpy."

He lifted some strips of moulding. "Just tired."

"Oh." Then opening the paper bag. "Too tired to give me an opinion on something?"

"What is it?"

She dug into the bag and pulled out three carpet sample—duplicates except for color—then laid them on the work bench. "Brown, green or blue . . . which one do you like?"

He walked to the bench. "For down here?"

She nodded.

"I'm not very good at this. In fact, my sister claims I'm either colorblind or have incredibly bad taste."

"You have a sister?"

"Yeah. Carol . . . she left a message here once."

Victoria nodded slowly.

He went back to the moulding, stuck a short thin nail in and hammered it. "Anyway, you're better off choosing your own rug."

Victoria picked up the samples and brought them to him. "Come on, don't be like that, just pick one. Any one."

He shrugged. "They all look fine to me."

"Please, Rusty, pick the one you like best."

A sigh, then, "Okay," he said pointing to the cocoa brown sample. "That one."

She smiled, then tossing the other two samples inside the bag, "Okay, then that's the one it'll be."

Rusty left the hammer on the floor and stood up. "I don't get it, Victoria. What difference does it make if I like the color or not? It's your goddamned room."

"You built the room, Rusty. And you picked everything else out. So why not the carpeting, too?"

"May I speak to Attorney Kagan, please."

"Who may I say is calling?"

"I'd rather not give my name at this time."

A sigh, then, "Okay, ma'am, just a moment." The secretary buzzed Brad's office.

"Yeah, Sandy."

"A call for you on line two . . . one of those no-names. Maybe you've got a live one."

"Not if Uncle Henry has a say. Okay, I'll take it." He pressed the second button. "Bradley Kagan speaking."

"Mr. Kagan, I need a lawyer desperately, a criminal lawyer, and your name was referred to me."

Brad sat forward in his chair—his first fuckin referral. Uncle Henry wasn't going to get this one. "I see. Well, why don't I make an appointment for you to come to my office. I have some free time, say tomorrow afternoon." Hell, aside for doing research and paper work for Uncle Henry, that's all he had was free time.

Silence.

"Hello, ma'am, are you still there?"

"Yes, but I'm afraid I can't come there. You see, I don't want to be seen, at least not until I've had some good legal advice."

Brad's eyebrows arched. "Well, where do you live? Maybe I can see you there."

"Oh, would you, I'd so much appreciate it. And I prefer it if it could be at night. I might sound overly cautious, but the less the neighbors see at this time and the more confidential I can keep this, the better. I'm afraid I've gotten myself involved in a situation that doesn't look very good for me at all. In fact, Mr. Kagan, I've never been so frightened in my life."

"Don't you worry about anyone finding out anything, our meeting, and whatever we discuss together lies within the strict boundaries of lawyer/client confidentiality."

"Then you mean, not even the office staff will know about this meeting?"

"No one, at least not yet." He picked up a pen. "Give me your name and address, ma'am. And from what you say, the sooner you get that legal advice, the better. How about tonight?"

Brad put down the phone and sat back in his chair, his arms folded onto the soft leather upholstery in back of his head. He couldn't be sure, of course, one could never be sure, but from the sound of that conversation, he just might have a homicide on his hands. Goddammit . . . his first fuckin case out of law school and he was about to luck out totally. A murder!

Victoria was so elated, she could hardly contain herself. She closed the bedroom door behind her and ran to get her black book. Then checked off the name, Bradley Kagan.

"We've done it, Rosalie," she declared triumphantly, facing the doll perched on the windowsill. She had them all. Of course, there was still Elaine but she was as good as here. Then there was Rusty . . . She shook her head—to think she had been worried for nothing—Carol was nothing more than his sister! But there *was* that other girl . . . Well, what difference did it make now: the new plans had already been made. And Rusty would pay just like the others.

Victoria grabbed hold of Rosalie's hands, and squeezed her eyes shut, picturing the playroom . . .

"What will my playroom look like when it's done, daddy?"

Her father crawled into bed beside her, running his fingers through her hair. *"It'll be big and cheery and have lots of toys for Rosalie to play with."*

"And I can have parties there? Say yes, say yes!"

"Oh yes, princess, whenever you want."

"And Mama or Auntie Agnes can't come down there at all. Only me and you, right? And we can even live there, daddy. Just me and you together."

He smiled, that wonderful smile that told her she was the most special one of all. *"Well maybe we'll let them down sometimes, okay?"*

She nodded her head.

He got up out of bed, pulled the covers to her back, tucking them under her chin. *"Go to sleep, princess."* He leaned over and kissed her forehead.

Yes . . . Rusty had built her the very same playroom her father would have built if he had lived. Only, of course, her father hadn't lived. "I love you, Daddy," she said.

It was after five when Brad Kagan headed into the law library with a stack of folders under his arm. "Uncle Henry's got you going, huh?" Sandra said, zipping her woolen jacket to her neck.

He made a face and she followed him into the library. "What was that no-name?"

He looked up. "A client, a referral. And by the looks of it, a big one."

"Really? Well, well, congratulations are definitely in order. Do you want me to open a file on her?"

"Tomorrow will be soon enough." Brad suddenly remembered. "Sandy, do me a favor before you leave, pull the Agnes Mills file for me, will you?"

"Sure." She went back to her office, then returned with a manila folder. "Don't work too hard, Brad."

He sat and opened the file onto the conference table, then went through the papers. Finally he closed the file, shaking his head. No wonder the firm had agreed to handle a minor bookkeeping matter for the lady. Agnes Mills had been a client of Uncle Henry's eighteen years ago.

Uncle Henry had defended her, getting her off scot-free. For the murder of Alexander Salino.

Brad didn't know if this would mean anything to Rusty or not. But he'd call him and tell him anyway. After he got home from his appointment.

Rae's long hair hung free past her shoulders. She leaned forward studying the recipe again, then sprinkled some more oregano and grated cheese into the steel pot, then put the cover back on.

"I could help, you," Rusty said, coming up in back of her, wrapping his arms around her.

"No you can't," she said, turning in his arms, facing him. "I mean, how hard is it, to make spaghetti sauce? Besides for better or worse, it's almost done."

He looked over at the book, red blotches dotting the page, then looked at her, shaking his head. He leaned forward and kissed her, slowly pulling her toward the sofa. "Maybe I'm not so hungry for spaghetti," he said, nibbling her ear.

She pushed him onto the sofa, leaned over him, tracing his jawline with her fingers. "What about that line I'm always hearing about the way to a man's heart being through his stomach."

"That's just *one* of the ways."

"Well, maybe you can teach me about the others after we eat."

He gave a mock frown. "When will it be ready?"

"The directions say eleven minutes." She stood up and went back to the kitchen where a box of Prince spaghetti lay on the counter. She tore the box open, took out two handfuls of spaghetti and broke them into the boiling water.

"You do agree with me about Rosalie Salino, Rae, don't you?"

"I guess so. You are right about one thing. Even if Mrs. Mills *is* lying, it doesn't prove Rosalie has anything to do with the disappearances. And then too, there's Carol's skating incident and my loss of brakes . . . No connection there." She was silent a moment. "Unless, of course, someone thought that Carol and I both . . . and was jealous. No, that's crazy . . . everyone knows Carol is your sister . . . Don't they, Rusty?"

No answer.

She looked over at Rusty lying on the sofa—he was asleep.

Brad carried his new leather briefcase up the stairs. When she had told him the address, it hadn't dawned on him at all. But now that he saw the house, he remembered being here at that party. What a coincidence—here he was just yesterday talking to Rusty about Rosalie, then today he learned that Mrs. Mills was accused of Mr. Salino's murder. Now here he was, going into that same house.

What was it they said—everything happened in threes—and he guessed, whoever "they" were, were right. He hadn't even thought about that girl since he'd last seen her in high school. Now he couldn't seem to get away from her . . . He rang the bell and waited.

Victoria opened the door. "Mr. Kagan?" He nodded. "Oh, thank God you're here, come in."

He walked in and shook her hand. She was very attractive, not the type he expected to be mixed up in a criminal situation. Then again, weren't those the types people killed other people over.

"Please come into the kitchen, I've already got tea poured. We can talk there."

"That sounds fine to me."

Victoria pressed her hand over her chest as she led him to the kitchen. "Oh, you don't know what a relief it is to have someone to count on, to take care of things for me . . ." She stopped at the doorway, "Go ahead, sit down, I'll be right with you. Please help yourself to a pastry with your tea."

He nodded, then sat, laying his briefcase on the table. He opened it, pulled out a yellow lined pad and a couple of pens, then lifted the cup of steaming tea to his lips. He couldn't remember once them telling him about this in law school: the rush of adrenalin that courses through every inch of your body when you know you're dealing in a life or death situation. And to know that you're in charge. Completely.

He'd have to remember to ask her, who it was that had referred him . . .

CHAPTER TWENTY-ONE

VICTORIA had long ago decided on a theme for the party: Remember the Good Times. She had spent the rest of the week trooping through gift and party shops, purchasing the necessities: napkins, paper plates, a tablecloth, food. And also, one indulgence—a huge poster that would stretch across almost the entire back wall, featuring a string of sappy-looking people, each with a gigantic mug of beer raised in salute and a pile of stiffs—presumably the effect of one toast too many—passed out at their feet.

Meanwhile, a barrage of strangers marched through the house, each with a mission: plumbers, carpet and wallpaper installers and finally the furniture men. Rusty worked frantically to finish the room.

"It looks splendid, don't you think?" Victoria said as she watched Rusty put the finishing touches on the bar.

He looked around and nodded, quietly pleased as he always was, at seeing something he had actually built with his own hands.

"You do like it, don't you?"

"Sure I do, I built it."

"Is it the kind of place you'd like for yourself, I mean if you could, would you live here?"

Rusty shook his head with annoyance. "Tell me, what kind of asinine question is that?"

Then in a small voice, "I guess it *was* a silly question."

Rusty leaned on the bar. "Look, I'm sorry, I didn't mean to snap like that. I'm tired . . . and I've got some things on my mind."

"What kind of things?"

"A couple friends of mine are missing."

"Oh, how awful. That's the type of thing I expect to hear happened in New York, not here."

Silence.

"You know, Rusty, this may not be the time to bring this up, but then again, maybe it's just what you need."

"What's that?"

"Well, I'm throwing a party here Friday night. Sort of a celebration of the playroom. And since you're the one who's responsible for all this, well, why shouldn't you be here, too. I suspect you might get some offers of jobs when the guests see what you've done here."

"It's a nice gesture, really. But I can't, I've got other plans."

"You mean to say, you won't even sacrifice one night for the sake of business?"

He picked up a thick strip of wood and held it against the bottom of the bar, then grabbed a handful of screws. A few weeks ago, he might not have been so quick to turn down a chance to drum up business. But nothing was going to foul up his plans for *this* Friday. He and Rae had reservations at the Chateau—a remote little restaurant he had come upon accidentally a couple years ago while in New Hampshire: a renovated log cabin with two-inch deep carpeting, a floor to ceiling fieldstone fireplace, a superb piano soloist and excellent food. Rae and he had made a vow: not one negative thought or word the whole evening . . . Not about Bobby, or Millie, or Penny. Not even about Carol.

"Rusty!"

He looked up at Victoria, startled.

"What's wrong with you? I was asking you about the party. I was saying that—"

"I heard you, Victoria. No, I'm afraid not. Not even for business."

Victoria studied him a moment then headed for the stairs.

"Hey, wait a minute." He put his hand in his jeans pocket, drew out a small envelope and tossed it to her. "Before I forget—the keys to the playroom."

*   *   *

Wednesday night Mac's father called Rusty.

"Lenny McDermott here. What's going on, Erlich? You changed your number and the only way I could get the new one is through R&E Construction."

"My kid sister was being harrassed. I changed the old number and had it unlisted."

"The whole fuckin world must be going crazy."

"Then you know about Bobby being missing . . . and the girls?"

"Yeah, I know. Add some more to that list. Mac and Gena!"

"What? That's impossible, I just spoke to Mac Saturday."

"What time Saturday?"

"About eight-thirty."

"Well no one's spoken to him since. He didn't show up for work Monday. I didn't think much of it, you know, with the wife expecting . . . But when he didn't come in yesterday, I went over there. I found an empty house. Now no one's gonna tell me they took off on a vacation with the wife being two weeks from delivery. Especially some ass wipe cop!"

"Then you went to the police?"

"I went, that's when I found out about the girls and the one-man mickey mouse investigation they've been running. So I sat down with Malcolm Donnely, the chief—nice guy but not too bright. I've known him since I was a kid. I drew out the connection for him, and he assigned three more guys to the case. A fellow named Spanski is in charge."

"Then they are working on it?"

"Yeah, they're working on it, not that I'd give the whole force put together a combined I.Q. of a hundred. That's what you get for trying to save the taxpayer's money." Then taking a deep breath, "What I want to know from you, Erlich, is what you know about this?"

"Not much more than you do. I checked around looking for Bobby but I came up with zero. There is one thing, Mr. McDermott, I don't know if it means anything, but when I spoke to Mac Saturday, he mentioned that Gena was at a children's book show. But I have no idea where . . ."

"You don't know how much I'm looking forward to tomorrow night," he told Rae on Thursday as he slammed down the telephone. He had called a dozen or so classmates at random on the chance that someone in town had seen Bobby or the others.

Rae came over in back of him and put her hands on his shoulders, rubbing them.

"We need to get away from this, even if only for a few hours. There's not a day goes by, that we're both not asking ourselves a hundred questions, trying to figure out answers that aren't there." Rusty stood up—Rae's hands fell away—and went to the window, then slipped his hands in his back pockets. "You know, I'm getting obsessed with this. Every day, I drive Carol to school. I don't let her go anyplace unless she's with someone, I telephone her every hour . . . The other day she wanted to go up the street to a friend's house to study, and I actually insisted on driving her. Can you imagine—one lousy block? Then last night after Mac's father called—"

"What about last night?"

"I feel like an ass."

Rae went over to him, linking her arm through his. "Tell me."

A pause, then, "When you got off from your late shift, I was out in the parking lot, watching you, then followed you, making sure that you got home all right."

"You *were*? Why didn't you say something?"

"Two reasons: one I felt like a fool and two, knowing how self-reliant you like to be, I figured you'd slug me."

Rae bowed her head, then looked back up at him. "I won't."

"You won't?"

She shook her head, then he smiled, putting his arm out and drawing her close.

"Well, at least the police are involved in this now, Rusty."

"Yeah, Spanski. Why does that not give me solace?"

*   *   *

A sleepy voice, "Hello."

"Elaine, this is Victoria."

A few moment's pause, then, "Christ, it's two o'clock in the morning, is something wrong?"

"Oh no, nothing. I'm just calling to remind you . . ."

"What?"

"The party silly. It's tomorrow."

"I haven't forgotten."

"Maybe you'd like to come early? That way you can help with the preparations."

Another pause. "Sure, what time did you have in mind?" she said finally.

"Six."

"I don't close the shop till six. How's seven, seven fifteen?"

"Okay. You won't forget now?"

"Of course not. Want me to bring anything?"

"No, nothing. Wait . . . what do you like to drink—that is, besides beer?"

"God, you are too much, Victoria—it's two o'clock." Then, "Seabreezes—vodka, cranberry and grapefruit juice."

Elaine put down the telephone and rolled back onto her pillow. Just what was Victoria's problem? She woke her at this hour on a weeknight just for that? If Elaine didn't know better, she'd think that the sophisticated lady from the big apple was actually nervous about that party . . .

Victoria still couldn't get to sleep—she reached into her nightstand drawer and took out the black leather book, then opened it to the picture. She stared at the photograph, studying the faces. Suddenly her mind drew an image of a little girl . . . and other pictures.

The woman was standing in front of the little girl. It was Mrs. Mills, but the gray hair was brown—short hair softly framing her face. And the little girl was Victoria. No, no, not Victoria . . . Rosalie.

"*But I only wanted to see the pictures, Auntie Agnes.*"

"*You don't simply take things, Rosalie. First you must ask.*"

"*Can I?*"

"*Not these, dear, these are private.*"

The little girl looked at Auntie Agnes, bewildered.

"*Private, my dear, is when a person has a special secret, and he wants to keep it just to himself.*" She came over and lifted the album from the child's hands. "*I'll show you other pictures.*"

"*No, I want to see these.*"

"*Let me show you the picture of daddy and Rosalie riding up on a big horse. Do you remember when daddy and Auntie Agnes took you to the animal farm?*" She lifted another album from the box on her special cellar shelf, opened it onto the sofa, then sat down, lifting Rosalie onto her lap. "*Come dear, let me show you.*"

The little girl looked at the horse picture. Auntie Agnes turned to more pages, other pictures of Rosalie and daddy, but still, no matter how much she tried to stop them from doing it, her eyes kept moving back to the cellar shelf, to the secret box . . . She wanted to see *those* pictures. Why wouldn't she let her see those? She would come back another time, another time, another time . . .

Victoria thoughts snapped back. Had Rosalie gone back another time? She snatched the doll from the windowsill and pulled her onto the bed. "Tell me, Rosalie. Did you see those pictures?"

Since last Sunday when the young man and his girlfriend had made their surprise visit, Agnes Mills had been having trouble sleeping. Later that night she had gone to find the photograph album, to look at those special photographs of Agnes and Rosalie.

She saw the way Rusty's girlfriend had inspected the pictures on the wall—so interested, *too* interested. Why, if the young man hadn't grabbed onto her arm and pulled her along, she might still be standing there looking.

And those questions he asked Agnes about Rosalie, trying to pry out information from her. She hadn't believed his explanation for a moment, though she didn't let that on to him. There had been a 1981 high school class reunion last year, Agnes had seen the write-up and pictures in *The Bradley Sun* herself. If her classmates were so anxious to have Rosalie attend, why hadn't someone come around asking questions then?

Chapter Twenty-Two

WITH the playroom complete, Rusty worked all day Friday outdoors, replacing rotted gutters and boards —that is, aside from the twenty-minute lunch break he took when on an impulse he stopped at a florist and purchased one long-stemmed red rose. At three-thirty, Victoria came outdoors and called up to him on the ladder. "Why don't you call it a day, Rusty?"

He looked at his watch. "It's still a little early."

"You *do* have plans for tonight, don't you?"

"Yeah, but not till eight-thirty. No rush."

"But still, I insist. You go home and rest, you've put in enough hours these past two weeks."

A hesitation, then he began to climb down, "Actually it doesn't sound like such a bad idea." He grabbed the ladder and tools under his arm. "I'll leave these in the garage for Monday." He began to go, then turned, "By the way, you have a good time tonight at your party."

"We will, Rusty," she said softly as he headed for the garage. "Oh, we will."

"What's his name?" Rusty asked Carol.

"Charlie Finnigan."

"Why haven't you ever mentioned him before?"

"Simple, I didn't know him. He just moved to Bradley two weeks ago."

"How'd you meet him."

"Well, it was like this. I was on my way to a Student Council meeting. I went through the auditorium—the band was having practice . . . And there he was, this cute guy blowing into a big tuba. Blue eyes, dark skin and a hairy chest."

Rusty's eyes narrowed.

"His top two shirt buttons just happened to be open, so I could tell."

"Just happened to be open, huh?"

"Well, it's not exactly a crime. So anyway, I stayed around awhile and watched . . ."

"Then he asked you out?"

"No, not then. At lunch. He came over to our table and introduced himself."

"I'm not so sure I like this, Carol. Going out with a guy you hardly know."

"But I do know him. He ate lunch with us, and I found out a lot about him. His father's a doctor and Charlie drives a silver Camaro."

"Is that suppose to make me feel better?"

Carol pulled a towel from the linen closet. "I don't know, maybe not. Well, look at it this way, how much of a bad guy could a tuba player be?" She went into the bathroom and shut the door.

Elaine hated to rush dressing, but this time she had no choice: she had promised—albeit half asleep—to help Victoria with the preparations. Still in all, the image in the mirror looked damned good. Her hair shook out into hundreds of golden ringlets. And the new red silk dress with halter top, exposing plenty of skin, looked stunning. She would certainly give Victoria a run for her money.

She was only ten minutes late when she drove up to the Queen Anne and parked. Rosalie Salino's house? Oh my god, this must have been the one Rusty was working on, the one he was telling Sammy about. She got out of the car and rushed up the steps. Could it be possible? After all, Victoria didn't know that many people in town. Would Rusty Erlich be one of her guests?

*   *   *

Victoria had been busy most of the day: preparing the food, installing the equipment, decorating the room, then fixing up the guests, sponging their faces, brushing their hair. No one balked much—even when she took the sockballs from their mouths. Of course the drugs she had given them earlier hadn't yet worn off. Then, too, their incarceration had probably instilled a certain submissiveness. She hoped they'd regain their spirit for the party.

Now, though, it was time for her and Rosalie to get ready. A long hot bubble bath, a blow dry, then into their new outfits. It took some doing but finally they were done. Victoria took Rosalie downstairs and propped her against the bar lamp, then came back upstairs to wait for Elaine. So it wasn't so strange that she was standing right by the window when the car pulled up . . .

Victoria opened the door and Elaine came right in.

"That outfit does do you justice," Elaine said grinning. "Now where did you get it?"

"The question is, where did *you* get yours?"

They laughed together, then Victoria rushed into the parlor and picked up a glass. "Oh, you must try this right now, I made it special."

Elaine took a sip of the Seabreeze, then, "Perfect, you definitely are a pro, Victoria. So tell me, when are the other guests due?"

"Oh, at least an hour yet, we have some time. Come on downstairs, I'll show you the playroom."

Elaine followed after Victoria, sipping her drink and babbling along . . . "You know, you're not going to believe this, but I went to a party here once. Why, I'll never know. It was put on by this strange girl, but you know how kids are—a party's a party. Turns out though, it was a real drag."

Victoria led her into the playroom. "Well, what do you think?"

Elaine's mouth fell open. "It's fantastic . . . the room, the decorations, everything." She gestured to the balloons overhead, the long table, filled with platters of hors d'oeuvres and cheeses, covered chafing dishes, and the shelves above the bar stocked with liquor and mixes. "And here I thought you needed *my* help."

Victoria laughed. "I couldn't wait so I did it myself."

Elaine walked around the room, looking into every corner, finally she turned to Victoria. "When I was last here, this place was simply a grungy cellar. What you've done to it, or I should say what Rusty Erlich has done to it . . ."

"Oh, you know my carpenter?"

Elaine took another swallow of her drink. "Vaguely," she said, her eyes communicating a different message.

"Now don't tell me he's the one from high school, the one who you used to—"

"You never cease to amaze me with your quickness, Victoria. Yes, he's one and the same. I saw him a couple of weeks ago, and he was telling one of the guys he was working here. Of course I didn't realize that it was *your* house, not until I pulled up here." Elaine took a deep breath, then crossed her fingers and closed her eyes. "Okay, Victoria, now tell me, by any chance he—Rusty Erlich—isn't one of your guests, is he?"

"The guest list is a secret, a surprise," Victoria said heading for the stairs. "So don't try and pump me because I'm not talking."

Elaine stamped her foot. "Tell me, Victoria."

"Uh-uh." Victoria pointed to the pitcher on the bar. "Seabreezes, at least a dozen of them," she said. "Now, I still have one thing to take care of, so I suggest you have another drink and relax. You'll be the first to know when the guests arrive."

Elaine walked to the long table, inspecting the bubbling mysteries in the chafing dishes, slicing a sliver of cheese and tasting it . . . As she walked around the room, she noticed steel circles, about three inches in diameter attached about three feet from the bottom edges of the walls at regular intervals . . . then another track of circles standing up from the carpet, another three feet or so from the bottom moulding. She bent down and tried to pick one up. It didn't budge. It apparently had been screwed into the floor. What in the world were they for—a game? She'd have to remember to ask Victoria about them.

She smiled, taking her empty glass to the bar and refilling it. What a twist that would be, her and Rusty being brought together again by a stranger. And if she was correctly interpreting Victoria's innuendo, that was just what was about to happen. She put down the pitcher, then noticed the tattered doll facing her—an unlikely decoration for such a party. She pressed the doll's flat, ugly face with her fingers, then pulled them away. Uch . . . the silly thing was sopping wet!

Elaine looked over at the huge poster on the wall. "Remember the Good Times." What an odd theme for her to use for her party, considering she didn't really know any of her guests. Oh, well, whatever made her happy.

She picked up her freshly poured drink, took a swallow, then went to the sofa and sat down. Maybe she'd better ease up on the drinking—that is, if she wanted to take full advantage of this opportunity to win back Rusty. It had been a long day at work, and then with Victoria phoning and waking her at two in the morning . . . She could already feel the weariness seeping through her . . .

Elaine rested her head back against the sofa, looking up at the balloons. It was hard to tell, the letters were so very small, but if she wasn't mistaken, there were names on those balloons . . . If that was so, she supposed one of those balloons was for her. And just possibly, another was for Rusty.

Rusty had given Carol a one o'clock curfew: a movie, meet some of the kids at HoJo's, then home. Charlie seemed okay, maybe a bit too smooth for a tuba player though. He watched the two of them climb into the silver Camaro, then looked at his truck, parked next to it like an ugly stepsister . . . No justice at all. He looked down at his watch—7:45. Finally, the shower was free. He'd call Rae, then get ready . . .

Now out of the shower and almost dressed, he stood at the mirror, knotting his tie, always a slow process. For a moment, he thought about Bobby and Mac, then consciously pushed the thought aside. *Not tonight, Erlich, not tonight* . . . Finally done, he grabbed the phone directory, quickly ran through the yellow pages till he came to restaurants, and jotted the number of the Chateau on a pad, along with a message: "The Chateau—don't call unless it's important!" Then tossing the note on the television, and grabbing his navy sport jacket from the doorknob and the rose from the kitchen table, he headed for the door.

The phone rang.

He looked at it, then closed the door dismissing it.

It rang again.

He hesitated again—dammit, it could be Carol. He pushed the door open, rushed over and lifted the receiver. "Hello?"

Silence.

"Who is this?"

"Rusty, this is Victoria." The voice sounded out of breath.

He tilted his head up and closed his eyes, wondering why he had answered.

"Are you there, Rusty?"

"Yeah, I'm here."

"I tried to reach you earlier, but your number was disconnected. Finally I tried information and got your new number through the business name. And then I thought maybe I'd missed you."

"Well, you didn't. What is it?"

"Listen, I need you to come over here."

"Sorry, Victoria, I'm on my way out the door this minute."

"You must come, Rusty, I don't know what I'll do if you don't."

"What's wrong?"

"Some shelves have loosened in the playroom, over the bar."

"That's impossible, Victoria. There's no way that would happen. Those shelves could support five hundred pounds."

"I'm telling you, Rusty, they look like they're about to fall. Now you know I'm having a party tonight, and you know how important it is to me. The very least you could do is stop over for a minute and take a look at them, and if there's some small thing you need to do to fix them, do it. I can't take the chance that they'll fall and maybe hurt someone . . ."

He looked at his watch; it was 8:10. If he made it quick, he would still make it to Rae's on time. "Okay, do me a favor," he said, "take whatever you have on those shelves off now. And I'll be right over."

Victoria hung up the telephone. The change of telephone number had thrown her . . . suppose she had not been able to reach him? She wiped the thought from her mind. The fact was, she did reach him and he was now on his way . . .

Suddenly she had to see it all once again before Rusty arrived. Elaine had passed out in record time, giving Victoria plenty of time to drag her to the wall, pull her into a sitting position and cuff her hands and feet to the appropriate ring. Then she had gone into the wine cellar, released the ropes securing the others to the overhead pipes, pulled the adhesive and sockballs from their mouths, and one by one dragged them into the playroom and shackled them in place.

She went back downstairs and looked at them . . . Suddenly, a white-hot tingle of excitement swept through her, growing in intensity until she felt forced to cling to the wall for support. There they were . . . finally. The group most likely to succeed. All ten of them, propped up neatly against the walls, their ankles and wrists handcuffed securely to three-inch hooks. And facing Rosalie.

Just waiting for Rusty so the party could begin . . .

CHAPTER TWENTY-THREE

THE first thing Rusty saw when he rounded the corner of Valley was Elaine's flaming red Dodge Dart parked in front of the house. He hadn't known she'd be here, and now that he did, he had an overwhelming urge to turn around and leave. But, of course, he had already agreed to fix whatever it was Victoria was complaining about . . . Still he couldn't imagine how those shelves could possibly loosen.

Hopefully he'd get in and out before Elaine or Victoria had a chance to annoy him too much. He pulled his truck into the driveway, retrieved his toolbox from the garage, then grasping the handle, carried it through the back entrance of the house.

Victoria met him in the kitchen, two glasses in her hand. One she held out to him. "Thanks for coming, Rusty. Come on, join me in a drink."

He ignored the offer and headed for the basement stairs. "Let me see about those shelves before the rest of your guests arrive."

"No wait!"

He turned. "What is it?"

She put down the glass and shrugged. "Nothing. I just wanted you to wait for me."

He gave a look of irritation and headed for the stairs. As he took them two at a time, Victoria followed behind, trying to keep up with him.

He stepped into the playroom, gasped: the toolbox fell from his hand . . . Only a half second passed as the scene in front of him tabulated into his brain, then suddenly he spun around to face Victoria.

But by then the nightstick she was holding was already in motion, targeted at his head. And when he regained his balance, she was holding a gun.

*   *   *

Rae had never in her life taken so long to get dressed for a date. In the few short weeks she had known Rusty, he had not once seen her in a dress. So when he did, she wanted him to feel it was an experience worth waiting for. She had gone out yesterday and bought a black and white print with a full-skirted jagged hemline and spaghetti straps.

Now she glanced at her reflection in the mirror, liking what she saw. No longer was she that scrawny little girl she had been in high school. She went up closer to the mirror and lightly brushed on eyeshadow . . . Rusty had kept to his word, he had held back, not pressuring her to do more than she was ready to do. So aside from caressing and kissing . . . She closed her eyes, remembering, feeling his cool hands on her bare skin . . . Tonight would be different though . . . tonight she didn't want him to hold back.

Suddenly she felt a sinking feeling. How could she possibly be having these thoughts when Bobby was still missing? She looked at the kitchen clock—it was already 8:45—then went to the front window and looked out over the darkened street. Come on, Rusty, come.

"Rusty, Rusty . . . wake up, Rusty."

His eyelids fluttered.

"The party, Rusty, it's time for the party."

His body jerked, then his eyes opened. He was sitting, propped up against the wall, his arms spread-eagled, and Victoria kneeling in front of him. He tried to move his arms, then his legs, but they wouldn't budge. He turned his face to one side, the other side, then to his feet: his ankles and wrists were cuffed to steel pegs!

Suddenly, he remembered the others—and with wide, bewildered eyes hesitantly scanned the room, inhaling deeply as he saw his nightmare confirmed. He looked up at Victoria, his face red with anger. "My God—you're crazy! What have you done?"

Victoria backed up. "Now there's no need to get excited.

They're fine, everyone's fine. Wait, you'll see." She stood up and went to kneel beside Bobby. His cheeks looked sunken—a raw patch of skin had formed around his mouth as though something had been stuck there, then pulled away. Victoria lightly slapped his face. "Okay, Bobby, it's time to wake up."

Nothing.

"The party, Bobby. Wake up."

His eyelids lifted and his head rotated.

"Bobby!" Rusty yelled. "It's me, Rusty!"

No response.

"Come on, Bobby, please!" Rusty shouted.

From farther down the row, in a low unfamiliar voice, "I hear you, buddy."

Rusty's eyes went to Mac. "Okay, Mac, okay, buddy . . ." He could feel his eyes become wet. "We're going to get out of this. Me, you, all of us."

"Gena, the baby," Mac said.

Rusty looked over at Gena: her eyes were sunken, deep red rings around them, and her features were distorted in pain. "The baby," she said, her voice so weak it could hardly be heard. "Oh God, I think I'm in labor."

"First labors are long," Victoria said. "You'll have plenty of time to enjoy the party first."

Rusty sucked in his breath, then riveted his eyes again on Victoria. "Who are you, who the fuck are you?"

At first it was annoyance, then it was anger . . . Rae stood there with the receiver in her hand listening to the long, smooth bleeps pouring from the other end. Rae hung up the phone. Now, she was frightened . . .

Rusty had phoned her before taking his shower. "A half hour to forty-five minutes," he had told her. He was now more than an hour late. Where could he be? If something came up, surely he would have called, wouldn't he? But maybe an emergency . . . Carol. Rae slipped on her coat, picked up her purse and car keys and headed out.

She wasn't really sure where she would go. Maybe the truck

broke down on the way or maybe he *was* still home. Hurt and unable to answer the phone.

Victoria had gone around the room with a sponge and pail of water, drenching their faces with cold water. One by one they responded, opening their eyes and looking around the room. Some spoke, their first words coming out fuzzy as though their tongues had forgotten what direction to take in the process. When Elaine came to, she began to scream, but Victoria slapped her face several times until she was silent. Gena took deep breaths, every once in a while her body jerking and her teeth digging into her lip, trying to muffle any outburst. Finally, Victoria went to the center of the room and announced, "Game time."

"If we're going to play, you'll have to free us," Rusty said.

Victoria ignored him and went on. "I'm sure you've all noticed the theme of this party by now," she said, gesturing with a sweep of her arm toward the poster. "Remember the Good Times. And from what I understand, you people had some real good ones."

Rusty looked at Elaine, sitting next to him with her wet, eyeliner-blotched cheeks staring blankly ahead . . . had *she* told her that?

"Of course I wasn't a part of all that. But I thought it might be nice to reminisce a little tonight." Victoria held up her finger. "Now, the one rule is, when you're asked a question, you've got to be absolutely honest. If one of you refuses to answer or I catch you in a lie, then I'll ask one of the others to set the story straight. And those who lie or don't cooperate, will, of course, have to accept the consequences. It's really simple—all we're seeking here is the truth. So I'm sure we'll have none who refuse to go along with the fun, will we?"

Rusty swallowed hard, he couldn't believe what was happening. She was out there, giving instructions for a game as though this really were a party. He looked around again at each one of his friends, trying to choke the sobs rising in his throat.

"You crazy bitch," he suddenly cried out, "let us the hell out of here!"

"And we will not tolerate any spoil sports," Victoria said, ending her speech.

The apartment was locked, only one small light was on in the parlor. And no one answered when Rae banged on the door. Was it possible he was in there?

She leaned over the porch railing, trying to peek in the window. Finally, she climbed onto the railing edge, little chips of peeled wood sticking into her knees, and grabbed with one hand onto a tree branch. With the other hand, she pushed open the window. She stretched her right leg—a run in her stocking—onto the windowsill, then bending and ducking low, pushed herself forward, falling into the living room head first over the radiator.

She stood up—her dress was torn, the skirt and one spaghetti strap had snapped.

"Rusty," she called. No answer. She ran through the kitchen, into the bathroom, then the bedroom. Finally, she came back to the parlor and spotted the note on the television.

She picked it up and read it: "(603) 555-1830. The Chateau—Don't call unless it's important!" She threw down the note. Dammit, Rusty, where are you?"

Victoria went behind the bar and came back with a long stick, a sharp nail protruding from its end. She held it up. "This is a balloon breaker," then looking overhead, "and those are *your* balloons. Since all of you are my guests, I'll volunteer to do the honors. Okay . . . who wants to start?"

Silence.

She shook her head. "It's hard to believe, a fun-loving bunch like yourselves and not one of you raring to volunteer. All right, if you're going to be party poopers why don't I choose for you?" She looked around the room at the now tense faces. "Okay Mac, you start."

Victoria went over to a red balloon with Mac's name

imprinted on it, raised the stick and used it to puncture the balloon. It popped, and the deflated balloon sailed to the carpet. She stooped down, ripped it open, and retrieved a tiny piece of paper from inside, then unfolded the paper and stood up, taking it to Mac. She held it up in front of him, "Here, it's your message. You read it."

"Let Gena go," he said.

"What . . . and have her miss all the fun?"

He stared at her, then the message. He took a deep breath, then, "Remember the basketball playoffs—1980? Bradley High was defeated in the seventh game. Where did you go directly after that game?" Mac's eyes widened as he stared at Victoria.

"Well?" she said finally.

He licked his lips. "A party, I guess. We had a party."

Victoria looked at Elaine. "Will you be kind enough to correct that lie for us?"

Elaine swallowed hard, then in a shaky voice. "There was a party, but Mac didn't show up."

Victoria reached down, grabbed hold of Mac's shirt and ripped it up the front, the buttons popping onto the floor. "Why not, Mac?"

Silence.

"He was sick," Gena said, her words coming in spurts. "He didn't feel well, that's why."

"That's true," Barbara said. "We didn't know why till later. I remember Gena was crying when he didn't show."

Victoria smiled at Mac. "Why don't we tell them all the truth." Then turning to the others: "The reason he wasn't there was because he was with the basketball coach. In the coach's car, parked behind the school. While everyone waited for him at the party, the coach comforted him . . . in his big strong arms."

A few gasps, one from Gena. Mac stared down at the carpet between his legs, his mouth drawn into a tight line.

"Why are you doing this?" Rusty cried out. "What the hell is the purpose of this?"

"No purpose," Victoria said, looking first at the doll sitting on the bar, then at Rusty. "Can't you tell, it's only a game. Now let's see, who's next?" She popped a blue balloon with Bobby's name on it, took out the paper inside, and brought it over to him. He looked at it, then shook his head.

Victoria lowered the stick down to Bobby's face, running the nail along his jaw. "Come on, Bobby, don't be like that."

He squeezed his lips together . . . again shaking his head.

Victoria pressed harder, and a bubble of blood, popped up and ran down his chin.

"Dammit, Bobby," Rusty said. "Read the fuckin thing!"

Bobby glanced at Millie, then back at the paper. His voice crackled: "Remember when . . . when Millie got an abortion in sophomore year—"

Several gasps from around the room and Millie began to sob quietly.

"Why were *you* the one to take her to the clinic?"

Victoria looked again at Bobby.

Silence.

"Why do *you* think, Rusty?"

"I . . . I don't know. I didn't know . . ." Then, "How did *you?*" Then to Millie. "Why don't you tell us?"

Millie sucked in some air, then in a whispery voice, "It was Bobby's baby."

Victoria gazed around the room at the stunned faces. "See, I told you this would be fun. Now was I lying?"

Victoria ripped off Bobby's shirt, then stabbed at another balloon: Elaine's. She took out the paper and brought it to her.

"I don't want to play," Elaine cried. "Please don't make me!"

Victoria put the paper in front of her, smiling. "Why, Elaine, of all people, I never suspected you'd be the one stick in the mud." She lifted the stick.

"No, no, don't do that! I'll play." Then she looked at the paper, sniffling. "Remember the time . . . you took on two guys at once in the boy's locker room. Who were they?"

Victoria looked at her, waiting . . .

"Brad . . . and Sammy."

"See that was easy, wasn't it? Now don't you feel better getting it out into the open. Especially to Rusty. Why I bet he was foolish enough to believe that you were true to *him*."

Elaine started to sob, and Rusty tilted his head back and closed his eyes.

With both hands Victoria reached down and grabbed the part of Elaine's red silk midriff that covered her breasts . . .

"No, don't, please!" Elaine cried. "I told the truth, I did!"

"I know, but this is for other things." Victoria tore the midriff slowly until the upper torso was fully exposed. Then the silk skirt. Victoria stood up finally and threw the material behind her, leaving Elaine naked and sobbing.

"Uh-oh, should have worn underwear," Victoria said, as she poked the stick at another balloon. It fell into her hands. "Okay, Roxanne," she said turning, "this one's for you." She pulled out the message, carried it to Roxanne, and held it up for her to read.

"Remember the time you were caught shoplifting . . . tell us about it." Finished, Roxanne stared angrily ahead. "It was in Gimbels . . . I stole a blonde wig."

Some nervous snickers.

"Why did you steal it?"

Silence.

"Answer me!"

"Because I wanted to look like Elaine . . . okay?"

Victoria glanced at Elaine, tears were dribbling down her cheeks. Suddenly Gena jerked forward, her arms straining against the ropes. "Oh God, help me! Someone do something . . . please!"

Mac sat stiffly, his head still hanging down and his eyes squeezed shut.

"Look, Victoria," Rusty said. "What would it hurt to untie her? She couldn't do anything, not in her condition. Just let her loose."

Victoria turned to Rusty, ignoring his plea. "What about you, Rusty . . . ready for your turn?"

Silence.

"Well?"

He nodded. "Yeah, I'm ready."

"Good." She punctured a purple balloon, took out the paper and brought it over, holding it up for Rusty to read.

"Remember the time the eighth grade boys dragged Rosalie Salino in back of the school . . . into the fields." He sucked in his breath, then looked up at the woman standing in front of him. Rosalie . . . my god, *she* was Rosalie! Two tears bubbled onto her eyelids, then skidded down her cheeks. He forced his eyes back to the printing on the paper. "You saw, Rusty, didn't you? Why didn't you do something to stop it?"

Suddenly there were tears in his eyes, too. He had seen kids surrounding Rosalie, teasing her . . . Sure, lots of times. But what she was suggesting now . . . No, he had had no idea . . . "I didn't know, I swear it," he said.

"Then you should have known. Rosalie counted on *you* to watch out for her."

He just stared at her.

Victoria kneeled down beside him, and peered into his eyes. "Rosalie loved you . . . for all that time, Rosalie loved you. But you turned out to be just as bad as the rest of them."

CHAPTER TWENTY-FOUR

AROL jumped from the car, slammed the door behind her, and the Camaro whizzed away. The entire night Charlie's hot, tuba-thick lips roamed around, searching for a mouthpiece, but he soon discovered, it wasn't going to be Carol. Nix for tuba players.

Rusty's truck wasn't in the driveway, not that Carol expected it to be. Tonight was her brother's first real date with Rae, and considering how much he seemed to like her, she expected it would be a late night.

She pulled her house keys from her shoulder bag and went up the walkway. Even though the skating incident had been only two weeks before, the stitches were out and her face was healed, and the whole terrible night seemed almost like it had never taken place. And then, too, Rusty's idea of changing the telephone number turned out to be a good one. She hadn't gotten a crank call since.

She walked up the front stairs, feeling those slight jitters that always came when she walked into an empty house at night alone. The parlor was lit—thankfully, Rusty had thought to leave on a light. She slipped the key in the lock and pushed the door open.

"Rusty?" a voice called out.

Carol's hands flew up.

Rae stood up. "It's me, Carol, Rae." Then going over to her. "I'm sorry, I didn't mean to scare you."

Carol stared at her. "Your dress—what happened?"

Rae ran a hand over her dirty, ripped dress, then gestured to the window. "I came in the easy way, through the window."

"Why? Where's Rusty?"

"I don't know. I was hoping maybe you would."

"But didn't you two go out?"

"Come on, sit down." Rae took Carol to the sofa and sat beside her. "Rusty called me just after you left, he was about to get into the shower. And that's the last I heard from him. I thought maybe he was hurt, so I came over. When there was no answer, I climbed in to see for myself, then I thought I'd stay and wait."

Carol's hand cupped over her mouth, and her voice came out breathy. "What are you saying . . . that Rusty could be missing like the others?"

"Let's try not to jump to that yet, maybe there's some other explanation. Is there anyplace at all you can think of that he might go, someone close to him, anyone. Even another girl. If there is, tell me."

"No, honest. He used to be mad about Elaine—she had him wrapped around her little finger—but that was years back. Before he grew up. I mean, she still bugs him to get together again, but he's not interested at all."

Rae ran her tongue over her lips. She had already called the hospital and even the police to check on accidents. But neither Rusty nor his truck had been involved in an accident. No, there wasn't another explanation. Not for Rusty. He would never have just gone off . . . Leaving Carol, leaving her.

Rae stood up and slipped on her coat, then took hold of Carol's hand. "Come on, we're going to the police."

Before Victoria left the playroom, she had fed those who had wanted food and drink. Rusty had taken nothing. Then she had put Donna Summer's "Last Chance for Love" on her old stereo and turned up the volume. Finally she took the rag doll and placed it on Rusty's lap. "I'll be back," she explained, then she slid her hand into Rusty's pocket for his keys. "I've got to get Elaine's car and your truck safely back."

"Wait, don't go yet, Rosalie," he said, shouting over the disco music. "Let's talk, I know we can talk about this."

"Oh, no, Rusty, you've got it all wrong. My name's not Rosalie, it's Victoria." She pointed to the doll. "That's Rosalie, you talk to *her*." She went upstairs, grabbed up Elaine's red silk purse, then left.

His head was still aching from the swipe on the head, now the music blasting in his ears only made it worse. What time was it? It seemed like he had been here for hours. Rae would be worried, so would Carol . . . They would get help. But from where—certainly not the Bradley police.

Neither Carol nor Rae would have an inkling of where he was, and they had no reason to suspect Victoria. He looked around at his friends. So much had come out about them, things even *he* never knew. How had she? He studied their faces, faces he had seen a thousand times over . . . yet why did they now look so foreign to him? Most of them slept, a few stared ahead, their eyes blank as if they'd been drugged. Even Gena seemed to have fallen off . . . She cried out every few minutes, then fell back, closing her eyes. How much longer would it be till the baby was ready to come?

The questions raced on in his head so fast, he had trouble keeping up with them. Had Victoria . . . no *Rosalie* planned this from the very beginning when she first called him to do the job? And what about Carol's skating accident and those crank calls? And Rae's accident? Was Rosalie responsible for that, too? But why, to punish him? What the fuck did she want, to keep them all trapped there forever? She had insisted on removing the windows, installing a door with a lock, soundproofing the playroom. And he had been the fool who did it all!

Like a puppeteer, she had been tugging their strings right along, his most of all. Here they were, strung up in a cage, a cage he himself built. He looked down at the dark-haired doll, her blue chipped eyes staring up at him. It was the same doll that had been in her bed . . . The doll that she now called Rosalie.

He began to pull at his hands, twisting and tugging and rotating them . . . he had to loosen those rings.

"I want to see Lieutenant Spanski," Rae said.
"Why don't you grab a seat, he's on break."

"I don't want a seat, I want to see him now."

"Listen, the guy needs a few minutes off," the officer said scratching a yellow patch of hair that sprayed like a dandelion from his head. "Now why don't you be a good girl and—"

"What's your name?"

"McKinney, why?"

"McKinney, you go call your boss and tell him I want to report a missing person. This disappearance is related to some others you've had. Bobby Cole, Millie Carton, Penelope . . ." She looked at Carol.

"Penny Burns and Gena and Mac McDermott," Carol said.

The officer's smooth pale face crinkled in a frown and he sifted through a bunch of papers, then lifted one. "Add Bradley Kagan, Roxanne Miller, Sam Regis, and Barbara Belmontie to that list."

Carol drew in her breath. "That's all of them, Rae, all that hung around together that still live in Bradley."

"Except for Elaine," Rae said. She turned back to the officer, "Do I get to see him now?"

The officer picked up a phone and pressed a button. "Spanski, I'm sending some people in." He looked up, but Rae and Carol were already gone.

Carol followed Rae into Spanski's office. He looked at his watch. "Two in the morning. Aren't you ladies up a little late?" He focused on Rae. "I remember you, you reported that Cole fellow missing last week."

"Do you remember Rusty Erlich? He was with me."

He nodded.

She laid her hand on Carol's arm. "This is Rusty's sister, Carol. And we're here to report his disappearance. From what the officer at the desk says, this now makes ten missing from the same crowd."

Little lines deepened around his mouth. "Sit down." He took a paper from the drawer. "When was he last seen or heard from?"

"Last night, just before eight," Rae said. "He was due to pick me up at my apartment 8:30. He never came."

"Any signs of struggle at his house?"

"No, none."

Spanski raised an eyebrow. "Normally, you know, we can't file a report till someone is gone twenty-four hours. Of course, under the circumstances, I'm going to override that policy and add him to the list. However, keep in mind, it *is* possible that Mr. Erlich might of just went out, stopped at a bar and hung one on."

"No, that isn't possible," Rae said.

Spanski put out his hands. "Look, I'm not saying that's how it is, I'm just saying it's possible. What I'd like you ladies to do is—if this fellow is still missing tomorrow—come back here with a picture of him and a list of any friends of his you can think of. Business acquaintances, neighbors, whatever. That way, my unit can add him to the investigation."

"Have you found any clues . . . with the others?"

He shrugged. "So far nothing. But we're gonna keep going after it till we do. You know, this isn't a big city—we've never had anything quite like this happen before. I'll be up front with you ladies, it's got us dumbfounded. Of course if this were a little different story—say if all of them disappeared at one time, then I'd be saying: okay, here we got a bunch of kids who hung out together, grew up some and wanted to roll the clock back. So they take a place in the boonies for a few weeks and raise hell. People do those kind of screwy things."

"Unfortunately, lieutenant, that's not the scenario."

"No, I guess not," he said, scratching his head. "The way it reads now is, one by one they drop out of sight, almost like pieces of a chain. One end falls into a hole of quicksand, and the rest—link by link—follow along.

Carol and Rae sat in the car for five minutes before either of them spoke. "Let's drive by Victoria Louise's house to look for Rusty's truck," Carol finally said.

"Why there?"

Carol stuffed her hands in her coat pockets. "I don't know, just that the cop said something about checking into business acquaintances. But not until tomorrow, of course. So why shouldn't we start now? Besides, he didn't seem too swift to me. I get the impression that we could do as well ourselves."

Rae turned the ignition.

Rusty had lost track of time. All he knew was, when he opened his eyes, the music was off and his wrists burned. Victoria was pouring some liquid down Sammy's throat. He watched as the red liquid dribbled down his chin, remembering the harmless bit of information Victoria had disclosed about Sammy. It turned out that back in high school Sammy had tried electrolysis on several occasions. The group had always razzed him about his extreme hairiness, but he had seemed to take it in stride. At least, that had been Rusty's impression. Apparently, though, it hadn't been funny at all to Sammy. He looked at the others: all sleeping quietly, except for Gena whose body seemed to be undergoing a series of slow convulsions. A low, deep moan was coming from her throat.

Victoria went around the room, giving each of the others a few swallows of the drink. Mac was the only one who refused. Finally she came to Rusty, holding the partially full cup out to him. "Thirsty?"

He shook his head. "When are you going to let us out of here?"

She shrugged. "When the party's over."

He sighed. "Don't you understand, Rosalie, Gena's got to get to a hospital."

"Victoria," she corrected him.

"Right . . . Victoria. Well, what about Gena?"

"Babies can be born at home, too. Rosalie was." Suddenly she put her hands to her temples and rubbed them. "I don't know, I think she was."

"Could you let my arms free for a while, they're hurting."

She shook her head.

"Why are you doing this?"

"Doing what?" Her voice was higher suddenly—like a child's.

Rusty stared at her intently, then gestured with his head around the room. "This. I know you've been hurt . . . more than you should have been. But that *was* in the past. Look at yourself now, you're bright and beautiful."

Victoria gave a cautious smile. "Do you really think so?"

Rusty nodded.

"My daddy used to say I was beautiful. He used to call me 'princess.' Can you say that?"

He nodded again.

"Go ahead, say it."

Silence, then, "Princess."

She giggled. "You say it just like him."

"What I'm trying to say is, we were all kids when these things happened. Stupid kids. But kids grow up . . . What good will it do to punish us all now?"

"Oh, but I must punish you. Don't you understand, I promised Rosalie, and I can't go back on my word to her. Not that I'd want to, of course. I saw what happened, all the mean, hateful things you did to her." Victoria tilted her head, looking down lovingly at the doll. "Besides, look at her now—after all this time, finally she's happy."

Neither Carol nor Rae had been there before, but once they found the address, Rae parked in front and both of them stared up into the huge darkened house. "Well, that idea wasn't too good," Carol said.

"It's almost three, and there's no cars here at all, not even hers," Rae said, then noticed the double garage set way in back. She looked at Carol and sighed. "Maybe we ought to get some sleep."

"Will you stay over?"

"If you want me to."

Carol nodded, then glanced past her out the window. "Look Rae."

Rae turned quickly and looked across the street to where Carol was pointing. But she saw nothing, only a darkened apartment window. "What was it?"

"No big deal, I guess. Just someone staring out at us from that apartment. But whoever it was turned the lights off and left."

Rae looked again at the window: it was the side window of Mrs. Mill's apartment. Why would she be spying? Well, she did live here once . . . Maybe she missed it, maybe keeping her eye on the house made her feel closer to Alex Salino. And Rosalie.

The moment they turned the corner onto the street, they saw the battered truck in the driveway. "Rusty's home!" Carol shouted.

They pulled up next to the truck, got out, looked in the cab—empty, except for one red rose—then rushed inside. They ran around the apartment calling his name. Finally they went to the front window, pulled the drapes aside and looked out. "How . . . ?" Carol asked.

Rae shuddered as if the warmth in her body had suddenly been suctioned out. "I don't know," she whispered.

CHAPTER TWENTY-FIVE

VICTORIA had never driven a truck before, but she had used a stick shift, so it wasn't too difficult to get the truck back to Rusty's driveway. What had made her uneasy was the Honda parked in front of Rusty's house until one o'clock. She had been patient though, parking up a side street and waiting till the car left. That's when she knew that the redhead was still alive.

Not that she supposed it mattered much now. Everything had worked according to plan—the party had been a great success. And though it was now all put on hold for the moment—she had turned the music off to let her guests sleep—they were all waiting for it to begin again tomorrow. Of course it had to end eventually . . . she wasn't foolish enough to think it could go on forever, but it would end only when Rosalie decided that they had suffered enough. That they had truly paid.

Rosalie. Victoria turned and hugged the pillow. As happy as she was now, there was one thing that kept it from all being perfect, and it was something she hadn't even thought about until this very moment: ever since she could remember, she had slept with her best friend at her side, but now *she* was with *him.* Oh, Victoria could ask her to come back, to sleep with her, but Rosalie would never agree to that. Not so long as she had Rusty.

Rusty had slept fitfully on and off. Now he woke up to Gena's screams. The others were up too, their eyes wide and terrified. Mac's normally ruddy face looked pallid, even ghostly in the dim light. "Do something!" Elaine cried out to no one in particular.

Rusty began to twist his hands and feet again, trying to

loosen the hooks secured to the wall and floor, but the burns already on his wrists only deepened. Finally he stopped and took a deep breath. "Push!" he said to Gena, wondering instantly if it wouldn't be better if she tried to hold it back. She was still fully dressed, her underwear still on . . . If the baby came now, it would die. And maybe Gena would too!

Suddenly he had to urinate so bad, he thought he would explode. What did Rosalie plan to do about that—simply let them all relieve themselves right on the carpet? He began to laugh softly, the off-pitch sounds mixing with Gena's cries. Here they were, captives of a lunatic, and Gena about to smother her own baby, and maybe die herself in the process, and what was he worrying about? Pissing on the carpet.

When Carol got up at six, Rae was already in the kitchen having coffee. "How did you sleep?" Carol asked. "I know the sofa's not great. Rusty's always saying—" She stopped and tears came to her eyes.

"Come on, have some coffee with me." Rae stood up, got a cup, and placed it across the table, then poured coffee into it. "We've got to come up with a plan, Carol," she said.

"What kind of plan?"

"Well, first off, find a picture of Rusty and make up that list the lieutenant asked for. We'll drop it off at the station. Then I think we should do some looking ourselves. We could ask the neighbors if they saw anyone bring the truck home. Or if they saw anyone around the house early this morning."

Carol nodded. "Maybe, too, it wouldn't hurt to call Victoria's house. I mean, for the past two weeks Rusty's spent more time there than at home. Maybe she knows something we don't."

"All right, Carol. Why don't I do that, and you check with the neighbors. They might be more open with you. And then I was thinking—" She stopped.

"What?"

"Well, I don't know if it's a good idea or not. Your brother didn't agree with us when this was brought up before."

"Tell me anyhow."

"Let me ask you something first. What would be the first thing you'd think of, if all the kids you hung around with at school met with an accident."

"That someone was out to get us."

"What kind of person—druggies, rough types?"

"Not necessarily. I guess I'd be more apt to think of someone jealous, someone on the outside who wants to be in."

"And would you immediately think of a boy or girl?"

Carol considered the question. "I don't know . . . a girl, I guess. They're more emotional, more apt to care about something like that. But I suppose it could be a guy, too."

"Maybe, but I tend to agree with you. For instance, it was a girl who kept calling you on the telephone, wasn't it?"

Carol nodded. "Do you think that's connected with all of this?"

"I don't know. Someone tampered with my brakes last week, too. The thing is, when Rusty and I looked through the class yearbook, there was one girl we came up with who I know wanted to be 'in' more than anyone I ever knew."

"And she wasn't?"

"No she wasn't. Her name is Rosalie Salino and the strange part is, she used to live in the same house Rusty is working on now. But she left town after graduation and later sold the house. Anyway, I convinced Rusty to talk to a lady named Mrs. Mills—she used to live in that house, as a boarder with the Salino family."

"What did you expect to find out?"

"That maybe Rosalie hadn't left town—or perhaps, she did, but moved back. I assumed Mrs. Mills would know where she was."

"And?"

Rae shrugged. "Oh, she said she didn't know much about Rosalie these days other than she *had* moved to New York after graduation. And since she did sell the house, Mrs. Mills suspected that she'd never come back."

"But you didn't believe her?"

"Not really. In fact, I believe her whole existence is tied to

Rosalie and Rosalie's late father. There were fifty pictures of both of them, minimum, hanging on her walls."

"That doesn't mean that Mrs. Mills knows where Rosalie is, or that Rosalie *is* living around Bradley."

"No, you're right, it doesn't. I just thought maybe . . . Well, what would it hurt to talk to her again?"

It had been at least an hour since Victoria had come in carrying the brown paper bag, and twice that long since Gena's screams had stopped. Gratefully, Gena had fallen into such a deep sleep that she didn't see Victoria lift Gena's skirt, pull down her underwear, take the scissors from the bag and snip the cord tying her to the baby. Nor did she see Victoria deposit the tiny, still object into the bag, her hand shaking as if the enormity of what she was doing had penetrated even her.

Mac had sat there, stiff and pale, his eyes blank and unseeing. Victoria stood up, the top of the bag rolled into her fist, and looked around at the hate on the faces staring back at her. "Sometimes these things just happen," she had said, then walked out of the room. When the door had closed, the girls began to sob. Penny began to scream. And Rusty felt the grip on his bladder finally release.

Now Rusty looked next to him. Ten feet away was Elaine—naked. He looked away. "Are you okay?"

"I guess. Did *you* know who she was, Rusty?"

"No, not till I read that message last night."

"She was dragged out into the fields by a bunch of boys?"

"Yeah, and I assume raped. How old are you in eighth grade?"

"Twelve, thirteen."

Silence.

"What are we going to do, Rusty?"

"I don't know yet."

"She's crazy."

"How observant of you."

Elaine looked down at the floor, then back up. "About that thing . . . me and the guys in the locker room, Rusty."

"I don't want to hear about it."

"But let me explain."

"No."

"I loved *you* Rusty, only you."

Rusty turned to her. "Don't you get it, Elaine? I might have cared at the time, but that was then, that was before I knew what I was about, let alone what you were about. Now it's different, now I don't give a damn."

Suddenly there were screams from across the room. "Let me go, let me go!" Roxanne wailed. "You fuckin crazy bitch, let me out of here!" Then just as suddenly, there was silence.

This was the seventh house Carol had visited that morning. She rang the bell and waited. Finally a thin woman with sharp features opened the door. "Hi there, Carol, what can I do for you?"

"I'd like to know if you or Mr. Lyman saw or heard Rusty's truck come home last night. Actually it was early this morning."

"No, I can't say I did. And Stanley sleeps like the dead—in fact, when we lived in L.A. he slept through earthquakes. Why do you ask, Carol?"

"Rusty's missing. His truck came home but not him so someone had to be driving it."

"Perhaps he drove himself home, then went off in someone else's car."

"Yeah, maybe."

"Well, I'm sorry I can't help you more. But you let us know if either Stanley or I can do something, won't you?"

"Sure, thanks."

That was the last one of the neighbors—at least, the last of any that might have heard or seen something. But no one had, unfortunately, not that Carol had really expected that they would. Most of the people in this neighborhood were career types, young people with no children who minded their own business. In fact, that was one of the things Rusty liked about the neighborhood. There was not one single window-watcher like old lady Krebbs who used to see every rotten thing Carol or Rusty ever did, then turn in graphic reports to their parents.

She rushed across the lawn toward home. Never did she think a time would come when she'd miss old lady Krebbs.

"May I speak to Victoria Louise."

"She's out now."

"Oh. This is Rae Lemkin. When do you expect her home?"

"Later."

"I see. Who is this please?"

"Princess."

A pause, then, "I'm looking for Rusty Erlich, he's doing the carpentry work there for Ms. Louise. I thought perhaps she'd be able to help me find him."

"He doesn't work here Saturdays anymore."

"Yes I know. Well, why don't I call back later when Victoria is home?"

"Okay." Click.

Rae put down the receiver and looked for Carol.

"Not home?" Carol said.

Rae nodded.

"Who was that you were talking to?"

"Some young girl named Princess. Did your brother ever mention that Victoria had a child?"

"Uh-uh. In fact, I thought he said that Victoria lived there alone."

"Well, maybe she's just visiting." Rae took a deep breath and stood up, then noticed Carol's beaten expression. "No luck with the neighbors?"

"Nope. There's no old lady Krebbs around this neighborhood."

"What does that mean?"

"Oh, nothing. At least, nothing important."

Rae put her arm around Carol's shoulder. "Let's get dressed," Rae said, then she remembered what she was wearing last night. "Do you think you have something that'll fit me?"

"Sure, let's look in my room," Carol said, leading the way. "I must have some jeans and a shirt you could wear. Where're we going?"

"First to the police station, to drop off the picture and list. Then to talk to Mrs. Mills."

"Can you let us up to go to the bathroom?" Rusty asked Victoria as she set down the full tray of food in front of him.

Victoria seemed to be thinking. "All right," she said in the little-girl voice she had adopted, "but first you've got to eat your breakfast."

"What about the others?"

"If they eat."

Rusty looked over at Mac, his body stiff, his eyes blank and unseeing. Somehow Rusty had to snap his mind back. The baby was dead, but Gena wasn't—at least, not yet. Somehow they had to get her to a hospital. Bobby, Sammy and Brad were either too hurt or too drugged to be of any help. "Hey Mac," Rusty called out. "You want bathroom privileges, you eat. You hear me?"

He didn't move.

"Come on you bastard, get with it."

But still no recognition.

"I'll eat," Elaine said in a weak voice.

Victoria looked around the room. "Anyone else?"

No answer.

Victoria held the spoon while Elaine accepted the thick, lumpy oatmeal into her mouth. "Done," she said finally.

Victoria took a key from her pocket and stretched toward Elaine's right hand while Rusty watched: one side of the cuff was attached to the steel hook, the other to her wrist. With a key, Victoria released the one circled cuff from the hook, then yanked Elaine by her cuffed wrist toward her other hand at the wall, forcing her to face the wall. Victoria attached the freed circle to her left hand, then released the other cuff from that hand. Elaine fell back against the wall, her hands now cuffed together in her lap.

Wait Elaine, not yet, wait till she releases your feet, then . . .

But suddenly Elaine looked like she could barely stay awake, let alone put up a fight. Victoria had drugged her.

Victoria studied Elaine's expression, then satisfied, knelt down at her feet and released her ankles. "Okay, stand up," she said finally.

Elaine forced herself up, but the moment she stood up, her legs buckled. Victoria grabbed her around the waist, then led her, with her head hanging onto Victoria's shoulder to the bathroom. Rusty leaned his head back, waiting, thinking . . . He was next. Once the drug took effect—and by the looks of Elaine, that gave him less than thirty seconds—he'd have no chance in hell to overpower Victoria.

Come on, Erlich, think! What should you do?

CHAPTER TWENTY-SIX

"**W**HO'S there?"

Rae glanced at Carol, then back at the door. "Rae Lemkin, Mrs. Mills. You remember me, I was here last week with Rusty Erlich."

Silence.

"Please, Mrs. Mills, I must talk to you. It's important."

"What is it about?"

"About Rusty . . . he's missing."

Slowly the door opened, and Mrs. Mills looked out.

"This is Carol Erlich, Rusty's sister," Rae said.

Mrs. Mills nodded to Carol, then looked at Rae. "I don't know anything about the young man," Agnes said. "The last I saw of him, he was with you."

"Can we come in? Please."

Agnes opened the door and led them to the sofa. "Sit down." She took the chair across from them. "Now what is it you want from me?"

"I came to tell you the real reason we were here last week, the reason we wanted to locate Rosalie Salino. It wasn't about a reunion at all."

"I'm not stupid, young lady. I figured that out for myself."

"I'm sure you're not. Rusty wasn't truthful with you because he didn't want to worry you with accusations that may have had substance only in *my* imagination."

"And now?"

"It may still be only my imagination."

"But *you* don't mind worrying me, is that it?"

Rae returned the woman's cold stare. "I don't know what else to do."

Agnes sighed. "All right, tell me."

"When Rusty was in high school, he hung out with a popular bunch of kids. I wasn't part of that, neither was Rosalie. But Rosalie wanted to belong to that crowd very badly. She used to follow those kids around, listening to their conversations . . ." Rae stopped and sighed. "I don't mean to put Rosalie down—I know how much she means to you—but, that's how it was. And the fact was, none of those kids were very nice to her. Some probably even treated her cruelly."

"Go on."

"Well, about three weeks ago, Bobby Cole, my cousin who was one of that group, disappeared. Since then others have been missing. Mrs. Mills, Rusty disappeared last night and from what the Bradley police tell me, that now makes ten."

"What are you insinuating?"

"Only that out of all the people in the 1981 senior class, there was no one who might have had more cause to be angry with that crowd. Maybe even want to strike back at them for putting her through what they did."

Mrs. Mills stood up. "You're saying you think Rosalie is behind these disappearances?"

"What I'm saying is that if she does live in town or in the vicinity, I think it is possible. If I could only talk to her, find out for myself."

"I thought I made it clear last time you were here—I know nothing about Rosalie. I was simply a boarder in the Salino household."

Rae got up and went over to the wall, her arm stretched out to the pictures. "I'm not stupid either, Mrs. Mills. If you were simply a boarder, you wouldn't have kept pictures like these."

Mrs. Mills walked to the door and opened it. "I think you'd both better leave. Now."

Carol stood up and followed Rae through the doorway.

"You know, Mrs. Mills," Rae said, turning back. "Rusty is . . ." Her voice began to break. ". . . he's a good person, so is Bobby. I don't know the others very well, but I'm sure most of them are now caring, responsible adults. Do you think it would be fair to punish them for what they did as children?"

The door banged shut in their faces.

Carol turned to Rae. "Was Rusty one of those that was so cruel to Rosalie?"

Rae shook her head. "No. But he didn't step in and stop it either, Carol, and it bothers him even now when he thinks about it."

Tears slid down Carol's cheeks, and she wiped them away with her fists. "He told you that?"

Rae put her arm around Carol. "Uh-huh, he did. Come on, let's you and me go talk."

Agnes watched the girls get into the car, then went back to the wall and studied the pictures. Rosalie and her father . . . so very long ago. The end had come far too soon for Alex. Now it was coming for Rosalie, too.

The young woman had mentioned the police. Soon they would be breaking down the doors of that house to get Rosalie, to lock her up. Because no matter how Agnes wanted to lie to herself now, she knew that the words spoken by that young lady were true. If someone were troubled enough to do what she described, it would surely be Rosalie.

Agnes remembered back to when Alex was killed, right downstairs in that house. The police had dragged *her* away then, off to a cell. She hadn't said much to Henry Kagan, her attorney, except that it had been an accident. Nor had she said much to the court. So it had looked pretty bad for her until Rosalie had come forth. Agnes had been as shocked as the jury when the lovely little six-year-old marched up to take the stand . . . Agnes had instructed Henry not to involve the child, but he hadn't listened to her. What would the child say, what would she tell the court?"

"Please tell us your name," her attorney said.

"Rosalie Salino."

"Do you know what is meant by the truth, Rosalie?"

"Yes. It's when you say what really was, not what you wish it to be," she answered, casting those big blue eyes up at the judge.

The judge nodded his head for counsel to go on.

"And do you promise to tell the truth today?"

"I promise. Cross my heart and hope to die."

"Do you remember the night your daddy was killed?"

Tears came to the little girl's eyes, making the jury fidget uncomfortably in their seats. The judge handed the child a tissue, and she wiped away the tears. Then she nodded.

"Will you tell the court in your own words what happened that night, Rosalie?"

The child stared at Agnes, for so long that Agnes thought she had gone into shock. But then she began to speak. "I went down cellar to say goodnight to daddy. My daddy calls me 'princess' and he's building me my very own playroom. I was just almost at the bottom of the stairs when I heard them talking, so I stopped."

"Who was talking?"

"Daddy and Auntie Agnes, silly."

Some snickering from the people in the courtroom.

"And what were they talking about, Rosalie?"

"They were saying things about the gun."

"What gun?"

"Daddy's gun, the one Auntie Agnes shot daddy with."

Gasps and jumbled voices.

"Tell us what they were saying, what they were doing, Rosalie."

Again the little girl looked at Agnes, then turned back to the lawyer. "They were sitting on the old sofa, and daddy was showing her how to use his gun." She looked at the jury. "My daddy is a policeman."

"Then what happened, Rosalie?" the attorney asked.

"Then daddy gave the gun to Auntie Agnes and told her to shoot it."

"He *told* her to shoot it?"

She nodded her head. "Yes, but she didn't want to, she said she was scared. But daddy said there were no bullets in it and that she could even point it at him and pull the trigger, and it wouldn't hurt." She frowned and shook her head. "I wouldn't have been scared if it was me."

"What happened then?"

"She pulled the trigger like he said to do, but daddy was

lying—it did have bullets in it!" She looked at the judge. "Can Auntie Agnes come home now?"

And Agnes *had* come home—to Rosalie. But nothing was ever the same since. The child began to address her as Mrs. Mills, she treated her with no more affection than she would a stranger. Mrs. Salino kept her promise to Agnes, to let her stay in the house, but the child never forgave her. And neither her father nor the story Rosalie told the court were ever mentioned again.

Now Agnes was sobbing. All she had ever wanted to do was to protect the child, and in a strange way . . . a very strange way, it was Rosalie who had protected her.

She went to the dresser, pulled open the drawer, and stared at the photograph album inside: the pictures she had never allowed the child to see. Agnes had to do something to get the upper hand, to gain her trust so she would listen to reason . . . And though she didn't know for sure if the pictures would accomplish that, what other weapon did she have? Now it was Agnes's turn to protect Rosalie—she could never allow them to lock her up.

Victoria helped Elaine back from the bathroom, secured her in place, then looked at Rusty. "Are you ready for your breakfast?" she said, holding up a spoon and saying it teasingly.

He nodded, thinking as he did that her speech and mannerisms were becoming more and more those of a child. She lifted the juice and he drank it in one long swallow, then quickly ate the oatmeal. "Make it fast, please," he said to her, "my kidneys are busting."

She took out the key, leaned over him, and released the right handcuff from the wall hook, then as she yanked the freed cuff to meet his other hand, he hauled off and swung his fist, slamming her in the face and throwing her backward to the floor. With his one free hand, Rusty stuck two fingers down his throat, then throwing his head to the side, vomited up the juice and cereal.

Victoria got up to her knees, holding her hand over her bruised cheek.

Rusty held up his hand, the empty cuff dangling from the one on his wrist. "Don't come near me," he said.

She backed away, then stood and ran toward the door, still holding her cheek.

Rusty looked down at the doll still in his lap, inserted his finger through the tiny rip in the doll's chest and grabbed it up. The rip widened, sawdust spilling onto the carpet. "And take this thing with you!" he shouted, hurling it forward. The sawdust flew through the air like tarnished snow, and the doll rammed against the wall, both eyes smashing. Shattered blue chips dumped onto the carpet.

Victoria gasped, then knelt beside the doll. Tears streamed down her cheeks. "Look what you've done!" she cried, lifting the sagging remains into her arms. "How could you?" She grasped the limp object to her chest, stood up and ran out, slamming the door as she ran.

He sat there, breathing heavily. He was tired, some of the drug had gotten into his system and was taking effect. He leaned back against the wall, looking down at his free hand. Now what? Now he'd try to use it to get the rest of himself free . . . Then free the others.

But even if he did manage to do all that, there was still the thick, soundproofed door . . . When it slammed shut after her, it released a double lock, only to be opened by a key from either side. Unless she came back, the room was sealed like a vault.

Victoria had run up the two flights of stairs, crying as still more sawdust flakes spilled from the doll's body. Once she reached her bedroom, she placed the remains on her bed, staring at it. "He didn't mean to do it, Rosalie," she said, although she knew that wasn't true at all.

She picked up the destroyed doll and squeezed it, but all there was left was a hunk of stained cloth. Rosalie couldn't desert her, not now, not before she told her the whole truth.

Victoria ran her hands over her eyes, wiping away the tears and wondering if that strange emptiness she felt would ever go away. Of all the vicious things that they had done to Rosalie, this was the worst. And she knew then, without having Rosalie tell her, that the party must never end.

CHAPTER TWENTY-SEVEN

CAROL rested her elbows on a table at the far end of the coffee shop, placing her hands over her face while Rae called the hospital and told her supervisor she couldn't report for the afternoon shift. When Rae slid in the booth across from her, Carol pulled her hands away and looked at her. "Well, was she upset?"

"Yes, but she'll find someone to cover."

Carol sat back, thinking. "You know when you were talking to Mrs. Mills about Rosalie?" Rae nodded. "I felt sorry for Rosalie. It's really weird, I don't even know her, yet I almost wish I did, at least then, when she was in high school."

"What would you have done?"

Carol shrugged. "I guess . . . just take time to be nice to her."

"You probably know other people like her . . ."

She thought about it a moment, then nodded. "Maybe even that girl who made those crank calls."

"Maybe. Sometimes people hurt so much, they have to strike out at someone else. Then there's others who learn from it, sometimes even become stronger because of it."

Carol was silent for a few moments. "But you don't think Rosalie was one of those people, the ones who got stronger?"

Rae shook her head. "But it could be that I'm just looking so hard for an answer. Perhaps I'm reading things into Rosalie's personality that just weren't there."

Carol sighed. "This isn't getting us anywhere. I just wish there was something we could do to find Rusty. I feel so . . . *helpless!*"

Rae opened her purse and pulled out some change. "Look, why don't you order yourself another coke. I'm going to make another call." She slid out of the booth. "And Carol . . ."

"Yes?"

"Don't give up hope. Somehow, we'll get to the bottom of this."

Rusty was still trying to loosen the steel hook that held his other hand to the wall when Victoria came back in the room. Damn. She was dragging a long thick chain with single cuffs on the ends. And holding the gun.

"What's that for?" he said.

"A present for you," she said simply.

She walked over to the lolli column and wound the chain around it, then brought the two ends closer to Rusty. She aimed the gun at him. "If I come near you, promise you won't touch me."

He nodded.

"Go ahead, say it, say you promise."

"Okay Victoria, I promise."

"Not Victoria, silly . . . my name's Rosalie."

He stared at her and she inched forward, then knelt down at his feet, bringing the two new cuffs to his ankles. Rusty jolted forward, his hand aiming for the gun, but she yanked it away in time and swung it at him, smashing the side of his head. He fell backward against the wall.

"I told you not to, Rusty," she said with annoyance in her voice. Quickly she fixed the new cuffs, removing the others attached to the floor hooks. Now he'd be able to walk, go to the bathroom, do all kinds of things. She looked at his other hand—the screw was now almost out of the wall. At least, he would be able to as soon as he got that out . . .

She had tried information. "Rosalie Salino in Bradley."

A few moments of silence, then the nasal voice crept back in her ear, "I have nothing at all under that name."

"What about in cities close by."

"That would include the rest of the Merrimack Valley. As far as other cities, you would have to be more specific."

"Thank you." It was only a shot, one she hadn't expected to

pay off. She looked at Victoria's number, written on the paper—she'd try her again later. Rae hung up the phone, stood there a few moments, then went back to the booth.

"What, Rae?" Carol said.

"Nothing. I just thought maybe I could find a telephone listing for Rosalie."

Carol rested her chin in her hands. "What about Victoria . . . did you try her again?"

"I thought I'd wait awhile. There's no point in talking to Princess."

They both stared blankly at each other for a few minutes, turning over possibilities in their minds.

"What I'm having trouble figuring out," Rae finally said, "is how the things that have happened to you and me fit into the overall pattern. I mean, supposing this girl Rosalie were involved. Why would she make crank calls to you or . . ."

"Push me into a wall while I was skating?"

Rae's eyes darkened. "Carol . . . tell me more about what happened that night at Zoee's."

"There's not really much to tell. I didn't see anybody push me, nothing like that. But I thought I did feel hands on my back. The next thing I knew, I was flying into the wall."

"And that's all that happened . . . the calls and the incident at the skating arena?"

"That's all . . . except, of course, for that car."

"What car?"

Carol leaned in closer to Rae. "The one that I thought followed me."

"When was that?"

Carol thought for a moment. "Before the accident. My girlfriend Franny and I had gone out. When I left to go to Franny's, I saw a car parked near the house. That night, I thought I saw the same car again, following me."

"Describe it to me, Carol."

"I don't know much about makes. All I remember was it looked pretty new, and it was blue."

Rae's face paled.

"Why, what's wrong?"

"It had completely skipped my mind, Carol. Until you just mentioned it."

"Tell me, Rae. What?"

"The day that my brakes failed . . . well, on the way to work that day, I thought *I* was being followed. But then when I pulled into the hospital parking lot and the car behind me kept on going, I decided it was just my imagination. So I didn't think much more of it. But that car was blue, too, Carol. And I do know makes . . . it was an '88 Honda."

"Do you think that the person driving it was responsible for your brakes failing? Or my getting pushed at the arena? Could it have been Rosalie?"

"I don't know . . . it doesn't make much sense . . . if only there was some way—"

"Rae, I don't know if this will help . . . I mean, there *are* lots of other places the car might have been bought. But Mac McDermott works in the Honda dealership in Bradley. It's the only one around, and his father owns it."

Rae grabbed up her purse and tossed a five-dollar bill on the table. "Come on, Carol."

"Rusty . . . answer me."

A deep sigh.

"Please . . . answer me, Rusty."

He opened his eyes, looked down at his ankles now being stretched by the thick chain attached to the lolli column, then turned to Elaine.

"Oh, thank God, Rusty, I thought you were unconscious. Bobby opens his eyes now and then. Roxanne screams a blue streak, then collapses, Mac just sits there staring into space. And then there's the others." She stopped, took a deep breath, then looked at Rusty's feet and the chains stretching from them to the lolli column . . . "What's that?"

"A 'present' from Rosalie. I just wish I could get my other hand free." He twisted himself toward his restrained hand, then reached over with his free hand and with his fingers turned the screw.

"What are you doing?"

"Be quiet, and you'll see." Five minutes later, he pulled the screw loose and sat up. Done. Then he stood up slowly as though he weren't quite sure that his legs would hold.

"You're free?"

"Yeah . . . as far as my ball and chain goes."

"But it's something. See if you can reach me, Rusty."

He tried, falling a few yards short. He walked over to the table near the bar, pulled a cloth off of it, then walked back toward Elaine. He tossed the cloth over her.

"Thanks, Rusty."

He looked at Mac. "If only Mac would snap out of this . . ."

"Then what?"

"I don't know. But he's a strong bastard. I wouldn't mind having him working on our side."

Elaine sniffled. "Do you think we'll ever get out of here?"

"How should I know?" Rusty said irritatedly.

"You don't have to be angry."

"Well, don't ask me stupid questions. Does it look like I'm in a position to know more than you?"

"Well, your hands *are* free, and you *are* walking. And you did build this damn room, didn't you?"

Silence.

"Well, didn't you?"

"Shut up."

A few minutes of silence, then, "Where do you think the rest were . . . I mean, before the party?"

"There's another room . . . a wine cellar. Probably there."

"You mean to tell me, you were working here, building this damn hole while all the time, the rest of them were in the next room?"

Agnes had put the photograph album in a shopping bag. If only she could jolt the girl's memory so she'd know who she was. And the pictures could do that. They could do more too, they could enable Agnes to convince Rosalie that she must let those young people go. Even if the police did get involved at some point, Agnes knew that Henry Kagan would go to court and fight for Rosalie. Just like he had fought for her.

And if Agnes testified for Rosalie, guaranteed the court that she'd take full responsibility for Rosalie in the future, then maybe they'd set her free. Agnes could picture it now—she would move her belongings back to the house and care for the girl. She'd watch her every move, twenty-four hours a day if she had to. Whatever she had to do to keep Rosalie from causing harm to herself and to others. Perhaps, she could even get the girl the kind of psychiatric care those school counselors had always told Mrs. Salino she should have.

Just so long as Rosalie hadn't yet hurt anyone, Agnes could make things right again.

CHAPTER TWENTY-EIGHT

RAE and Carol walked through the display area, ignoring two salesmen headed their way, and stopped at a window marked 'Office.' One girl was sitting at a desk at the far end of the office, another at the window. "Is Mr. McDermott here?" Rae asked the girl near the window.

The girl stuck a ball of gum in her mouth, then looked up through thick, smudged glasses from the stack of papers on her desk. "Which one, senior or junior?"

"Senior. Wait a minute. Is Mac here?"

"Nope."

"Then it's senior I want."

"Sorry, he's not here either."

Rae began to say something then stopped. Finally, Carol said, "Where is he?"

The girl shrugged. "Home maybe, he's not been around much this week. Some kind of personal problem he's attending to."

"We're friends of Mr. McDermott," Carol said. "Could you get him on the phone for us? It's very important we speak to him."

She studied Carol a moment, then shrugged. She picked up the receiver and began dialing. "What's your name?"

"Carol Erlich. Tell him, Rusty's sister."

The girl raised one shoulder, crushing the receiver to her ear while she penciled in some forms. Finally, "Mr. McDermott, Sally here. Don't like to bother you, but there's two girls here want to talk to you. They say it's important. One says she knows you . . . Carol Erlich. Rusty's sister."

A pause, then, "Okay." Sally handed the phone through the window to Carol.

"Hi, Mr. McDermott."

"This is a bad time, Carol. I'm just on my way out to question a couple of my son's college buddies. So if you could make this quick."

"I will. I'm down here with Rusty's girlfriend, Rae. We're trying to find out names of people who bought '88 Hondas. Could we look through your sales' records?"

"I don't get it, why would you want to know that?"

"Because Rusty's missing now, too, and we're trying to piece some things together so we can find him."

"Holy Jesus." Then a sigh, "You'd better tell me what kind of things you're talking about."

"Well, I don't know how much Rusty told you, but for a while someone was harassing me on the telephone."

"He mentioned it."

"I had a skating accident, too. Only I don't know that it was really an accident."

"Go on."

"A couple days before the accident, I was followed by a blue car ... Rusty's girlfriend had an accident not long ago—her car brakes were tampered with—and that same day she thought she was being followed. The car following her was blue, too. And it was an '88 Honda. So we thought—"

"I get the picture, Carol. If you find anything out, let me know. I'll be coming down there right after I see these guys."

"We will, I promise."

"Put Sally on."

"He's coming here later," Carol whispered to Rae as she handed the phone to Sally. Sally listened a few moments to Mr. McDermott's instructions, then hung up and gestured to the door. "Come on in." Carol and Rae went in and Sally led them to a wall of filing cabinets, running her hand down three drawers. "The '88 models came out last fall. Any sales would be in these three drawers."

Rusty had searched the bar area and the bathroom, trying to find something sharp, sharp enough to file away the cutts on his ankles, but all he came up with was a dull-edged bottle opener and a couple of nails and screws he had extracted from the shelves. After twenty minutes of scraping, he pulled the tool away—not even a slight ridge in the thick link attaching to the cuffs.

He looked over at Mac . . . if only he could reach him. If only he could reach *one* of them, he'd surely be able to release those hooks holding them. But apparently Rosalie had measured out the length of chain carefully before attaching it to his ankles.

Rusty picked up a plastic pitcher from the bar, went to the bathroom sink, and filled it with cold water, then came back and picked up a paper cup. He poured some water in the cup, then with a jerk of his arm, sent the liquid sailing to Mac. It splashed onto his face. "Come on, Mac, force your mind back."

He threw water onto Bobby's face. Bobby jerked, but kept his eyes closed.

Then Roxanne.

"God damn you, you bitch?" she screamed. Then softer, "My arms hurt so much . . . Won't you please . . . please. Won't you please." Suddenly, silence.

Rusty looked at Brad and Sammy. Aside from Elaine, who he might as well let sleep, the others were too far away to reach with the water. He dropped the jug and cup onto the bar, then picked up the bottle opener and screw. Right now, this was his only shot.

He thought of Carol and Rae. Then he thought about his dad. Carol was right—he should have phoned him. He ran the heels of his palms across his eyes. *Yeah, the story of your life, Erlich. So why didn't you?*

Rae was calling off the names and addresses and Carol was sitting at an empty desk taking them down—they had checked the color charts and agreed to eliminate all but cobalt blue Honda Accords. "Twelve so far," Carol said. "What will we do with this list once it's done?"

Rae closed a folder and tucked it back in the file. "I think our best bet would be to bring the names to the police and have them run a check on them."

"But will they do it?"

"They'll do it, even if I have to—" She sucked in her breath. Carol got up and went to the filing cabinet. "What is it?"

Rae picked up the next file in the drawer and held it up. "Carol, look at this!"

Carol read the name off the flap: "Victoria Louise?"

Rae sat on the edge of the desk and opened the folder. "Honda Accord, cobalt blue. She bought it last month."

"But it doesn't make sense, Rae. Why would she . . . ? She doesn't even know us."

"I don't know. Unless . . ." She thought about that one time at Morgan's. "I saw her once, Carol, I was with Rusty. And it was quite clear that she liked him. Maybe she was jealous of me being with him."

"I suppose that's possible, but what about me? You're not saying she was jealous of me, too, are you? I'm his sister."

"Maybe she didn't know you were."

Silence, then, "It would be so crazy, even if she were jealous. I mean, what kind of person goes around hurting people just because she happens to like a guy . . . and a guy she hardly knows?"

"A sick one," Rae said, her voice falling to a whisper. "A very sick one."

"Okay, even if all that is so, what about all the rest of Rusty's friends. Victoria doesn't know them."

"You're absolutely sure of that?"

"Yes . . . I suppose she could have known one or two of them slightly, but that's it. Rusty said she just moved here."

"Did he tell you from where?"

Carol thought about it, then shook her head.

"I guess you're right, she couldn't have known them. Maybe Victoria has nothing at all to do with the disappearance of Bobby and the others, but she does know Rusty. And it *is* possible that for some reason he had to stop at her house last night . . ."

"Victoria wasn't home this morning when you called. Maybe she convinced Rusty to take his truck home, then go off with her in her car."

Or maybe she forced him to, Rae thought.

Carol picked up her purse. "Let's go see if she's home yet. If not, we'll talk to Princess . . . maybe she'll know where she went."

Rae hesitated. "I don't know, maybe we should wait for Mr. McDermott. He could come with us."

"Mr. McDermott may not be here for a while yet. And Rusty might need us right now. The sooner we get over there and question Princess, the closer we're going to get to him. Besides, what's to be afraid of . . . she's only a little girl."

Rae thought about it a moment. "You're sure that Mr. McDermott is stopping by here when he's through seeing Mac's friends?"

"That's what he said to me."

Rae pulled a pen and paper from her purse and quickly scribbled a note: "Mr. McDermott . . . we found a name that may be linked with both our accidents: Victoria Louise, Seventeen Valley Road, Bradley. She has a connection to Rusty. We're not sure about Mac and the others." Rae signed it, "Carol and Rae," then went over and handed the note to Sally. "Mr. McDermott is expected to stop by here soon. Would you see to it that he gets this note—it's very important."

"Okay." Sally took the note, and dropped it into the pile of papers on her desk.

"You won't forget now?"

She crackled her gum and shook her head.

Agnes slipped the shopping bag under her arm, put on her coat, then turned out the one dim apartment light and headed out the door. When she got to Seventeen Valley Road, a half block away, she stood in front of the house, looking in. No cars there tonight. Rosalie's, she suspected, was in the garage.

Agnes walked up to the front door and knocked. No answer. Finally, she turned the knob and let herself in. She went through the front hallway, past the living room into the kitchen, then stopped: dirty pots and pans stacked high in the sink ... Rosalie turned from the counter, flour dotting her face and blouse. "What's going on here?" Agnes asked.

"Auntie Agnes!" Rosalie cried out.

Agnes dropped her purse and shopping bag to the floor, then lurched forward, catching hold of the chair for balance. Had Rosalie finally remembered ... had she forgiven her?

"I've made pizza, I just now put it in the over." Then looking at the bag on the floor. "Is that for me?"

Agnes nodded.

"What is it?"

"You'll see later. What's this I hear about you having some people here?"

"Who told you that?"

"That's not important. Is it true?"

"I'm having a party."

"Where are the guests?"

"In the playroom. Waiting for me."

"Your friends must go home, Rosalie."

She stamped her foot and squinched up her face like an angry child. "No, not now. Not till the party's over!"

Agnes stared at Rosalie, then went over and ran her fingers through her silky hair, pushing strands behind her ears and remembering how often she had done that to her as a child. Then she remembered those awful temper tantrums when Rosalie would turn blue with rage. Whatever Agnes did, she must avoid bringing on one of those tantrums. "Then you'll let them go ... after the party?"

She nodded her head.

"You promise, Rosalie?"

"Honest to god, hope to die."

Agnes looked toward the cellar door. "You go clean yourself up and I'll wait here."

"Okay, but don't go to the party without me." Then she put her hand over her mouth and giggled. "You can't anyway cause I got the key."

Then she ran upstairs, and Agnes sank into a kitchen chair. Dear God, she had the young people locked up. Agnes had surely done the right thing in coming, there was no doubt of that. Rosalie needed her now more than ever. For so many years, Agnes had wished for the past to come back, to have Rosalie's love and affection, but she hadn't meant for it to happen like this.

Tears of pain began to spill from her eyes; she picked a dish-towel from the counter and wiped them away. There was no time for that, not now. First things first . . . she would go downstairs with Rosalie, oversee the party, then see to it that the young people got safely home.

Rae's main reason for stopping at her apartment was to phone Lieutenant Spanski. But when he wasn't there, she found herself looking through the apartment for something, anything that would serve as a weapon. She picked up one of the legs from the stereo cabinet, still unassembled, then just as quickly dropped it back on the floor. She couldn't very well walk in with that. Besides this was silly . . . what would she need it for? Finally, she ran back downstairs and got into the car beside Carol.

"What took you so long?" Carol asked.

"Well, for one thing I tried to call Lieutenant Spanski."

"Did you reach him?"

"No, he won't be in for another hour. So I left a message telling him where we'd be." She shrugged, and leaned forward to release the emergency brake. "I'm probably just overreacting, Carol, but I figured it wouldn't hurt."

"Is that all?"

"What do you mean?"

"You were gone almost ten minutes. I was about to come in and get you. What were you doing?"

Rae pressed her lips together, then sighing, "Do me a favor, Carol. Open the glove compartment."

Carol turned, pressed the button and released the hatch. "Okay, now what?"

Rae hesitated, then, "Reach in the back . . . there's a jackknife there."

Carol reached in, pulled out the thick, black-handled knife and handed it to Rae, staring at her.

Rae examined the knife—even if she had to, could she actually use this? No, never. She looked at Carol, her face coloring. "My mother bought it for me. It's got everything imaginable . . . a bottle opener, a spoon, a corkscrew, a nail file . . . I used to take it camping with me. Fishing."

"But a knife . . . ? Calling the police and now this . . ." Carol sat forward in her seat, staring at Rae. "You think that the little girl is lying, don't you, Rae? You think Victoria really *is* home."

CHAPTER TWENTY-NINE

ALLY stood up, picked up her purse, and called to the gray-haired lady typing, "I'm going to the ladies room, Mrs. Kurtz. Be back in a while." She pointed to the wire basket. "If Mr. McDermott comes in before I get back, give him that message."

Mrs. Kurtz nodded. "Still having cramps, dear?"

Sally made a face. "Give me change of life any day."

Lenny McDermott hadn't found out anything from Mac's college buddies that he hadn't already known. Another dead end. He pulled into the back parking lot and came into the office through the service area. "Where's Sally?" he barked.

Mrs. Kurtz jumped, her hand going to her chest. "Oh my goodness, Mr. McDermott."

"Where's Sally?"

"The ladies' room."

"Who the hell's running this office?"

"Why I—" She stopped and cleared her throat. "Perhaps I could do something to help you?"

"Two girls were here going through the files."

Mrs. Kurtz wasn't sure if it was a question or a condemnation. "Uh yes. I do believe so."

"Where'd they go?"

She looked over at the filing cabinets. "Yes, it seems they went off."

"The question is *where?*"

"I don't know."

"When did they leave?"

"Oh, I'd say a while ago. I can't say I noticed the time."

"Did they find anything?"

"Well, I really don't know. Sally will be back in a few minutes." She began to stand up. "Why don't I go and find—"

"Don't bother," he said. "Tell her to cancel my appointments for next week."

She picked up a pen and wrote it down. "Would that be all of them, Mr. McDermott?"

"Forget it." He went to the door. "Maybe you can handle *this*, tell her to call me."

Lenny snuck out, evading the shop manager who always had a load of questions for him. Goddamned help. Sally pisses all day, and that woman, whatever her name was, is as thick as shit.

Only a week ago everything was going his way: his boy in the business, a nice little daughter-in-law and a grandkid on the way. And now, nothing . . . *Where the hell are you, son?*

Rosalie had showered, changed and come downstairs. When she came into the kitchen, she picked up the brown paper bag and peeked in: the picture book!

"I told you, that was for later," Agnes said, noting the child's clothing she was wearing.

"But it's for me, you said so yourself."

Agnes sighed. Had she said that? Was she so sure that this was the right thing to do? But it made little difference now either way—Rosalie pulled a gun from her pocket, Alex's gun, and dropped it into the bag. Then picked the bag up and tucked it tightly under her arm.

The woman stared at her, a shudder invading her entire body. In spite of the changes, it was Rosalie, *her* Rosalie . . . Then why was Agnes so frightened?

Rae had parked a few houses away, and they both walked quietly to the house, up the front stairs. Rae rang the doorbell.

The door opened, and Rae's eyes narrowed. "Mrs. Mills! What are you doing here?"

"I don't see that it's any of your business, young lady." She began to close the door, but Rae forced the door open and stepped in with Carol following. "I'm not here to see you, Mrs.

Mills. I'm here to see Victoria Louise or Princess. Are either of them home?"

Agnes stood frozen.

"Please, Mrs. Mills, if I have to, I'll search this house."

The woman laid cold hands on Rae's arm. "No, you mustn't do that, you mustn't. Please go home," she whispered. "You're mistaken, there are no such people living here."

"But there is," Carol said. "My brother works here for Victoria, he built her a playroom. And we're not going home till we see her."

"Do you wanna see my playroom?" the childlike voice asked.

Both Rae and Carol turned together . . . She was wearing a red, full skirted pinafore, a matching red ribbon in her hair. And was pointing a gun . . .

Carol grabbed Rae's arm. "Oh, God . . . who is she?"

Rae's mouth opened, about to say Victoria." But before she could, Victoria spoke. "My name's Rosalie," she said. "And I know who you are."

When Sally had gotten back from the ladies room, Mrs. Kurtz and most of the others were gone. She noticed the message still in her basket. Hadn't Lenny come? Dammit, why did everything always fall on her?

She picked up the phone, dialed Lenny's home number, let it ring ten times, then hung up. It was after six and it was Saturday night—the message could wait till Monday. She collected her purse, turned off the lights and went to the door, then stopped and looked back . . .

Shit! She switched the light on again, went to the basket, picked up the note and read it. Then she tossed it into her purse. If she got time, she'd try him again later.

Was it night, day . . . how long had he been here? He had spoken some to Brad—he complained of a sharp, cutting pain in his leg. It might be broken. Rosalie had brought down food several times, but Rusty had been too wary of the drugs it might have been spiked with to eat it. Now Rusty had an ache in his stomach that matched the one in his head.

Rusty went into the bathroom, cupped his hands under the running faucet, then splashed water onto his hair and face. He came back, sat on a stool at the bar, and began again to file at the chain.

The door opened, and he stood up . . . Carol and Rae walked in, followed by Rosalie, who was once again holding the gun. Suddenly his throat began to close, choking him. He swallowed hard, forcing his throat open. "Let them go," he said, finally. "Please."

"They wanted to see the playroom."

"Now they saw it. Let them go home."

"I'm going to let them stay till the end of the party. They'll like it, you'll see. Auntie Agnes is coming too." She pulled two wooden slat chairs forward and looked at the girls. "Sit down. Put your feet together and your hands in your lap."

They both sat, and Rosalie cuffed Rae's wrists, then her ankles. Finally she took a rope and tied it around her waist to the chair. Rae sat paralyzed as Rosalie repeated the process on Carol. Finally Rosalie stood up. "Want anything?" she asked Carol.

Silence.

"If you do, you tell me, okay."

"C-c-can I sit near my brother?"

Rosalie giggled. "Uh-uh, you didn't say, may I." She went to the door. "Don't worry, I'll be back soon. Then we'll get to eat and see all my pictures." She slammed the door behind herself and Rusty studied their faces—Carol seemed okay, but Rae was in shock.

"Rae," he said. "Talk to me."

No answer.

"Why did you two come here?"

"Don't be mad at her, Rusty," Carol said, taking short little breaths.

Rae's stare moved around the room, past the swollen, teary faces with eyes barely open, finally resting on Bobby.

"He's alive, Rae," Rusty said.

She remained silent, staring at Bobby.

"Well, what the hell *did* you come for?" Rusty shouted.

"Rusty, don't," Carol said.

But he glared at Rae. "You should have stayed home where you belong!"

Rae's head jerked around toward Rusty, her eyes growing larger and darker.

"Why'd you come here . . . to be in the way? To give me more to worry about?"

"Rusty," Carol said. "Why are you—"

"Dammit, you answer me, Rae! What are you doing here?"

"To help *you!*" she shouted, tears falling down her cheeks. "I came to help you!"

He sighed, then ran his hand over wet eyes, "Good, that's good. Then start helping me."

She looked down at her hands and feet, then back to him. "How?"

"Push yourself up onto your feet. Lean forward, let the chair lay on your back." He looked at Carol. "You, too."

Both of them did as he said. "Now take little steps, don't try to rush."

Inch by inch they moved their feet, finally reaching Rusty. He sat them down and unknotted the ropes around their waists. "You okay?" he said to Carol, hugging her.

She nodded.

He stroked Rae's face. "How about you?"

She took a deep breath. "I'm sorry, Rusty."

"Why're you sorry?"

"Because I forgot to tell you. Put your hand in my back pocket. There's a jackknife there."

Before she had walked in, Sally took off her glasses. Now it was doubly hard to find a seat in the dimly lit bar, let alone one near someone halfway decent.

She found an empty stool, ordered a drink, then squinting, checked her neighbors: two girls on one side and an old couple on the other. *Good work, Sally.*

Now was a good time to make that call. She picked up her drink and headed for the phone booth. She deposited change in the slot, then tried Lenny's number. Still no answer. She hung up, then dug out her glasses and put them on, doing a quick check of the bar. She spotted an empty between two hot-looking guys, then slipped her glasses back into her purse and headed over . . .

Even with the knife, the thick chain holding Rusty was impossible to penetrate. Finally he sent Carol and Rae to dig out the hooks holding Mac.

"I'd rather get Bobby free first," Rae said.

"Mac . . . we need Mac."

Rae took Mac's hands, and Carol his feet—he didn't move or look at them. "I don't know, Rusty, he's really out of it."

"Dig into the wood with the knife, then roll the screw around, loosening it."

"I got it," Rae said, heading for his other hand.

"How is the ankle going, Carol?" Rusty said.

"Okay, I guess. It'll be easier once I can use the knife."

"Done," Rae said a few minutes later as she watched mac's hand fall limply to his lap, one cuff around his wrist, another flapping freely against his arm. Then she kneeled down next to Carol and dug out the hooks holding his feet. She looked at Rusty. "Now Bobby."

"Leave Bobby alone, he can't be of help to us."

"But—"

He looked around the room. "Let's try to free Elaine next."

"About time," Elaine said.

"What about me?" Penny cried out.

"Me too," Roxanne said.

"Just wait and we'll get to all of you," Rusty said.

Carol and Rae started back to Elaine. Rusty heard the lock in the door . . . He pulled forward, and reached out, grabbing them, swinging them into their chairs.

Mrs. Mills came in first, carrying paper plates, napkins and pizza. Then Rosalie, carrying the brown bag and the gun.

CHAPTER THIRTY

THE pizza and paper plates slid from Agnes's hands to the floor. "Look what you did!" Rosalie cried, getting down on her knees, lifting the gooey cheese and tomato slices back onto the plate.

Agnes leaned backward against the wall, her eyes gazing around the room—they were shackled! Her eyes locked at a huge bloodstain on the carpet under one of the girls. And the stench of urine permeated the room.

Rosalie handed her the plates. "Here, you give these out."

"But their hands . . . they can't move them."

"Why do you spoil everything for me?" Rosalie shouted. "Just do as I say."

Agnes delivered the plates, her horror mounting as she saw how each of the young men and women had suffered at Rosalie's hands. One boy's leg twisted at an odd angle, another boy sat in stiff deathly silence while the girl lying in the puddle of blood moaned quietly at his side. Only a few in back looked alert—three of them she recognized immediately and avoided their eyes: Rusty, Carol and Rae.

"Found it," she heard Rosalie say as she placed the Bee Gees "How Deep is Your Love" on the stereo.

Agnes passed out the last plate and went back to Rosalie, suddenly feeling an overwhelming weight fill her body. She grabbed onto the wooden-backed chair and sank into it. Whatever hope she had held to save this situation was now dead. She looked down at the shopping bag holding the album and gun. What good would the pictures do now? She reached for the bag, but Rosalie slid it away.

"Oops, you forgot to take some yourself, Aunti Agnes,"

239

Rosalie said, kneeling down and picking up a handful of pizza from the floor and laying it in her lap.

Carol, Rae and the others watched the scene as though it was a horror movie, growing ever grimmer with each frame. Rusty pushed his chair in back of Carol's and Rae's. By the looks of it, Mrs. Mills would be little help to them. Rusty looked over at Mac, still staring ahead, then slid the knife out of Rae's pocket ... Rusty was the only one ... somehow he had to cut through the chain.

One of the guys had asked her for a match—not much, but a start. Sally stood up now, tapping the fellow on his arm. "Be right back," she said with a wide smile.

She hurried to the phone booth and dialed.

"Yeah?"

"Mr. McDermott, Sally here. I expected you in today."

"I was there, you weren't."

"Did Mrs. Kurtz give you the message?"

"What message?"

"From those girls." She sighed and pulled the paper from her purse and read it to him.

"What time did they leave that?"

"About four-thirty, five."

"Why the fuck didn't you give it to me then?"

"I tried to, but—"

Click—she looked into the receiver. *Good move, Sally. Leave a live one alone at the bar just to get your ass kicked.*

No one ate the pizza, except Rosalie. Finally satisfied, Rosalie put down her plate, went over and removed the needle that was now scratching along the ungrooved center of the record.

"Play it again," Rusty said, "I liked it."

She began it again, turning down the volume, then went back to her seat and lifted the bag off the floor. As she did, Rusty cut through one chain, freeing his right foot.

Rosalie peered inside the bag and took out a thick book. She held it up to the others. "See this? These are Auntie Agnes' secret pictures."

Mrs. Mills, whose eyes had become dazed, suddenly came to life. "No Rosalie, not now." She grabbed for it. "You give that back to me."

"No, I won't!" Rosalie yanked it backward, hugging it to her chest.

Mrs. Mills stood up and lunged at Rosalie, tugging and twisting at Rosalie's arms to free the book. Rosalie shoved the woman down forcefully, knocking her to the floor.

Finally Rosalie put the album on the seat and extended her hand. "You fell, Auntie Agnes. Let me help you up." She pulled Agnes to her seat, then lifted the album, sat down, and looked at the threesome—Rusty, Carol and Rae—huddled together. "Okay, is everyone ready to see the pictures?"

Lenny McDermott had been pacing around the reception area for ten minutes before Spanski walked in. "What the hell kind of operation you run here? According to these guys, you were expected here an hour ago."

Spanski looked up at the big man with blunt features: a vein twitched on his high forehead. "What is this, McDermott, someone appoint you acting chief?"

"My boy's missing. I was under the misconception that you were running an investigation here."

Spanski sighed. The guy was a loudmouth, but he *was* the chief's friend. Besides, how would he feel if it were his son missing? "Look," he said, forcing a calmness he didn't feel. "Why don't you tell me what you're doing down here."

Lenny ran his hand over his mouth and jaw. "I've got something I want you to follow up."

"What is it?"

"These two girls—Carol Erlich and a girl named Rae—"

"Hold it," the desk sergeant said, fishing through the messages, then handing one to Spanski. "Came a couple hours ago."

Spanski read it through, then looking to McDermott, "Go on, I know the girls you're talking about."

"They asked me to let them do some investigating at my dealership. Something about a 1988 blue Honda. So I let them. When I got back to the office, they were gone. A half hour ago, I get word from my girl that they had left a message for me."

"What was the message?"

"It seems they found a name that fit into their theory of the blue Honda. Someone the Erlich boy knows. Now I don't know if they're pissing in the wind or what . . . but these are two young girls out there alone, and they could be getting in over their heads."

"Does the name tie in with any of the others?"

"As far as I know, it doesn't." McDermott ran his hand over his peppered hair. "But then again, I don't know anything anymore."

Spanski glanced again at the message. "We talking about Victoria Louise, Seventeen Valley Road?"

"Yeah. That's it."

Spanski patted a hand over his shoulder holster, then with a nod of his head. "Come on, McDermott, you keep me company on this one. Let's go see."

Rosalie opened to the beginning of the book . . . On the top was written a date: January 8, 1964. *Her* birthday. She looked down at the first photograph, her mind suddenly whirling back to a time when she had done this before. Her jaw dropped—her hand clamped over her mouth.

She dropped her hand and looked at Agnes, then back to the first picture: a pretty lady with a big belly, lying on the bed. Daddy was sitting next to the lady, one hand holding her hand, the other resting on her swollen belly. The lady's blue eyes stared right into daddy's eyes.

Rosalie picked up the book and turned it around so the others could see. "See, that's Auntie Agnes," she said. She pointed to the date. "And that's *my* birthday."

Rusty looked at Mrs. Mills who was now staring down at her hands.

Rosalie pointed to the next picture: a woman in labor, then the next ones, step by step showing the birth of the infant. Always daddy was there. "Oh my, what a pretty baby," Rosalie said, bringing the picture up closer to her face. Then turning to Agnes. "Who took these pictures?"

"Mama," she answered softly. "Your mama."

"Where did the baby go?"

Silence.

"Did you throw her away?"

Again silence.

"Answer me! You had a baby . . . Where is it now?"

Agnes looked up at Rosalie, tears dribbling down her cheeks. "You know, don't you?"

In a small voice, "But I want you to tell me."

Mrs. Mills licked her dry lips. "You, Rosalie. You are that baby."

Rosalie began to cry—little-girl sobs that made her gasp for breath . . . Mrs. Mills reached out to touch her, but Rosalie swatted her hand away. Finally Rosalie lifted the skirt of her dress and dried her eyes. Then looked at her. "Why didn't you want her?"

"Oh I did want you, but I had promised . . . and then it was too late. You see, your mama couldn't have babies. She and your daddy came to me, they pleaded with me . . . And there I was, alone and not getting younger. I was thirty-five, soon it would have been too late for me."

"Did they pay you money?"

Agnes swallowed hard. "Once you were born, I refused to take it. Instead I insisted that they let me stay, to be with you, to watch you grow. You see, by then I loved you."

"And daddy, too?"

Agnes nodded. "Yes. Daddy, too."

"Then why did you kill him, Auntie Agnes?"

Silence, staring . . .

Rosalie pulled the gun from the bag and pointed it at Agnes. "Tell me why you killed my daddy!"

Agnes's eyes bored into Rosalie. "It . . . it was an accident. You remember, you said so yourself. In court."

"No, no, I lied! You know I—" Rosalie stopped. A memory flitted by, then came back again, this time more slowly so she could watch. She squeezed her hands into fists and bit down hard on her lip.

The little girl had heard the footsteps coming down to the playroom . . . She wasn't supposed to have been looking through the picture album—Auntie Agnes had warned her about that—but she *was* looking. And she had seen something naughty, something shameful: a picture of daddy taking a baby out of Auntie Agnes' privates. What if mama ever found *that* out?

The steps came closer . . . She closed the album and ran and hid in back of the boiler. The steps came into the playroom, then there were voices: daddy's and Auntie Agnes' voices. But the little girl couldn't even listen to the words—she was too frightened to listen. It was dark and dirty in back of the boiler . . . slimy, crawly insects and sticky webs played with her face. If she didn't get out soon, she would die!

The moment she peeked out, she saw them—arms and legs all wrapped together on the sofa. And with their clothes off! On the floor, next to the sofa was daddy's police uniform rolled into a ball, and daddy's holster. And daddy's gun. She tiptoed over to the sofa and picked up the gun. And aimed it!

Now Rosalie plucked the gun from the bag and jumped to her feet, her arms flapping frantically through the air. "It was me," she screamed. "I killed daddy!"

Agnes jumped up, trying to grasp onto her hands. "No, no, Rosalie. It was an accident, a child's accident."

Rosalie lifted her hand and brought it down again, cracking the butt of the gun against Agnes' head. The woman sank to the floor, then Rosalie, her lip dripping blood, moved toward Rusty . . .

Carol sucked in her breath. "Oh God . . . what is she going to do?" At that moment, the last link cracked—his left foot was free. Rusty stood up. "It *was* an accident, Rosalie," he said.

She lifted the gun, aiming it at him. "I had to do it, daddy. You understand, don't you?"

"I'm Rusty, Rosalie. Not your father. And it was an accident, he knows that. Now put down the gun. Please put down the gun."

"I loved you so much, and I believed in you. But you lied to me. All that time you lied to me. The playroom wasn't really for me . . ." She gestured to the woman now lying on the floor. "It was for her. For you and her!"

Carol jumped up in front of Rusty. "That's not your father, it's my broth—" Rae turned and reached out, trying to drag Carol down, and Rosalie turned the gun toward them.

At that moment, Rusty leaped toward Rosalie. But before he reached her, the gun fired.

Rusty fell to the floor. "Rusty!" Carol shrieked, scrambling over to him. Rosalie pointed the gun at them and Rae threw herself over Carol, "No, don't . . . *please!*"

Suddenly there were footsteps, running, a scream . . . Rae looked up. Mac was standing there, holding Rosalie off the ground, then with a deep cry from his throat, he hurled her. Her body thudded against the wall, then fell to the ground.

Rae crawled over Carol to Rusty, and with her cuffs still on, ripped open his shirt.

Carol lay with her face in the carpet, sobbing.

"He's going to be okay, Carol. It's his shoulder." Then putting her face down to his. "You hear me, Rusty?" she asked, her voice catching.

He nodded.

She pressed her hand over the wound and put her face to his. "It's over, it's over, it's over . . ."

Then there was banging on the playroom door. "Bradley Police. Who's in there?"

Cries, screams . . .

Lenny's voice. "Break the fuckin thing down!"

EPILOGUE

RUSTY had just put down the phone when Rae came into his room. "Hey you, you're supposed to be resting," Rae said. She sat on his bed, leaned over and kissed him. "They let nurses do this kind of thing?"

"Only the good ones." She gestured to the phone. "Who was that?"

"My dad. He and mom are flying up next week to visit."

"That's nice."

"I suspect Dad's coming to meet you. I did tell him all about you."

Rae flushed, then smiled. "*All* about me."

"Well, almost all. I told him you were an ace mechanic and loved the outdoors . . . And judging by that jackknife you had in your jeans pocket the other night, for all I know you hunt and fish, too. You never told me about that."

Rae laughed. "No hunting . . . just fishing."

"Good, that's what I told my dad. And it was the fishing that really got to him. That's the thing he misses most out there in the desert. He figured maybe this summer he'd come up for a month or so, and you'd go out, do some deep-sea fishing with him."

"Sounds good, you coming too?"

"Only if you bait the hooks."

"A deal."

He stared at her, then, "Carol was up here earlier. Thanks for letting her stay with you."

"I love having her, you know that. I'll miss her when you take her home next week."

He reached out, putting his hand on her cheek, then running his fingers down to her lips. "You're not going to miss either of

247

us. I promise you that." Then his voice became more somber. "How's everyone doing?"

"Well, the girls are all home. Millie came in today to have the bandages changed on her ear. Bobby's in good spirits, except, of course, for his complaining about that strained food we feed him. Can you imagine losing twenty-five pounds in three weeks?"

"When does he make it to solids?"

"Another couple of days and his digestive system ought to be back to normal. Meanwhile Maxine managed to put a real smile on his face: she told him the news about his painting."

Rusty nodded. "What about Sammy's concussion?"

"He's going to be fine. He just needs a lot of rest and nourishment. And you should see Brad, he's getting around real well with that leg cast."

There was a short pause. "And Mac and Gena?"

Rae frowned. "Fortunately she got here in time, before any infection set in. God, if the afterbirth had stayed inside her much longer . . . Well, the D&C did the trick anyhow. Now it's just a matter of getting her strength back, physically and emotionally." Rae sighed. "Mac is still pretty much in shock. He's spoken some, but not much. He blames himself for the baby, that he wasn't with Gena when she went to the house. There's going to be a small, private funeral for the baby tomorrow. I thought I'd go."

Rusty leaned his head back against the pillow and closed his eyes. "Mac wanted a boy, too."

"I know, but at least Gena will be able to conceive again, she might not have had that. Mr. McDermott is thinking of having Mac transferred to a psychiatric facility for a few weeks where he'll be able to get some therapy."

"That's good, I guess." Then, "What about Mrs. Mills?"

"Mrs. Mills is still in a coma, she's not expected to make it. The thing is . . . well, the doctors say she's not really trying very hard. Maybe somehow she knows that Rosalie was transferred to that sanitarium . . ."

Rusty was silent for a few minutes. "It never should have

happened," he said finally. "None of it. You know what she said to me while I was tied up there. She said she had loved me, that she had counted on me to watch out for her." He shook his head, started to say something, then stopped. After a moment, he said softly, "Do you know how that made me feel, Rae? Like shit. Like I had really let her down."

Rae took hold of his hands. "Who knows, Rusty, you may have helped her out far more than you remember. She had to have had *some* reason for trusting you like she did. Besides, as we heard the other night, Rosalie's classmates weren't her only problem."

Silence.

"Hey, let's talk about something else. Something a little more cheerful."

He looked at her, then pulled her hand up to his lips and kissed it. "Go ahead, start talking."

"Well, there *was* something I wanted to ask you."

He waited.

"You remember that stereo cabinet I bought at the lumber company?"

"What stereo cabinet is that?"

"Come on."

"Okay, I remember."

"I thought maybe . . ." She took a deep breath. "Come on, do I have to spell it out for you?"

"Absolutely."

She stared straight ahead, now avoiding his eyes. "It's sitting in my bedroom, partially assembled—I keep on coming up with three extra pieces. Now I want you to understand, I don't just ask any guy into my bedroom . . ."

He studied her face, her dark eyes now meeting his. "But you're asking me?"

She nodded, and he drew her close to him, wrapping his arms around her.